A Heron House Affair
An Eastport Beach Romance

Tara Ryan

Above Average Press

ISBN 978-1-967758-04-3 (Paperback) 978-1-967758-03-6 (eBook)

This book was inspired by my sweet friend, JeanAnn, and her love of dancing.

Anything I got wrong is on me, because I have two left feet.

YOU ARE CORDIALLY
INVITED TO

A HERON
HOUSE

Affair

A GRAND RE-OPENING

SATURDAY
9-20
6 PM

55 RIVER RD, EASTPORT BEACH, NC

Chapter One

Ada noticed the invitation as soon as she entered her mother's Soho loft. Not the soot coating the cabinets above the stove or the melted pile of goo that may have been a spatula. Nor the puddles of water remaining on the brushed concrete floors and the lone plate on the counter—a soggy piece of wheat toast as its centerpiece.

Ada's mother didn't believe in displaying photos, or appointment reminder cards, or the A+ her only child got on that American History exam. As far as she knew, her mother didn't even own a magnet.

Yet, there it was. Stark white and black in design, art déco font and trendy tropical leaves centered on the stainless-steel refrigerator door. A magnet advertising a Chinese restaurant offering delivery and a free egg roll with every order held it in place.

So, as Ada took in all the evidence of the kitchen fire, saw Gertrude, her mother's Pothos plant, barely clinging to life, and found several paintbrushes left in dirty water next to her work in progress, it was the placement of the invitation that most signaled something was wrong with Charlotte Maddox.

Stepping to the refrigerator, Ada reached out and traced the raised lettering with one finger. Her mother had always been up for a party, but had she really considered traveling to North Carolina? Not that it mattered now, because Charlotte's days of jetting around the world had come to a screeching halt.

They still didn't know exactly how the fire had started, only that her mother, THE Charlotte Maddox, now had second-degree burns to both hands and a brand-new diagnosis of early onset dementia. If the neighbor hadn't heard her screams, if the fire extinguisher wasn't three steps from her door, if Ada hadn't taken that job in Virginia. There were too many what ifs.

She turned and leaned against the counter, suddenly unable to support her own weight. Her mother's New York loft boasted large windows facing the east—*absolutely the best light*. Her mother's eclectic tastes filled the space—the purple velvet sofa (eggplant, not plum, Charlotte insisted), the rattan chair with a cushion the color of mustard, the textured rug from India, or Burma, or Indonesia. Ada couldn't keep up with her mother's travels.

Now Charlotte would be confined to a 10' x 14' white box. It was unfathomable.

Her eyes settled next on the large canvas propped on an easel. Deep greens and blues signaled water churning. Dark storm clouds towered over the water, threatening and ominous. The piece was unfinished and a departure from Charlotte Maddox's usual work. The piece reflected the turmoil within the artist as her own mind betrayed her.

Ada's phone rang, and without looking, she knew Paul would be on the other end of the line. He always seemed to know when she needed him. Attending a dance recital because her mother was out of the country or buying her a backpack filled with school supplies because Charlotte felt inspired and wouldn't leave the house—she wondered if all managers helped raise the orphans of their artists. Because even when her mother was around, she was never really present.

"Did you make it okay?"

"Yes, I'm here. The whole place feels, I don't know, off." She opened the refrigerator door. Eggs, fancy water, a few random condiments and a plate of stinky cheese. Ada couldn't tell if it was stinky on purpose or had come to this refrigerator to die.

"I'm sorry I can't be there. I've got an opening tonight, and this kid is green. He's currently freaking out because the hardware we used to hang his paintings is burnished gold, not nickel. I'm too old for this kind of drama."

Ada smiled, feeling some of the tension drain out of her, just hearing his voice. "You live for that kind of drama. Without it, you'd just shrivel up and die."

"Maybe. All artists have their peculiarities, I know, but this younger generation—I'm not sure it's worth it. I'd take your mother's over-the-top attitude any day."

She closed the refrigerator door, staring again at the invitation. "Paul, what is Heron House?" She slid the card out of the magnet's hold and flipped it over. The handwritten note was addressed to Charlotte.

"It was a retreat of sorts. Your mom went there in the late 90s, maybe. I guess it was right before you came along." His voice became muffled, but she thought she heard him tell someone they could shove the gold hardware up their ass for all he cared.

"Well, apparently, it's reopening, and they wanted Charlotte to come down. And they had a question about one of her pieces."

"If you give me the number, I'll handle it. I haven't had time to put out a press release, but eventually, we'll have to let people know."

"Paul, you've already gone above and beyond. You were here when I wasn't. You got her settled in a care facility, and you're handling the financial end. I couldn't do this without you." Her eyes scanned the apartment, mentally cataloguing everything she'd need to do to get it on the market. "I'll call and let them know she won't be attending. You worry about Mr. Green and his nickels. I'll worry about Charlotte."

"And I'll worry about you."

"Guess very little has changed."

"Love ya, kiddo."

"Back at you." Ada disconnected from the call and started assembling boxes.

***

She'd packed up most of the kitchen and living room when her phone rang again. The disruption alerted her stomach to the fact that it was after six and she hadn't eaten anything since the bag of salt and vinegar chips she'd bought at a gas station five hours ago.

As soon as she got Miranda off the phone, she'd be putting her mother's magnet to good use. "Hey Randi."

"You were supposed to text me that you got to New York okay. Either you forgot or you took a detour to Canada."

"I'm in the city and before you ask, yes, I've eaten today." *Chips count as a meal, right?*

"And stay hydrated. You're going to be using all your muscles moving boxes and furniture. Do you have some Powerade?"

"How was class, Randi? Did you tell the girls I'll be back soon?" She had only started at the dance school three weeks ago, but she was already getting attached to the students. As scholarship kids, they really appreciated the chance to learn how to dance.

"Yeah, so about that."

"What happened? Did someone get hurt? I bet it was Elsie. She's a little wild." The seven-year-old had spent half of the last class sitting in the corner after she kicked another student in the head while cartwheeling across the room.

"Someone got hurt, but it wasn't a student."

"Are you okay?"

"I'm fine. It's Susan."

The director of the school was a little odd, but she had taken a chance and hired Ada despite her lack of teaching experience. "Oh no, what happened?"

"She was riding her unicycle when a chipmunk ran out in front of her. The chipmunk is fine, but Susan has a broken hip."

"That's awful. I can help cover her classes as soon as I'm back." She'd have to dig deep into her memory banks to recall her tap and hip-hop skills, but it was like riding a bike, right? She'd steer clear of unicycles, though.

"Hold your horses—there's more. And please don't shoot the messenger."

Her worst nightmare. Fired. She knew leaving so soon after arriving would cause issues. But she couldn't see any way around it. It had always been just her and Charlotte. She held her breath, waiting to hear the dreaded words.

"She's closing down for the semester."

"Closing? What about all the students? What about the grant? If we cancel the program, we'll lose the funding." Ada had worked tirelessly on the application for the arts grant to offer classes to underprivileged kids. She'd assured Susan that she'd take care of everything, it would be great PR for the school, and most of all, it would help more little girls gain the confidence that dance had given Ada when she was little, and her mother couldn't be bothered with a child.

"They pulled the funding."

"What the hell? Can they do that?"

"Some uppity-up in Congress killed the bill that funded our grant and thousands of other arts projects. So, if you need to get your anger out, stop in D.C. on your way back."

Ada squeezed her eyes shut, spots spinning behind her lids. She tried to control her breathing to calm the anger threatening to explode out of her. What about her plan? Without a job, how would she pay her rent? She was so proud of the program she had started at Susie B's Dance Academy and now it was gone?

But she would not scream at Miranda. It wasn't her fault.

"I guess you can stay in New York a while longer. Hang out with your family, eat great pizza." She laughed awkwardly.

"My mom barely knows who I am. I'm packing up her apartment so her manager can sell it. We need the money to pay for her care."

"What about your father?"

Ada had known Miranda for less than a month and hadn't felt the need to share her dysfunctional family situation with her over tutus and leotards. She let out a sigh and plopped down on the sofa. "I don't know my father." She was tired, pissed off, and hungry. She didn't have time to fill her friend in on her childhood and semi-famous mother. It had never been convenient for Charlotte to have a daughter, and now she'd conveniently forgotten that she had one at all. "I have no reason to stay here."

"Where will you go?"

"I have no idea."

Chapter Two

As Trip made the turn onto River Road, his phone rang and the bags in his passenger seat slid toward the floor. He could either save the produce or decline his mother's phone call.

His car decided for him as it answered on the second ring. *Traitor.*

"Carlton? Are you there? Honey?" Two seconds in and she wanted something. Hence, the "honey."

"Yes, Mom. I'm in the car. I just picked up some groceries for Riley."

"I thought your friend's name was Chesnee. Who is this Riley fellow?"

Rolling his eyes, Trip turned the volume down. Not that it would make his mother any less screechy. "*She* is the owner of Heron House. Where I've been living and working for the last two months?" *Any of this ringing a bell?*

"Of course. I'm sure she's going to miss having you around to help out." Karina Westinghouse paused, drawing out the silence before she dropped the inevitable bomb. "When you come home."

And there it is. "The grand re-opening is this weekend. She's counting on me. I'll be home after that." *Unless my wish comes true, and I discover that I was abducted as a baby, and this isn't really my family.*

"Yes, speaking of the party. I thought I'd drive down and join in the celebration. I would love to see what you've been up to all summer."

Trip was so startled, he momentarily veered into the other lane. Thankfully, it wasn't a heavily traveled road. "Mom, it's just going to be some artists and locals. No one you'd care to meet."

"Now, Carlton, you know how much the arts mean to me. I may want to purchase a piece at the auction. I'm still redecorating the pool house."

He ran the guest list through his head, trying to determine who had his mother wanting to schlep down here from Virginia. "I'll check with Riley and see if there's room." He turned onto the driveway leading to Heron House. "I've got to run, Mom. Talk to you soon." He disconnected the call before his mother could remind him anyone would be honored to have her at their party.

Circling the fountain, he pulled up in front of the steps. He'd unload the groceries and then move his car around back. Last week, he and Ben had created an extension to the gravel driveway that wrapped around the house and allowed for more parking.

If someone had told him a year ago he'd be sanding woodwork and slinging gravel, he'd have laughed in their face. If they'd told him he'd be enjoying it, he would have declared them insane and suggested they seek professional help.

He lined his arms with the reusable shopping bags from the local market and climbed the steps to the front door, toeing it open with his sneaker.

"Trip? Is that you?" Riley's voice filtered down the stairs.

"Yup. I bought out Murray's for you." He continued down the hall to the kitchen and heaved the bags onto the counter. Within seconds, Ansel had his head stuck in one of the bags, snooping for food. "No cat treats today, buddy." He ran his hand along the cat's back and was rewarded with a purr. Ansel didn't offer affection liberally. But he'd decided early on that Trip was okay for a person.

"Come upstairs when you get done. Third floor."

He wondered what project Riley had in store for him today. If they were working on the third floor, it would probably involve moving boxes and taking more donations to the church.

The second floor of the house was nearly ready for guests, and they'd already had a couple groups utilizing the first floor. Manny from the bait shop ran a poker game on Monday nights, and the Henry sisters were hosting their monthly book club in the parlor. Trip had accidentally walked in during their last meeting and discovered that their preferred genre was monster romance. His nightmares that night hadn't been about mythical creatures in love, but rather about seventy-year-old women chasing after the monsters.

Trip put the perishables away in the refrigerator, snagging a Granny Smith apple to tide him over until lunch. He bit into the tart apple as he ran outside to move his car. Driving to the back of the house, he parked beside Ben's car. If Riley had convinced her boyfriend to stay home from work, it likely meant she had a massive project in mind. As Trip headed back into the house and up the stairs, he found himself excited for whatever she had up her sleeve. Anything was better than what was waiting for him back in Virginia.

"Riley? Where are you?" As he ascended the narrow staircase to the third floor, he heard muffled laughter.

"Second door on the left."

The hallway looked normal, except all the doors were closed. He wasn't sure what he was walking into, but Riley had tried to scare him more than once in the massive house. Maybe he'd turn the tables on his boss. Swinging the door open, he leapt into the room. "Baha!"

"Surprise!" Riley and Ben screamed in chorus, drowning out his failed scare tactic.

The sound died on his lips as he looked around the room, which had been transformed from a storage area into a modest bedroom. His duffel bag sat on the bench at the end of the bed, and his golf clubs leaned against the far wall. "Is this for me?"

Ben stepped beside him, clapping him on the back. "We weren't going to make you go back to sleeping on Chesnee's couch."

Riley bracketed him on the other side. "This is your home, as long as you want to stay here." She squeezed his arm and beamed up at him.

Trip wasn't the type to get sentimental, but he had to swallow before he could speak. "I can't believe you did this." He cleared his throat to chase away the emotion. "I mean, I can't believe you did this without me. I'm usually the one moving furniture around." He forced a laugh.

Luckily, Riley laughed along and didn't seem to notice the strain in his voice. "Don't worry, we've got another room to set up, so you'll get to join in the fun."

"You're putting another bedroom up here? Is it for when Ben's in the doghouse?"

"That's what the boat's for." Ben winked and laughed. He still technically lived on his sailboat that was docked next door, but ever since he and Riley made things official, he'd spent most nights at Heron House.

"Gina's going to use the room across the hall, just until she gets her roommate situation figured out." Riley patted Trip on the back. "I'll leave you fellas to it. I've got descriptions to write for the auction."

The couple shared a quick kiss, and Riley clopped down the stairs.

"I've got a petition due by the end of the day, so let's get to it. Riley was less than helpful getting your new bed up the stairs. I'm sure you'll be more help with the next one." Ben followed his girlfriend down the staircase.

Trip stared around the room that would be his temporary home. He'd moved around a lot since graduating from law school. Home to Virginia until his mother drove him crazy about what was next. Then a quick trip to Cozumel for a buddy's bachelor party, where he ran into Chesnee, who suggested he crash with him for the summer. He really liked Eastport Beach, even if his 6'3" frame hated sleeping on a couch every night.

So, when Riley had asked him for help fixing up the house she'd inherited and offered him an honest-to-goodness bed in exchange, he couldn't pass it up. Now, Ben and Riley had become some of his closest friends. It had been a great summer.

He didn't want to leave. Riley's offer was so tempting. Life in Eastport Beach was laid back and easy. The exact opposite of what he would find when he went home.

But that was the deal. Take the summer to goof off then back to his responsibilities. It was a deal with the devil.

***

"Riley, where do you want this?" Trip balanced the bust of some Greek goddess against his chest. He didn't consider himself a weak man, but this thing weighed a ton.

She looked up from her desk, her eyes going wide. "Can you handle that alone?"

"As long as I can put it down very soon."

"Oh, sorry." She jumped up and led him into the dining room. "Set it on this pedestal in the corner. It should be big enough."

At least the next time he moved it, he wouldn't have to carry it down two flights of stairs. "I've got one more stack of paintings. You want them in here or the study?"

Her mouth twisted as she considered. "The study. I need to nail down the information for the auction catalog today." She headed back down the hallway.

"Have you eaten?" Trip had learned that his boss often forgot trivial things like food and water.

"No time." She disappeared through the French doors leading into the study.

He grunted. She was stubborn, that one. He'd grab the last of the art from the third floor and then make them a couple sandwiches. Ben would be upset if he knew Riley skipped lunch.

Jogging up the stairs, he passed the room they had set up for Gina. There were several bags of all shapes and colors piled on the bed. She must have dropped a load off while he developed a statue-induced hernia.

He liked Gina. She was upbeat, spunky and gorgeous. But she was also off-limits. Chesnee had it bad for her, though he refused to admit it. His friendship with Chesnee was too valuable to risk over a hookup.

As much as his mother would like him to settle down, Trip had zero intention of fulfilling her wish anytime soon. It was bad enough he had to suffer under the weight of his family's obligations—he wouldn't subject anyone else to it.

In the room at the front of the house, five or six paintings leaned against the wall. Riley had already sorted through what they would auction off, and the rest adorned the walls of Heron House.

He thumbed through the pieces. Landscape, landscape, fruit, green glob, ballerina, lighthouse. He flipped back to the dancer.

The piece was stunning. The girl, possibly in her late teens, posed with pointed toes and arched arms, her face in profile, her hair in a bun with wisps framing her delicate features. She wore a pale pink leotard and tutu, and the background was only a few shades darker, which gave the entire picture a hazy effect. The artist was obviously very talented, but the subject made it easy. She was effortlessly beautiful.

For a split second, he considered bidding on the painting.

Then he remembered that couch-surfers don't own art.

Trip stacked the paintings and carried them down to the study. "Last batch."

Riley looked up from her laptop. "Great, just lean them against the wall. I'll go through them in a minute."

"I'm going to grab some lunch. Can I interest you in a tuna salad on rye?"

She caught his eye over the screen, and a smile formed on her lips. "Sure, I'll force one down."

"Coming right up."

Chapter Three

The GPS announced her destination was 0.4 miles away. Ada blew out a sigh of relief. Her muscles had cramped up hours ago, and her stomach had been growling for the last hundred miles of barren landscape. Did they not have restaurants in coastal North Carolina?

She hadn't been desperate enough to stop at the ancient gas station/BBQ place at an intersection in the middle of nowhere. There obviously wasn't a hospital close enough if she needed it.

With her GPS counting down the feet until her turn, she slowed her car and switched her blinker on. Not that there was anyone around to need her signal. She hadn't seen another vehicle since she'd left I-95. She seriously doubted this plan.

A discreet wooden sign assured her she was in the right place, so she turned onto a winding gravel driveway. As she traveled around a bend, a huge white house loomed ahead, framed by large, gnarled trees covered in Spanish moss. A sparkling expanse of water lay beyond, a wide river snaking through tall grasses. There was a picturesque gazebo on a grassy crest above an inlet with a small dock jutting into the water.

Ada felt all the tension of the past week and the hours of driving leak out of her limbs. It was perfect. For the first time, she understood something her mother had done. Charlotte had spent several months here, painting and growing as an artist. According to Paul, at least.

As she drew closer to the house, the driveway curved around a grand fountain with a bronze bird perched on top. The namesake, she supposed. Hope blossomed in her chest. Maybe she would find some answers here. And even if she didn't, it was a lovely place to figure out her next step.

The screen door opened, and a smiling woman about her age stepped out onto the porch. Her strawberry-blonde ponytail bounced as she bounded down the steps.

Ada got out of the car and watched in amazement as a real blue heron flew overhead.

"Hi! You must be Ada Maddox. I'm Riley."

"Do you have the birds trained to appear when guests arrive?"

Riley craned her head back and watched as the graceful bird disappeared over the house. "Ha, I wish. I've tried to get a picture for the website, and I think they're camera shy."

Movement down by the river caught Ada's attention. She looked over the other woman's shoulder just as a man jumped from a kayak and waded to the shore. He was tall, with an athletically lean body. After pulling the boat onto land, he shucked his life jacket and stepped back into the river to dunk his body in the water.

"How was your drive down?"

"Fine, although the last bit was a tad boring." Ada took a step to her right just in time to see the man breach the water.

Riley turned, catching Ada watching the now very wet man. She smiled in a conspiratorial way. "That's Trip. He helps out around here in exchange for a room. I'm sure you'll meet him later."

Ada tore her attention away from Trip's toned, tanned, and dripping torso. "Oh, okay, I was just wondering if we can rent the kayaks."

Riley snickered. "The kayak is Trip's, but I'm sure he'd let you borrow it."

Heat crept up Ada's cheeks. She was so busted. "It's no big deal." She opened her trunk to get her bags out. "If you'll point me to my room, I'd like to freshen up." Right now, she just wanted to escape her humiliation.

"Ada, you don't have to be embarrassed. He's a good-looking man. And single." Riley winked and took the smaller of her guest's bags.

She wondered how Riley got anything done with a distraction like Trip. "Do you have many guests right now?"

Riley wrapped her arm around Ada's shoulders and led her up the porch steps. "You are my very first guest. I mean, other than family."

So much for blending in with a crowd and avoiding the sexy man that worked on the premises. Ada hadn't had time to date since starting her new job, but thanks to some tight-fisted politician, she didn't have to worry about that anymore. Anger welled in her chest. Man, if she could get that jerk alone in a room, she would give him a piece of her mind. Senator Westinghouse was a rich, entitled, pompous ass who only cared about money and power. Not about little kids who wanted to learn how to plié and pirouette. "I'm sure you'll fill up for the grand opening."

"Oh, yes! We're completely booked for the next two weeks. Most people will arrive closer to the weekend. Hope you don't mind being a bit of a guinea pig." Riley opened the screen door and gestured for Ada to enter.

A gleaming wooden staircase with a carved banister rose to the second floor, and a sparkling chandelier caught light from the sunlight pouring in through tall windows, casting a prism of color that danced around the foyer. "Riley, this is stunning. You must have killed yourself doing the renovations." She continued to take in her surroundings. A formal sitting room lay to the left with multiple sofas and chairs and an enormous fireplace. On the right was a grand dining room with a table long enough to seat her entire dance troupe.

Riley beamed at the compliment. "I had a lot of help, and most of what I did was cosmetic. My uncle Archie loved this place and took excellent care of it." She started up the stairs. "After you get settled, come back down and I'll fix you some fresh-squeezed lemonade. Then I want to hear all about your mother."

Ada followed her hostess up the stairs, her hand sliding along the polished banister. Even without her mother here, this trip was already all about THE Charlotte Maddox. Just as it had been her entire life.

She followed Riley down the hall to the last door on the left. On the wall was an engraved plate which read "The Maddox Suite." *Just bash me over the head with it.*

Riley pushed the door open, her face bursting with excitement. "I saved this room, just in case your mother could attend." Her face dimmed appropriately. "I'm so sorry about what you're both going through."

Ada bit her lip. "Thank you."

"But I'm so glad you're here." Riley embraced her like they hadn't just met downstairs.

Tears threatened, but Ada wasn't ready to cry in front of her new bestie. It was nice to have someone acknowledge that her mother's dementia affected her as well. When Paul released the statement on social media, messages had poured in expressing concern for Charlotte and the art world as a whole. But only a few people had reached out to see how Ada was holding up.

If she could find answers here, maybe she could finally understand why her mother was the way she was. Why art was more important than her only child. And if there was someone else out there Ada could call family. Riley stepped back and set the bag on a nearby chair. "This room has its own bath. There are towels in the cabinet under the sink. If you need anything, please don't hesitate to ask." She started to leave the room but then turned around. "Feel free to explore the house and the grounds. There are surprises everywhere you look." She winked and pulled the door closed behind her.

Ada realized she had been clutching her suitcase the whole time, so she relaxed her hand and let go of the handle. Looking around the room, she realized she was completely surrounded by her mother's art. She sighed and flopped back on the bed, wondering if she would ever be anything other than Charlotte Maddox's daughter.

Chapter Four

After stashing his kayak in the storage shed behind the house, Trip decided a shower was in order. Riley was counting on him to keep an eye on Manny's game later. Hopefully, he wouldn't lose any money this week. It might look like a table full of geriatrics, but the old geezers were poker sharks.

Nope, this time, Trip was in charge of refreshments and wouldn't be joining the game, no matter how much the guys harassed him.

He climbed the main stairs to the second floor and ducked into one of the shared bathrooms. While his bedroom was on the third floor, it had originally housed only studios, so there were no bathrooms on that level. The second floor had three bedrooms on each side of the central hallway. Coming up the stairs, the first one on the right had its own ensuite bathroom, and that's where Riley had stayed until she cleaned out the master suite on the main level that had been her uncle's room. The next two rooms had a shared bathroom sandwiched between them. The left side of the hall was flipped, with the suite at the far end of the hallway, near the stairs to the third floor.

After a quick shower, Trip wrapped a towel around his waist and gathered up his clothes. He'd seen a strange car outside, and he knew they were expecting their first guest today, so he didn't want to leave anything in the bathroom.

He popped his head out the door. The hallway was empty, so he made a dash for the steps to the third floor. He should really get a robe, or better yet, bring fresh clothes next time he showered. It wasn't a good look for Riley to have naked men running down the hall where her guests were staying. As he neared the stairs to the third floor, the door on his left opened and someone rushed out—colliding with him and sending his wet swimming trunks and dirty t-shirt flying.

The woman teetered, thrown off balance by the collision. Without thinking, Trip reached out to steady her by the shoulders. Startled, she flailed her arms, knocking against his hip, and inconceivably, grabbed his towel as they fell into a heap on the floor.

"I'm so sorry!" Her voice quivered with surprise. "I didn't expect anyone to be right outside my door."

Their limbs tangled together, with Trip's left arm bent at a painful angle underneath her slender frame. He froze for a minute, trying to figure out how to extricate both of them from this awkward situation.

Naked.

It was a good thing he was leaving after the party, because Riley would *so* fire him if she found out about this. She was generally pretty easygoing, but there had been a whole pseudo lecture about making a good first impression on the guests.

Not that he didn't look good naked.

This scenario was likely at the top of Riley's worst things that could happen this week list.

He snagged the first piece of material he could grab and covered his manhood. The wet bathing suit shocked his heated skin. He'd only gotten a quick glimpse of the woman he was now in a compromising position with—but his body had already decided that being naked with her wasn't the worst thing ever.

Focusing on civility and not the fact that he'd had a particularly "dry" summer in that regard, he gently extracted his arm from behind the woman's back and tried to turn her away from his nudity.She had long, straight brown hair, with a hint of red, and it cascaded over her slim shoulders like silk. He wanted to run his fingers through it, but considering he didn't even know her name, it seemed inappropriate.

Even if she had already seen him in the buff.

"It's completely my fault. I shouldn't have been running." He pulled his leg from between hers, separating them. He spotted his towel and reached for it, hoping she would keep her back turned long enough for him to cover up.

"No, really, I should have been looking where I was going." She glanced over her shoulder, her gaze lingering on his blue striped swimming trunks that barely covered his alert member.

He drew the towel across his lap, trying to tie it around his waist, which was almost impossible from his seated position. "Um, could you..." He twirled his finger in the air, hoping she'd take the hint and stop staring at his crotch.

A faint blush rose across her high cheekbones, and she bit her top lip as she swiveled her head back around, facing away from him. "You're Trip, right? Riley mentioned that you help out around here."

Her back finally turned, he rose to his knees and secured the towel, then stood up, testing its closure. "Yeah, you must be our first guest. Um, welcome to Heron House." He stepped in front of her and held out a hand to help her up.

She tilted her chin up, meeting his eyes, and he got the distinct feeling that he knew her from somewhere. "It's Ada." She placed her hand in his, her long, graceful fingers wrapping around his palm, then levered herself up with very little effort. She was lean and toned and obviously had amazing core strength. He basically stood there gawking instead of helping her up.

After an awkward staring contest, Trip realized he was still gripping her hand. And still standing there in only a towel. Turning their handholding into a handshake, he tried to figure out how to salvage this cringe-worthy first impression. "Ada, that's a lovely name. I'd love to stay and chat, but I'm a little underdressed, and honestly, there's a draft coming from the screen door."

She grinned, her gaze once again sliding below his waist. "I'm sure I'll see you around. Maybe even in a shirt—although it'll be a shame." She dropped his hand and headed for the main stairs.

Trip stood there stunned by the enchanting beauty who had just openly flirted with him. He briefly considered heading back to the bathroom for a cold shower, but a quick check of his watch told him he'd better get dressed before Manny got there—because most Monday nights he ended up losing the shirt off his back in the poker game.

Chapter Five

The half-naked man she'd seen hauling his kayak onshore looked good enough to eat. The fully naked man she'd just run into in the hallway made her want to sit down at an all-you-can-eat buffet.

Ada fanned herself as she hopped down the stairs, praying her face didn't look as flushed as it felt. She slipped outside, closing the screen door quietly behind her so she could have a moment to herself.

It wasn't like her to flirt with a stranger, but the encounter had left her skin covered in goosebumps and her insides on fire. That had to be the reason she'd been so brazen. Either that, or her mother's younger spirit had possessed her, and she'd become a wanton hussy.

While packing up Charlotte's things, Ada had found a case full of journals dating back to well before she was born. The earlier tomes detailed her mother's carefree escapades as she flitted around the world, looking for inspiration and, apparently, a good lay. She'd always known Charlott was a flirt and a serial dater, but reading her mother's recounting of her many flings was like picking up a smutty romance novel.

She never named the men she was with, only referring to them by a distinctive trait or possibly an initial. Like her romantic picnic with "sideburns" or her rendezvous during a double feature with "T."

According to the journals, these trysts often inspired her work. The first painting she'd ever sold was "Good Genes." Ada now knew Charlotte had painted it after a weekend in Italy with a local barber who had amazing bone structure. That piece recently sold at auction for close to a hundred thousand dollars.

Unfortunately, her mother didn't bother to date the journals, so Ada had to jump around, attempting to put them in some sort of order based on events she was familiar with. She'd yet to find one from the time Charlotte spent at Heron House. But Paul had implied it was just before Ada came along. Was it possible she was conceived here? Would she finally learn the identity of her father?

Her skin had returned to its normal temperature, so she headed back into the house to find Riley. Maybe she would have some of the answers Ada sought.

She followed the sound of voices down the hall to a bright kitchen, where she found Riley with a handsome man in a suit. So far, Eastport Beach was full of attractive men.

His tie was loosened and his hair tousled, almost like someone had just run their fingers through it. Her hostess's cheeks turned bright pink when Ada cleared her throat to announce her arrival.

Riley grinned and hopped off the counter, grabbing the man's hand and jerking him forward. "Ben, this is Ada—Charlotte Maddox's daughter." She licked her swollen lips. "Ada, this is my boyfriend, Ben." The pink spread to the tips of Riley's ears, and she giggled like a teenager.

Ben reached out to shake Ada's hand, smiling at his girlfriend like she was the homecoming queen, and he hoped to be her loyal serf. "Great to meet you, Ada.

And thanks so much for coming. Your mother's work will be the highlight of the auction."

It was obvious to Ada that the two were in a fairly new relationship and completely gaga over one another. She was thrilled for them, and only 10% jealous. Briefly, she flashed back to her romp in the hallway with Trip. It had been a long time since she'd been gaga about a guy, and that had not gone well. She pushed aside thoughts of the opposite sex and returned Ben's handshake. "I'm excited to be here and hopefully learn more about my mother's time here. She's never been very forthcoming with details about her life, and now, even if she wanted to, she can't remember them."

Riley reached out to pat her shoulder. "It must be so hard."

"My mom and I have never been particularly close, mostly because she wasn't around much and as soon as I was old enough, I spent all my time dancing." Ada was used to her mother being absent in her life, but this felt different. She wasn't even sure how yet because it was still so new. "But thank you."

"Ben, will you take her to the study and show her the pieces we've pulled for the auction? I'm going to make us a batch of lemonade." Riley tossed a lemon in the air and caught it.

He led Ada back to the hallway and through a set of French doors. "Archie acquired a number of your mother's pieces over the years. He must have thought very highly of her work. Riley chose the ones that are in your suite to keep at Heron House, and we've got the rest here for the auction."

The room was packed tight, with a desk, loveseat and dozens of paintings leaning against the walls. They weren't all her mother's, but her eyes lit on Charlotte's stack immediately. She remembered the landscape in the front—a tableau created after a week-long jaunt to Napa Valley, which prevented Charlotte from seeing Ada's debut in the Nutcracker when she was nine. She could have caught the last show after she arrived home, but "inspiration is a fickle beast, and I must capture it when it shows its head." It wasn't the first time Ada had learned her mother's art was more important than her only child—and it hadn't been the last.

She thumbed through the pile, recognizing most of the pieces and feeling nothing. Not bitter, not nostalgic, just nothing.

When she got to the last piece, her breath caught in her throat, causing her to choke. She covered her mouth with her hand, letting the paintings fall back to cover up the piece she'd never seen before.

"Looks like I'm just in time." Riley slid a mason jar full of lemonade into Ada's free hand. The drink was the perfect blend of sweet and tart and soothed her scratchy throat, if not her shocked reaction to seeing herself on canvas.

Ben accepted a glass with a kiss to Riley's cheek. "We've found the provenance of all the pieces except the ballerina. Archie did a great job organizing everything until he got sick, so it's likely here somewhere. If we can't find it before the auction, we'll probably hang onto it. I did shoot Charlotte's manager an email, but he wasn't familiar with the piece."

It was rare for any piece not to go through Paul and his gallery. "It's possible it was a gift, because normally Paul would have a record of the sale." Feeling a little more prepared, Ada flipped to the last piece again, pulling it out of the pile. She looked around the crowded room. "Is there somewhere I can lay this down to get a closer look?"

"Of course." Riley led the way into the dining room and moved a few things to clear a space on the enormous table. "You don't think it's a fake, do you?"

Ada traced the gilded frame with her index finger, studying the lines of the painting, recognizing her mother's distinct brushstrokes. But the subject of the piece made her certain. Her teenage self stared back at her, posed mid step, wearing one of her favorite costumes. "It's definitely one of hers, even though I've never seen it before." It didn't make any sense. By that time in Ada's dance career, her mother had basically dropped out of her life—no longer pretending to be interested in her daughter's activities.

Riley looked from the painting to Ada and then back again, her face dawning with realization. "It's you, isn't it?"

"Yes, I traveled with a company throughout my teens, touring North America. Honestly, I don't remember my mother ever attending a performance." There was always something more pressing than watching one of her "little shows." Ada's breath got shallow, and her hands clammy. Before she realized what was happening, a drop of moisture fell onto the painting, just above her mother's signature.

"She obviously loved you very much. And captured you perfectly." Riley hooked an arm around Ada's shoulders and gave her a comforting squeeze. "You should keep this."

"No, no." She pushed away from the table and swiped at her eyes, angry that her emotions had betrayed her. "It's part of the estate. You can keep it. Or sell it." She stared through watery eyes at a girl who had felt so alone in the world. Her chest felt tight, and her throat was clogging up again. "Excuse me."

Ada rushed from the room and fled outside. She'd learned from an early age that crying over things you couldn't control didn't solve anything. It was better to keep those emotions sequestered inside and then draw on them when needed to make a dance sequence come to life. She didn't cry, let alone in public.

On the porch, she scanned the vista that lay before her, looking for a place of solace, a place she could collect herself and stuff down these unwelcome feelings. Seeing the gazebo in the distance, she scrambled down the stairs and across the green expanse of lawn, praying that Riley wouldn't follow her and ask what was wrong.

Because how did you deal with the realization that your mother wasn't completely closed off? That, maybe, just maybe, she felt love for the daughter that messed up all her big plans.

Chapter Six

He was halfway down the main stairs when Ada rushed out the front door. Riley stood in the doorway to the dining room, a confused look on her face.

"Everything okay?"

"I think she got a little emotional seeing her mother's work." She took a step into the hallway, but then backed up again, indecision evident in her demeanor.

He could see Ada running across the lawn, her hair flowing out behind her like a cape. She stopped at the gazebo, circled one arm around a post and stared out at the river. Something compelled him to follow her. Make sure she was okay.

A series of honks shattered his deliberation and the quiet of early evening. Manny's pickup truck lumbered up the driveway, followed by a parade of classic 70s and 80s automobiles. "Is it already seven?"

Riley checked her watch. "Nope, they're early. Must have been a slow day at the bait shop."

"Luckily, it'll take them twenty minutes to catch up before they come inside." The group of men had likely spent most of the day shooting the breeze at their local hangout—Manny's Bait & News—so Trip wasn't sure what they still had to talk about, but invariably, the men would linger around their cars for a while before coming inside to talk while they played poker. He'd never met people who enjoyed talking as much as these men—and Trip grew up in a political family, so that was saying a lot.

Ben appeared in the hallway. "Did I hear the guys pull up?"

"Yeah, you got some money burning a hole in your pocket tonight?" Trip ribbed his friend.

"Heck, no. I was just going to offer to help set up and then get out of here before the sharks start circling."

Riley laughed and patted Ben on the ass as she passed by him on her way to the kitchen. "I'll grab their snacks. Then I'll find a way to keep Ben occupied that won't cost him a dime."

Ben watched Riley enter the kitchen, an appreciative expression on his face. "Let's get this over with. I've got plans, apparently."

Trip shook his head and chuckled. He had watched as Riley and Ben fell in love and became each other's whole worlds. Admittedly, he was a little jealous of their easy affection. He hadn't been serious about a woman since Jennifer, and his mother had been more in love with her than he had.

He flashed back to his run-in with Ada and his body's immediate reaction to her. She was beautiful for sure and had even seemed interested. Out the screen door, he could just see the top of her head as she sat in the gazebo, her back to the house. He'd get the guys set up and then he'd go check on her. Maybe there could be something there.

"Who you moonin' over, boy?" Ralph, a retired football coach, pushed through the door, shoving a six-pack of light beer into Trip's arms. "You can get laid on your own time. My beer's getting warm."

And that was why Trip shouldn't play poker with these particular senior citizens. They could read him like a front-page headline.

Four more men streamed through the door, shoving their miscellaneous beverages at their host for the evening. The decibel level in the house immediately rose by a factor of five old farts.

By the time Trip had stashed everyone's BYOB in the fridge and returned to the parlor with a round of drinks, the poker table and six folding chairs were set up, and Ben had disappeared.

"Come on, young man"—Irwin patted the empty chair beside him—"this seat's getting cold."

"Oh, no, I'm not falling into your shark tank tonight. I'm just here to make sure you have what you need, and you don't get too rowdy."

"Rowdy? Please. You haven't seen rowdy until you've taken a weekend pass in Singapore with your platoon!"

A not un-rowdy cheer went up around the table.

Looks like the drinking started early tonight. Trip backed out of the room toward the front door. "I'll be back in ten. Try not to burn the place down."

The blue sky was dotted with a few fluffy white clouds, which would make for a stunning sunset, but that was still a while off. The air was warm, but September had turned the humidity dial down a notch, so combined with a breeze off the water, it was nearly the perfect temperature.

He crossed the lawn toward the gazebo, his shoes sinking slightly into the plush grass. With Google's help, Trip had coaxed this neglected expanse of green into the perfect setting for the upcoming party, which would relaunch Heron House to a new generation of artists and guests. As someone who grew up in a household with hired help, the satisfaction of hard work paying off in such a tangible way surprised him.

His mother couldn't show her face at her annual garden party because her disgraced son had spent the summer tending the lawn. His father was so checked out, he barely noticed. The true head of the family—Senator Carlton Westinghouse, Sr.—his grandfather, had asked him why he even bothered to get a law degree if he was going to squander his intelligence and pedigree.

The weight of his family's expectations weighed heavily on Trip. It was why he finished law school, despite the niggling in the back of his mind that he wanted nothing to do with his family's position in political circles. He'd assured them all he just needed the summer to decompress after eight intensive years of education. Then he'd buckle down and "make something out of his life."

This summer in Eastport Beach had shown him how other people lived. A genuine sense of community, not just showing up for the media and letting others do the hard work. The satisfaction of manual labor, the pride of figuring out how to solve a problem and seeing the end result. How real family cares for each other, even when there's no blood relation. He wanted to stay here, outside the Westinghouse bubble.

He slowed as he neared the gazebo, not wanting to catch Ada off guard. She stared out at the water, her knees pulled up, her arms wrapped tightly around them. Her face showed no emotion, but the sunlight glinted off a single tear on her cheek.

He cleared his throat, and her hand flew up toward her face, slashing at the dampness there. By the time she turned her head toward him, she had mustered up a weak smile. It didn't reach all the way to her eyes, but he was well-versed in fake smiles. His mother could have won an Emmy for hers.

"Can I join you?" He put one foot on the single step to the gazebo, hopeful she would at least allow him into her immediate vicinity, if not the depths of her emotions.

"Of course." She unfurled her limbs and scooted over to make room for him beside her.

The bench went the entire way around the hexagonal gazebo, so he took it as a sign she was open to sharing space with him.

"The nights here are the best. It cools down, the fireflies come out, and the moon's reflection off the river will take your breath away." He sat next to her, leaving more room than lovers but less than a stranger. She had seen him naked, after all.

"I came here straight from New York, and the air is so fresh and clean. It's like I can't breathe enough in."

"Is that where you live?"

"Not any longer. I was getting my mother's loft ready to be sold. I recently moved to Virginia because of a job, but now I'm not..." She trailed off, turning her head away from him. A small sniffle betrayed her, but he could tell it was important to her to hide her true emotions.

He slid an inch closer. "My family lives in Virginia as well. I'm supposed to go back soon, but I dread it."

"You don't like Virginia?"

"Virginia's fine."

Her hand moved from her lap to the space between them. He mimicked her movement, placing his own hand within an inch of hers.

"Family is hard." She spoke like a woman who knew this truth down to her very core.

He twitched his pinky in her direction. "My family is suffocating."

"Is the opposite any better?"

They sat in silence for a few minutes, staring out at the river, the air between them heavy. When the side of her hand met his, the contact raced up his arm and rocketed through his body. Just touching this woman's finger had him ready to throw her on the floor of this gazebo and get naked with her for the second time today.

"Do you have any plans for tomorrow?"

She turned her head, facing him. "No. I have zero plans."

"Can I show you around Eastport Beach?" The sun was sinking, the sky warming to a vibrant orange. He watched her face transform from neutral to crinkled eyes and upturned lips bathed in a warm glow.

"I would love that."

He slid his hand fully over hers, and she rotated her wrist, tangling their fingers together. He'd never felt such a perfect fit. "I've got to go babysit some potentially destructive old men now, but I'll meet you on the porch at ten tomorrow."

She laughed, and her face lit up brighter than the sunset. "What's the dress code?"

"I'll be fully clothed, but I can almost guarantee some nudity. This town will surprise you."

Chapter Seven

Sleep evaded her, and as the sun's first light penetrated the edges of the window shade, Ada gave up. She'd spent hours the night before scouring her mother's journals, trying to find anything about her time at Heron House, or something about the portrait she had hidden from her daughter. Charlotte's scribbles were as cryptic as the way she'd addressed Ada's questions growing up.

When asking about her dad at the age of six, after a particularly difficult Father's Day craft in school, Charlotte just waved her hand and said they would talk about it when she was older and could understand adult things.

At age nine, when she wanted to play soccer with her friends, but her mother couldn't be bothered to get her to practice on Saturday mornings because Friday nights were gallery nights—and oh, the wine, so much wine—Ada insisted that her father would take her, if only she knew him. He would make time for his daughter. Charlotte ended the discussion by explaining that in nature, most males of the species had little to do with rearing the offspring. Ada had spent the next year researching every type of creature that left their young to fend for themselves, because she knew, even then, that she was on her own.

She'd been riding the subway to her ballet classes for over three months before her mother even realized she was missing every Tuesday and Thursday for two hours after school. When Charlotte asked how she had paid for the classes, Ada explained that Paul had started giving her an allowance out of her mother's sales at the age of five when he discovered that the young child often had to fend for herself on nights when "inspiration took over" and her mother didn't bother to prepare dinner. Thankfully, they lived in a city where anything could be delivered, even if ordered by a kindergartener.

That was also when her weekly sleepovers started. Paul's wife, Elaine, would pick up Ada from school on Friday afternoons, and they would spend the weekend baking cookies and watching musicals. Ada loved anything with dancing in it. The couple had two older boys, so Elaine enjoyed her time with the little girl, which left Charlotte free to spend her nights gallery hopping with other artists.

When Ada was thirteen, she asked the now famous artist why she had her at all. Obviously, she was just in the way. Charlotte replied, "People told me a child would keep me grounded."

Not hard to read between those lines. Having a child had held her back.

At some point, Ada stopped inviting her mother to recitals. If she needed something for dance, she asked Paul, and he would take care of it. When she got her first period, she took a cab to Elaine's and spent the evening curled up on the couch eating rocky road ice cream and watching *Singing in the Rain* on a continuous loop.

Her talent allowed her to attend a residential fine arts program in high school. She traveled the country performing, including a major role in *Giselle*. To her knowledge, her mother never saw the show. Yet somehow, she painted Ada mid-step in her costume.

If anyone would know what it all meant, it was Paul. And Ada knew he and Elaine rose with the sun every morning, read a (legit) newspaper, and shared French press coffee.

The phone rang once. "Ada, sweetheart, is everything okay?"

"Yes, sorry to call so early, but I figured you'd be up. Tell Elaine I said hi." She heard him relay the message and then Elaine's cheerful voice echo back, "Good morning." Not for the first time, she wondered why she couldn't have been born to two wonderful parents like the Mallorys.

"Are you in North Carolina?"

"Yes, I arrived yesterday. Heron House is lovely. I can see why Charlotte liked it here."

"Yes, it's a beautiful setting."

Ada sat up a little straighter. "You've been here?'

There was a rustling noise, like he was moving around. "Yes, once."

She filed that bit of knowledge away for a later time. "Did you know about the painting?"

"The ballerina?" Paul had been Charlotte's manager from the very beginning of her career and knew her inside and out. He also knew Ada better than her own mother. Sometimes it was like he could read her mind. "I didn't, not until Riley sent me a picture of it."

"She never came to my shows, how did she... I mean, it's me, right?"

Paul sighed, like a man who had just unloaded fifty pounds of brick off his shoulders. "Of course it's you. And it's stunning." He paused, as always considering his words. "Ada, your mother was extremely proud of you. You had a dream, worked hard to achieve it and are a beautiful dancer. How could she not be proud? She's just in her own little bubble, can't always relate to what's going on outside her mind."

It had always been true, but now it was permanent. "Why hide it? And why is it here?"

"Who knows why Charlotte Maddox did anything. I know that's not a satisfying answer, but she loved keeping people on their toes and making them guess." He was silent for a few moments. "Ada, you deserved so much more than you got from her. You deserve everything wonderful in life."

This conversation was going to strange places, and she still had no clue when or how her mother had painted her. "How can we sell it without provenance?"

"Sell it? Why would you sell it?"

Tears threatened again. Ada didn't cry. Certainly not twice in a 24-hour period. "She hid it from me. She never intended for me to see it."

"Kiddo, don't decide right now. You have a few days, right?"

"Just tell me, Paul, please." She'd come here for answers, but now she wanted to run away from questions she hadn't asked.

He sighed again. "Pop the frame off. If she gifted the painting, she'll have made a notation under her signature. That will be good enough provenance. But promise me you'll at least think about keeping it."

"They killed my program."

"What?" He sounded shocked but didn't question the abrupt subject change.

"Some jerk politician pulled the funding for the arts grant. I don't have a job, I don't have a plan, and I have no place to hang a giant portrait of myself. But I'll think about it. For you."

"If you want to come back to New York, you always have a place with us."

She shook her head, even though he clearly couldn't see her. "No, New York is not my home." The city had taken too much from her, and she wouldn't go back. She'd thought she could make a new home in Virginia, but now she wasn't sure about anything.

They exchanged goodbyes, and Ada figured it was early enough that the occupants of the house might still be asleep.

She listened at the door and, hearing nothing, pushed it open a crack. As the only guest right now, the hallway should be, and was, empty. She tiptoed toward the staircase and once again strained to listen for noises. The first floor appeared as quiet as the second.

Being a dancer, she was naturally light on her feet, and the stairs didn't betray her as she descended. The main floor of the house was dark and quiet. She crept into the dining room, where she'd last seen the painting. Using the light on her phone, she found it right where she had left it yesterday.

Flipping the picture over, she examined it for any markings or notations. A thick, waxy paper covered the back of the canvas, and a simple notecard near the bottom read simply, "Charlotte Maddox, The Enjoué Period".

Paul might be able to narrow down the timeframe with this information, but it was clearly after Ada had danced in *Giselle*.

She tilted the painting up and studied the frame's construction. She would need tools to disassemble it. But maybe she could make do with a butter knife. As she laid the piece back on the table, her flashlight glinted off something glittery. Upon closer examination, she realized that Charlotte had added glitter to the tiara Ada wore in the painting. Her mother. THE Charlotte Maddox. The woman who once told her seven-year-old daughter that her picture portraying a hippopotamus wearing a tutu and a crown—a glitter crown, of course—was unexceptional and something the child of a normal parent would produce.

Just how long had her mother been suffering from dementia? Because the woman Ada knew would never allow glitter in her house, let alone on her art.

She flopped down in a chair, rubbing her tired eyes and trying to make sense of it all. The painting, the diagnosis, her job being ripped away, everything falling apart. It was lack of sleep that was all. No one could have perspective after tossing and turning all night. Ada didn't allow herself to feel defeated. She picked up the pieces and did what needed to be done. She was THE Charlotte Maddox's offspring, after all.

With a heaving sigh, she pushed up out of the chair and headed toward the kitchen. But when she stepped into the hallway, she ran straight into a bare, toned chest. Again.

Strong arms encircled her, steadying her. Trip's chest vibrated with laughter. "I'd like to point out that I have pants on this time."

What a shame. Her face was pressed against a smooth chest, her hands rested against defined pectoral muscles. It felt nice. Safe. Comforting. She could just wrap her hands around his torso and return the hug. But something held her back.

Regretfully, she slid out of his arms and stepped away. He was wearing blue and green board shorts and nothing else. She allowed herself a moment to appreciate the fine male specimen in front of her. By the time her gaze landed on his face, the cocky smile there told her that he appreciated her appreciation.

"Going out on the water this early? The sun's barely up."

"I've got some lawn work to take care of, and I wanted to do it before it got too hot. This way, I can just jump in the river when I get overheated." He made zero effort to hide his lingering gaze as it roamed over her body.

Suddenly, she realized how little clothing she had come down in. Lack of sleep was definitely affecting her common sense. Who wandered around a strange house in tiny shorts and a thin tank top?

He reached out and slid the strap of her top back onto her shoulder. "Looks like the river might be my first stop, after all."

The heat in his eyes brought a flush to her cheeks. It had been a long time since a man looked at her like that. Feeling naked suddenly, she crossed her arms over her chest. Her nipples were trying to bore a hole through the gauzy material of her shirt. She gulped but held his gaze. "We still on for later, or do you need to stay here and work?"

His hand traced down her bare arm, leaving a trail of goosebumps in its wake. "Wild horses couldn't keep me away."

Relief flooded her. She couldn't remember the last time she was this excited to go out with someone. But was this even a date? Or just a friendly guy showing her around town? Was she reading too much into this?

Trip leaned forward, bringing his mouth close to her ear, and his sheer maleness overwhelmed her senses. "I hope you're as excited as I am."

His breath heated the sensitive skin of her neck and sent a lightning bolt down her body. She couldn't speak, so she just nodded.

He pulled back slightly, and she could see the grin spread over his fine features. "Good." He pressed his lips against her cheek, less than an inch from her mouth—and her knees buckled. Not missing a beat, he steadied her once again and led her toward the kitchen. "Let's get some protein in you. We've got a busy day ahead of us, and you'll need your strength."

Holy moly. What did he have planned? It didn't really matter, because those wild horses couldn't keep her away either.

Chapter Eight

What Trip wanted for breakfast was Ada. Her skimpy outfit showcased her lean, athletic body and left little to his imagination—although he was pretty creative and had some ideas.

He started chopping veggies and ham for omelets and threw a pan of bacon in the oven while she squeezed oranges using Riley's fancy new juicer.

"Do you always get up this early?" He'd never been an early riser himself, but it was worth it to get the yard work done before the heat of midday.

She covered a yawn with her hand. "No, I didn't sleep much last night. Maybe just adjusting to a new place, I guess."

He got the sense she wanted to say more, but she turned back to her task.

"I've got to be back here by three to help Ben with a project, so maybe you can get a nap in later."

"Yeah, maybe." She pulled her bottom lip into her mouth, her tongue peeking out.

His shorts were getting tighter by the minute. He might have to take a cold shower instead of dunking in the river. At least then he'd have a little privacy. "I don't really have a set schedule around here, so some days I pass out in one of the hammocks we have strung up in the live oaks behind the house. I can show you if you're interested."

"Sounds like a sweet setup. Kayaking, naps in a hammock, free reign of the kitchen."

He laughed as he flipped the first omelet. "Riley is pretty much a disaster in the kitchen. Her best dish is lemonade."

"I've had it. Best I've ever tasted."

"Yeah, well, the same can't be said of her cinnamon rolls. She hasn't mastered baking yet. Ben and I split the cooking. I'm not sure what they'll do when I leave. Riley might starve while Ben's at work."

She turned to face him, leaning against the counter. "You're leaving?" She snapped her fingers. "Oh yeah, back to Virginia."

"Unfortunately. I'm staying through the weekend, but then duty calls." Unless the universe intervened, and his grandfather and parents finally came to their senses. From the increasingly frequent phone calls, it didn't look promising.

"Duty?"

"I smell bacon." Riley's raspy morning voice preceded her into the kitchen and saved him from having to answer the dreaded question. She appeared, like magic, through the secret passageway her uncle, Archie, had built into the butler's pantry. Trip had never met the man, but his spirit lingered in every inch of this house.

He stepped away from the stove long enough to pour his boss a mug of coffee. "You're up early."

She took the mug from him and dug around the refrigerator for creamer. "So much to do, not enough time."

"Is Ben up?" He plated the first omelet, added two strips of bacon and slid the plate in front of Ada, who was seated at the kitchen table.

"Yes, but he went in early so he could be home by the time the truck gets here." She stirred her coffee and turned toward the table. "Gosh, I'm sorry, Ada! Where are my manners? Did you sleep okay? Do you want coffee?"

Ada smiled up at her, a bite of eggs poised halfway to her mouth. "No, I'm not a coffee drinker, but your juicer is amazing."

"I know, right? That thing saves me so much time and you don't waste a drop of juice. Ben bought it for me when he realized I was juicing a dozen lemons a day by hand. He's the best."

Trip watched as the two women bantered, continuously scraping the pan so the eggs wouldn't burn. Growing up with a live-in cook and housekeeper, he wasn't allowed to "play around" in the kitchen. His senior year of college, he and Chesnee rented an apartment and for the first time, Trip got to experiment with cooking. He took classes, scoured the internet for recipes, and eventually got comfortable creating his own dishes.

He slid the second omelet out of the pan and handed it to Riley.

"Trip, I'm going to waste away when you leave. I need you to fill up the freezer with your lasagna." She turned to Ada. "It's to die for."

"I've already put two pans in there and a hash brown casserole. With reheating instructions written on top." He had become very attached to Riley and Ben. Leaving them was going to be exceptionally hard.

"He cooks, he does yard work, he gets the groceries. Trip, you'll make someone a fine husband one day." Riley shoved a piece of bacon in her mouth.

He shook his head but smiled as he slid the final omelet out of the pan. Too bad his family would scare away any woman who might be interested. "Guess I need to find me a woman to pay the bills so I can stay home barefoot and pregnant."

"I know times have changed, but I don't think they've changed quite that much." His boss was halfway through her omelet, talking between bites.

He joined the women at the table and bit into a crispy strip of bacon. "Ada, you must think we're nuts." Riley had become one of his closest friends and they loved saying outrageous things to each other.

"I'm just over here trying to picture you pregnant."

They all laughed, then ate in silence for a few moments before Riley jumped up from the table. "Ada, would you like one of my cinnamon rolls?"

Trip and Ada exchanged a smile, and he felt warm all the way down to his bare feet.

***

He was throwing the last branch on the wheelbarrow when his phone rang. Tugging his work gloves off, Trip tapped his earpiece to answer the call. "Hello?"

"Trip, my boy." His father always called him "my boy" right before he asked him for a favor.

He steered the brush he'd cleared toward the spot he and Ben had set up for a bonfire later in the week. "Hey Dad. What's up?"

"I heard about your little party this weekend and I was hoping you could scrounge up an invite for your old man."

Why was his family suddenly so interested in Heron House? The last thing he wanted was to inflict the Westinghouses on the sweet town of Eastport Beach. "Are you coming down with Mom? Riley saved a room for her."

"I can never keep up with your mother's plans, son. I've booked a suite at the Hilton."

"The closest Hilton is an hour away in Wilmington."

"Good thing I have a fast car."

Trip dumped the debris he'd collected on top of the pile, then leaned against the wheelbarrow, trying to get back to the zen he'd discovered while he was clearing the land on Ben's property.

46

"Son?"

"Yeah, Dad, you're welcome to come to the party. It starts at six on Saturday."

A horn blared across the line. "That's my boy. It will be great to catch up."

"I'll be working the party, Dad. There won't be much time for catching up." Trip didn't believe for a minute that his father wanted to bond with his only son. There was an ulterior motive at play, and he wouldn't allow his family's drama to ruin Riley's big day. "Promise me that you and Mom will behave. This is a big deal for my friends. No scenes, okay?"

"Trip, give your old man a little credit. I practically do this for a living. Your mother and I can act civilized in public."

If history was an indication, this was a disaster in the making.

Chapter Nine

"Riley, do you have a minute?" Ada poked her head through the open door of the study. She had showered and dressed for the day, but she had a couple hours to kill before her date with Trip. Surely the almost kiss meant it was a date.

Riley was bent over her desk digging through a towering stack of leather books and loose papers.

"I'm sorry, you're obviously busy."

"No, no, it's fine. I was just trying to find something. About your mother, actually."

Ada inched closer to the desk but tried to curtail her hope of answers about her mother's time here. "Oh yeah? What's that?"

Her host waved one of the books through the air. "My uncle had a system. I just can't figure it out. Anyway, I remember seeing your mother's name—either in one of these journals, or a letter, or something."

"I wonder if the chaos is an artist thing, because Charlotte's journals are the same way. It's like she just picked whichever book was closest and wrote down gibberish that has no rhyme or reason. Everything is out of order."

Riley looked contemplative. "Maybe. I never got to meet Archie, so I don't really know much about him." She tossed the journal back on the pile. "Anyway, what did you need?"

Now Ada was itching to get her hands on Archie's journals as well and see if they would reveal anything about his relationship with her mother. "I spoke to my mom's manager this morning and he told me to take the frame off the ballerina piece to see if there's a notation. Are you okay with that? I've seen her disassemble and reassemble paintings so many times, I'm sure I can do it carefully."

"Sure, of course. Without provenance, it technically belongs to you as far as I'm concerned. What tools do you need?"

"A butter knife, or letter opener, to start. Once I get the backing off, I'll know more."

Riley brandished a bronze letter opener shaped like a feather. "Will this work?"

"Perfect."

The two women trooped down the hall and entered the dining room where the painting still lay on the huge table. Every time Ada saw it, her stomach clenched, and her head throbbed. How could she possibly display this and see it on a regular basis? She prayed they would find answers under the frame so they could auction it off and she'd never have to see it again.

Flipping it over, she let out a whoosh of air. *Let's get this over with.* Taking the letter opener from Riley, she carefully slid it under the brown paper covering the back of the canvas. She hoped to keep it intact, because it was doubtful a small town like Eastport Beach had archival grade paper available.

"There are all kinds of framing supplies in one of the rooms on the third floor. I'm pretty sure there's a roll of that paper." A fluffy gray cat jumped up on the dining room table to see what they were up to. Riley stroked its back, but the cat quickly moved to the other side of the table. "That's Ansel. He's nosy as hell, but a bit of a snob. He loves Ben and Trip, but he still hasn't figured out if I'm an acceptable choice of companion."

"Was he your uncle's cat?"

Riley nodded.

"Maybe he's just used to men. Was Archie ever married?" Ada carefully pried a staple out of the wood frame.

"That makes sense. Even though there were often guests here, Archie was his person. Ben said he never really dated anyone seriously during the time he knew him."

Another staple released its grip, and the paper backing pulled away from the frame. Charlotte always stretched her own canvas, and Ada was certain this piece was no different. She had also painted all the way to the edge of the canvas, another surefire way to authenticate the piece. But who was she kidding? There was no way this was anything but a real Charlotte Maddox. Her eyes staring back at her were all the proof Ada needed.

"Did you always want to be a dancer?" Riley sat in one of the dining chairs, staying close, but not crowding Ada as she worked.

"Pretty much. Our neighbor was a professional ballet dancer and when she was in town, she'd let me come over and watch videos of her performances. I loved the costumes and the graceful movements and the music. She taught me my first few steps one evening when my mother was late getting home. From then on, all I wanted was to dance."

"How old were you when you started?"

"At six, I started ballet. My mom was gone a lot, so I added more classes as I got older. Tap, hip hop, jazz, ballroom."

"Ballroom? Really?" Riley bounced in her chair. "Oh, my goodness! Can you teach me? I mean, us? Before the gala?"

Ada chuckled at her excitement. "Sure, I can give you and Ben a few pointers. What kind of music will you have at the gala?"

"We have a band. The playlist is a mix of classic rock, crossover country, a few more current songs, but nothing too wild or loud. More background music. You know, keep it classy."

"Okay, that's doable. There are a couple easy dances I can show you that will work well with most music. When do you want to do it?"

"How about tonight? We can move the furniture in the parlor to make a dance floor." She clapped her hands. "This is so exciting!"

"Ballroom dancing is so much fun and it's something that's really accessible to most people. You'll love it." Ada had done a few competitions over the years, but it was hard to find a consistent partner, so she had dropped off. It would be fun to dust off her dancing shoes again.

Returning to her task, she slid the letter opener between the canvas and the wood of the frame, and the painting popped free. The back revealed no information, so she braced herself before she flipped it over once again.

There was writing on the edge of the canvas, just below her mother's signature, but she couldn't make it out. "Do you have a magnifying glass?"

"I think I've seen one somewhere in the study." Riley hurried out of the room, leaving Ada alone with—well, herself—in painting form.

She squinted, trying to read what her mother had scrawled, but her eyesight wasn't great, and she hadn't taken the time to see an eye doctor in years. Something to add to her ever-growing list. Make a plan. Find a job. Sell the loft. Get eyes checked.

"Ta-da!" Riley reappeared, waving a brass handled magnifying glass.

"Awesome, thanks." Ada bent close to the edge of the canvas, holding the glass over her mother's slanted handwriting.

Archie—A reminder of what you helped create. Always, Charlotte.

Her mouth dried up, like she'd had oral surgery and the dentist had stuffed her cheeks full of cotton. Another thing she hadn't done in a while. Teeth cleaning—add it to the list. She leaned heavily against the back of her chair, suddenly unable to bear the weight of her own body.

"What's it say?" Riley leaned closer, trying to get a look.

Ada wordlessly handed over the magnifying glass, unable to process yet another of her mother's cryptic messages.

Riley pulled the painting closer to her and studied the words, then looked back to Ada. "What's that supposed to mean?"

Flinging her head back, Ada let out a gush of air. "Heck if I know. My mother had a habit of being clear as mud." Once more, Charlotte Maddox left her only child feeling completely lost and alone. She couldn't begin to formulate the thought that was banging around her head like a pinball. She was scared to even think it, let alone say the words out loud.

Could Archibald Kirkwood be her father?

Chapter Ten

After his second shower of the day, Trip was waiting on the porch when Ada came through the screen door ten minutes early. Maybe he wasn't the only one looking forward to this date.

She had changed out of her skimpy shorts into a flowing white dress that danced around her slender legs. Her hair was held back at her neck with a clasp and a curtain of shining brown hair cascaded over one shoulder.

He stepped forward, reaching for her hand. "You are stunning." He kissed her delicate knuckles, his lips lingering long after an appropriate amount of time. If her rosy cheeks were any indication, she didn't mind the extra attention.

"You pull off fully dressed quite well."

He chuckled and smoothed out the polo he had tucked into khaki shorts. "It's still early." He gave her a quick wink before descending the steps. He stopped short when he saw the bicycles parked beside the fountain. "I thought we could ride into town, but with your pretty dress, we can just take my car."

"No, I'll be fine. I can just tuck the skirt up. Riding bikes will be fun." She flowed down the steps and began to gather her long skirt. "Which one's mine?"

Trip was enjoying the view as the skirt rose higher and higher. "Um, either is fine." He watched in awe as she knotted her skirt and mounted the bicycle, making sure the material wouldn't catch anywhere.

"You coming?" She pedaled off down the driveway, leaving Trip standing like a slack-jawed fool beside the fountain.

Shaking his head to clear it, he jumped on his bike and pedaled after her. He should lead the way, but he was enjoying the view from behind far too much. Everything this woman did, she did gracefully. He called out, loud enough for her to hear. "We're going to go left when we get to the road. It's a straight shot from there."

She glanced over her shoulder, a huge smile on her face. "You sure you don't mind the woman leading? Most men want to be in control."

He was pretty sure he'd let her lead him anywhere. "There are some advantages to taking a backseat."

As if she understood his innuendo, she wiggled her bottom above the seat.

He was toast.

At the end of the driveway, Trip pulled alongside her, panting slightly from trying to catch up. Ada looked fresh as ever, no signs that the ride had winded her.

"Do you ride often?" He admired her long, strong legs.

"Not in a while. But it's like riding a bike, huh?" She laughed at her silly joke.

"I hadn't been on a bike since high school, but Riley bought a few last month for guests to use, so I've been riding into town instead of using my car. Unless I have to get groceries or something else for the house. I'd forgotten what a great workout it is."

Ada didn't hide her assessment of his body. "Kayaking, biking, whatever you're doing, it's working."

Before he could recover from the compliment, she'd turned onto River Road and was pedaling effortlessly away from him. Damn. He couldn't remember the last time a woman had made him feel this good.

The road was clear, so he took off after her. He was happy to chase her a little, because he felt pretty certain she wanted him to catch her.

They rode in silence until the road ended. At the stop sign, Ada waited for him to catch up. Trip pulled up beside her and stopped. He spun his backpack around and pulled out two bottles of water, handing her one.

"Thanks." She smiled and then tilted her head back and downed half the bottle.

The long line of her neck begged for his attention, but he couldn't very well maul her on Main Street. The entire town would know in two point five seconds. "Welcome to Eastport Beach." He chugged some water and returned both bottles to his bag. "We'll walk from here, because if you pedal through, you'll miss everything." He dismounted from his bike and pushed it over to a small park with a fountain, benches and a couple bike racks.

Ada followed suit, and soon he had both bikes secured to the racks.

"Which way?" She turned her head from side to side, looking both directions.

Trip saw an opening and stepped closer to her, placing his hand at the small of her back, and turned her to the west. "Well, if you go that way, you'll be out of Eastport in about a block. That's the way to fast-food chains and big box stores." He slid his hand farther to grip her waist, then spun her in the opposite direction. "This way will take us through the true Eastport Beach. When you hit the water, that means you've seen everything."

"I can see the water from here."

"Told you you'd blink and miss it." Eastport Beach might be small, but it was the first place Trip had ever felt happy, comfortable. He found himself even more excited to share it with Ada.

They started walking, and he was delighted when she didn't pull away, so he kept his arm around her waist and pointed out the highlights of downtown.

"That's Murray's. It's kind of a combination market, grocery and wine store. It usually has anything you need, unless a hurricane is coming to town, then the alcohol sells out immediately."

She laughed and leaned farther into his embrace. "It sounds like the bodegas in New York City. Everything you need and things you never knew you needed."

"Exactly, except you can't get a pastrami on rye. You'll have to hit The Spicy Mermaid for that." The diner sat next to Murray's and shared a parking lot in the back. "Lewis and Maude run the Mermaid, but everyone knows Maude's in charge. We can grab lunch on the way back if you want."

"Yes, please!" Ada stared in the windows of the diner where the fifties met an under the sea motif. "What time do they open?"

"They only serve breakfast on the weekends, and it's a real treat. During the week they open at eleven."

"I suppose I can make it 'til then. Someone made me a whopping omelet this morning." She looked up at him, her eyes twinkling.

Trip was tall, somewhere between 6'3" and 6'4" depending on his shoes, and it was hard to find women who fit his body well. Ada was tall and lean, he guessed maybe 5'9", and his arm landed at the perfect spot on her waist. He wouldn't have to stoop much to kiss her either. Which he was getting desperate to try out. And not just her cheek this time.

"I can't guarantee an omelet every morning, but I'll try to have a good breakfast option for you so you can avoid Riley's baking."

"How bad can a cinnamon roll be?" They continued down the sidewalk, pausing every time they came to another business.

Trip grimaced. "You can't say I didn't warn you." He pointed across the street. "That's Manny's Bait & News." He waved at the men clustered out front in camping chairs, but most of them were focused on their lottery tickets. "If you need to know what's going on in Eastport, that's the place to go. The rest of the world lags a little behind. The Wall Street Journal is from last week."

"Are those the rowdy fellas that were at Heron House last night?"

"Yeah, we host their weekly poker game. They were a little extra last night because Ralph won a $20 scratch off. Started drinking before lunch."

They reached a building that had paper over its windows. Ada pulled away from him to peek through a crack. "What's this place?"

Most of the buildings along Main Street were historic and this was no exception. The entry was inset between two plate glass window displays with mosaic tile lining the vestibule. "It was a gallery until about a week ago. The couple who ran it retired and moved to be closer to their grandkids. I'm not sure if it's been rented yet."

"I can see hardwoods and those old tin ceilings. It reminds me of the first dance school I ever attended. During tap classes, the sound would echo back off the metal. It was so satisfying. Like you could hear your own performance."

Trip mentally slapped himself. Of course, she was a dancer. It made complete sense. "Do you still dance?"

One side of her mouth quirked up. "Any chance I get. In fact, Riley asked me to teach her and Ben some moves tonight for the gala."

"Oh really?" He couldn't believe his luck. "Any chance you need a partner for the lesson? I learn quickly."

She propped one hand on her hip and appraised him openly. "I don't know, do you have any rhythm? Maybe a quick audition's in order?"

Dancing was his secret weapon, but he decided to save the bulk of the surprise for Saturday. If he hadn't swept her off her feet by then. So instead of a full display, he grabbed her and spun her around in a basic box step before dipping her.

She was laughing from the moment he touched her and by the time she was leaning back in his arms, the wattage of her smile could compete with the sun. "Well, aren't you full of surprises?"

"I like to think so." He set her back on her feet and took her hand before they continued down the street.

A second later, he heard a familiar beep beep and slowed so Ada could fully appreciate Eastport Beach's most eccentric resident. Sure enough, Captain Percy rode past them on his bicycle, complete with eyepatch and Sami, the stuffed parrot.

Ada stood, mouth agape, staring as Percy rode away. "Um, was that man naked?"

"Technically, the parrot covers the unmentionables, or else the sheriff will fine him, and Captain Percy is a tight wad. Doesn't like to share his booty with anyone."

"I'm pretty sure he's sharing his booty with the entire town."

Trip doubled over with laughter. "I suppose you're right."

The two clung to each other laughing. "Let me guess," Ada said between her guffaws, "he's the Eastport Beach version of The Naked Cowboy."

He nodded and they said in unison, "The Naked Pirate." They dissolved in another fit of laughter.

After collecting themselves, Trip indicated they should cross the road. "I did promise you nudity today."

"I guess I was just expecting fewer wrinkles." She wiped at her eyes, which were watering. "You look way better with your clothes off."

He leaned in close to her, hovering mere inches from her lips. "Just say the word, darlin'."

Her eyes grew and he realized they weren't green like he'd thought last night, but more teal, like the Caribbean Sea, and he wanted to drown in them. He was so fixated on her eyes that when she closed the distance between them and crushed her lips to his, it knocked him off balance and he fell backward, his arms flailing to gain purchase. He could only imagine his expression as he landed on his ass in the grass in front of Ben's office.

"Has it been so long since a woman kissed you that your legs gave out?"

He tilted his head back to find Chesnee standing on the porch of the old Victorian, phone in hand. Unfortunately, his friend wasn't far off the mark. He just wished he hadn't witnessed it.

"Don't worry, brah. I got it all on film." He held up his phone triumphantly. "By the way, I'm Chesnee."

Trip wasn't sure how he did it, but suddenly his manwhore of a friend was in front of Ada, gripping her hand between his and raising it to his mouth. *Oh, hell no.*

"You don't have to worry about me passing out if you feel the need to lay one on me."

Ben appeared on the porch. "Chesnee, the phone is ringing." He waited until the leech had released Ada's hand and was ascending the stairs. "Forgive my assistant, Ada. He can't control himself around a beautiful woman. But don't worry, he's mostly bluster." Ben waved and went back inside the house that he'd converted into his law office.

Trip finally gathered his wits and rose from the grass, dusting his shorts off. "I'm so sorry, you just caught me off guard."

She smiled up at him, smoothing his collar down. "It's okay, I was feeling a little impulsive. Do I need to worry about him posting that to the Internet?"

Chapter Eleven

At her performing arts school, the girls had outnumbered the boys eight to one. The competition to date one of the straight ones was fiercer than any audition. So, Ada never had the chance to stroll around town holding a boy's hand as a teenager. Walking through Eastport Beach now with an attractive man gripping her hand was fulfilling all those childhood fantasies.

The kiss had surprised even her, because she'd never been the one to make a move. Hopefully now that he knew she was interested, he'd take the lead and neither of them would end up on the ground next time.

As if he could read her mind, Trip squeezed her hand gently and smiled down at her. She loved his height. A lot of men that asked her out were shorter than her, and the height difference made her feel awkward. Nothing about her time with Trip had felt awkward, well, except for the whole naked thing, but honestly, it had been a great icebreaker and she guessed it was part of the reason she felt so comfortable with him. She hadn't been the naked one, after all. Now that would be awkward.

They passed a large white church with an attached playground full of screaming toddlers. The kids were happily swinging, climbing play structures and sailing down slides. It was a warm day, but the towering live oak trees provided shade for the children.

"I love the trees here. They have so much character."

"Yeah, especially with the Spanish moss. It gives it a spooky quality all year long."

"The whole town is ready for Halloween—no decorating necessary." They stopped in front of a tiny storefront that simply said "Candy" on the sign. "And here's the candy!" The shop was dark, but she pressed her hands against the window to see inside.

"This is Ida Mae's. She'll be open later. Her fudge is legendary."

"Ooo. I love chocolate." She clapped her hands together. Normally, she'd only allow herself a taste, but who knew what the future held? She might never perform again, so maybe she could indulge a little. And she wasn't just thinking about chocolate.

Trip laughed at her excitement. "We'll definitely grab some after lunch."

Main Street was slowly coming to life as they walked toward the water. It was so different from where she grew up. "It's so peaceful here."

"Yeah, nothing like the big city. At first, I thought it might be boring, having spent so much time in D.C.. There's usually something going on, but it's a slower pace and there's lots of opportunity to just soak in nature. I'm really going to miss it."

There it was again. She kept forgetting that he wasn't a permanent resident here either. She looked up at him. "It suits you."

He sighed and took her hand again, pulling her across the street to a cafe. There was a large mug decal on the window, with a sailboat floating on the wavy brown surface. "I know you don't drink coffee, but this place has the best pastries. I highly recommend the cream horns."

He obviously didn't want to talk about leaving, so she accepted the change of subject. "None of my clothes will fit if I stay here too long." She grinned up at him.

"Now you know why I kayak and bike and run all the time."

Without her job teaching dance, she'd have to find a new way to keep her trim form. Standing this close to a hot man like Trip, she could think of one way to burn a lot of calories. They'd both be gone in a few days, never to see each other again. What would be the harm in a little fling? She'd never done anything like that, but maybe it was what she needed to shake things up a bit. She would never stoop to her mother's level of sleeping with anyone with a Y chromosome, but one guy—one really nice, hot guy—couldn't hurt, right? She trailed her finger down his chest to his abs. "No evidence of pastries or fudge that I can see."

His eyes darkened and a salacious grin spread over his smooth jaw. "And you would have seen it."

She pushed up on her toes to get closer to him, but then a bell jangled, and a group of elderly women exited the cafe.

"Trip! How's everything coming along at Heron House?" A woman with hot pink streaks in her white hair placed her hand on his arm. "Does Riley need us to come help set up for the gala?" The woman, who was clearly old enough to be his grandmother, squeezed his bicep.

Ada covered her laugh as Trip's face turned bright red.

"No, thank you, Ms. Windsor. We've got it under control. But we're excited to see you there."

The older woman seemed reluctant to let go of her prize, but a shorter woman wearing a muumuu covered in flamingos grabbed her arm and pulled her away. "Leave that poor boy alone, Edna. Why would he need an old hag like you when he has this cute, young thing? I swear." She rolled her eyes and yanked Edna farther away. "Have some decorum."

"Some men prefer experience over youth!"

"All men prefer grapes over prunes, Edna."

Ms. Windsor huffed, and the group shuffled across the street to the church.

Once they were (hopefully) out of earshot, Ada leaned her head against Trip's chest to muffle her laughter. His chest vibrated with a silent chuckle and his hands slid up to rub her back.

"I'm sure I can find my way back to Heron House if you want to go after her." She could barely get the words out, she was laughing so hard.

"I gotta admit, I'm a little curious about her experience." He buried his face in her hair, his whole body shaking.

Ada pulled back, trying to collect herself. "You're right, Eastport Beach is really something else. Maybe you and Edna can double date with me and Captain Percy."

"Oh, got your eye on the Naked Pirate, huh? I'm not sure I can compete with the parrot."

She couldn't remember the last time she'd felt this carefree. She hooked her arm around his waist. "You're going to need a bigger bird."

***

After exploring the marina and then having lunch at The Spicy Mermaid, Ada felt more comfortable with Trip than she had with any other man she'd dated. Her only serious relationship had been intense and short-lived. The entire thing had been secret, stealing moments in between shows in different hotels, in different cities. She saw now that it never stood a chance. But then, the end had been devastating.

Trip was the opposite of her former lover in every way. He was kind, and attentive, and confident without being cocky. He was taller, funnier, and more age appropriate. It was a shame that he could only be a fling.

They were crossing the street to Ida Mae's when a convertible pulled alongside them and honked. Trip said something under his breath, pulling her closer to him.

"You getting bored with my man, Trip, yet?" Chesnee slid his sunglasses down his nose and winked.

Ada snaked her arm around Trip's waist and leaned into him. "No, not yet. I've only seen him naked twice and I'm eager for a few more times."

Chesnee's mouth gaped. "Didn't you just get here yesterday?"

Trip squeezed her side. "Pretty sure that beats your record, bud." He turned and propelled them up to the stoop of the little candy shop. "See you later, Chesnee."

As they pushed through the door, she glanced over her shoulder to see a stunned Chesnee driving away. "I'm guessing he's the town playboy."

"He acts like it, but really he's got the hots for someone he can't have."

"Why not? He's good-looking and charismatic." She'd had charismatic and it wasn't a trait she desired anymore.

Trip shook his head and shrugged. "No one knows. Chesnee will talk to a wall, but he won't talk about what went down with Gina."

"Ooo, small town gossip. Sounds meaty."

"Yeah, for a place where everyone knows everyone else's business, Chesnee and Gina have done a remarkably good job keeping their past a secret. But whenever they're in the same room, it's like waiting for a bomb to go off. The tension is palpable. You'll see."

The candy shop was tiny, reminding Ada of the ice cream shop in her neighborhood growing up. NYC Scoops was little more than a lean-to at the back of an alley between high-rises—but its bubble gum ice cream couldn't be beat.

Ida Mae's was cleaner than Scoops, with walls the color of rainbow sherbert and a long display case painted purple. It smelled like warm chocolate, so intensely she thought she could taste it. Ada was drooling over the rows of fudge when a gnarled lady the size of a Keebler elf appeared from the back room.

"Young people! Welcome. I assume you've come for a sweet treat after a healthy lunch." Ida Mae was wrinkled but spry. "What'll it be today? I've got a fresh batch of maple walnut." She grabbed a purple box and eyed the couple with anticipation.

"The maple walnut is my favorite, so I'll take some of that, Ms. Ida." Trip slid his hand behind Ada, tweaking the side of her waist. He leaned closer to her ear and spoke in a low tone. "You can't go wrong with any of the flavors. If you want chocolate, maybe we can do a little trade."

Between the smell of heaven and Trip's breath tickling her neck, Ada was overcome with an influx of sensations. She breathed deeply, straining to focus on the fudge behind the glass and not the pinch of desire deep in her gut. Maybe she'd get to indulge in two forbidden pleasures this week.

"I'll have the turtle, please, ma'am." A thick layer of caramel over creamy chocolate was more than she could resist.

"Call me, Ms. Ida, honey. Are you new to town?" The older woman added a thick slab of the turtle fudge to the purple box.

"Yes, ma'am. Um, I mean, Ms. Ida. I'm visiting Heron House."

Ida Mae's face lit up, briefly smoothing out her wrinkles. "Lovely. Are you an artist, dear?"

"No, but my mother is. She studied here many years ago."

"Ada's a dancer, Ms. Ida. So, I'd argue she is an artist of sorts." Trip's grip on her waist grew tighter.

She tilted her head to the side and looked up at him. "You haven't even seen me dance."

"Oh, I can tell." His eyes twinkled and for a moment, it looked like he might lean down and kiss her right there in front of the candy maker.

The spell between them was broken when Ida Mae stepped from behind the counter and spun around in her orthopedic shoes. "I auditioned for the Rockettes. But they said my legs weren't long enough." She gave a little kick, which made it about four inches off the ground.

"Their loss, Ms. Ida." Trip released Ada's waist and grabbed the older woman, spinning her around the room. "You've still got plenty of moves."

The juxtaposition of the pair was more than Ada could handle, and she busted out laughing. Ida Mae hit Trip mid-chest, and she couldn't lean back far enough to make eye contact with him. Their dancing future was doomed.

As Trip dipped the older woman, Ada clapped and whistled. Ida Mae curtsied and went back behind the counter, her cheeks flushed with life.

"As lovely as that was, it won't keep the lights on. That'll be $16 even." No-nonsense businesswoman Ida Mae took over, her palm outstretched.

Laughing, Trip pulled out his wallet and placed a twenty in her hand. "Worth every penny, Ms. Ida. You have a great day." He winked, took the box, and grabbed Ada's hand. "The extra is for that fantastic dance. Highlight of my day."

"Hey!"

He smiled at Ada's indignation and pulled her out the door. "Guess you'll have to try extra hard to top that."

She narrowed her eyes at him. "See if I give you any of my fudge now."

"Whose fudge?" He held the box over his head, a teasing smile filling his face.

Stepping back onto the stoop in front of Ida Mae's, Ada easily nabbed the box from a stunned Trip. *Not used to a tall girl, huh, buster?* She ran with the box back toward the park where they had left their bikes.

About halfway there, strong arms reached around her, and she was pulled against a firm chest, her feet swinging through the air.

"Woman, I don't play around with Ida's fudge." His warm breath coasted over her neck, leaving goosebumps in its wake.

It felt so good to be locked up in his arms. And it was her downfall.

He snagged the box from her and took off.

Ada watched in disbelief as his long legs took him away from her. Damn, the man looked good when he ran. Long, lean lines, perfect form. Idly, she wondered if he ran track or cross-country in school. She was fit, but if she ran, it was only across a stage, so she shrugged and set a normal walking pace toward her destination. She'd just have to find a way to top dancing with an elf.

Chapter Twelve

By the time they returned to Heron House, the truck had already arrived. He hastily said goodbye to Ada, who grabbed the box of fudge out of his hand and headed inside. She shot a victorious look over her shoulder as she entered the house.

The battle was far from over.

And he was there for it.

He loved the fire in her, the immediate ease they felt with one another. He couldn't wait to see what she'd do next.

"That looked like one of Ida Mae's boxes." Ben appeared from behind the box truck, two folding chairs in each hand. "Did you bring me any?"

"Apparently, I didn't even bring myself any." Trip was still staring at the screen door, almost as if willing Ada to reappear.

"Women get away with effing murder." Ben laughed. "And we let them." He set out over the lawn, carrying the chairs toward the gazebo.

Trip shook himself, trying to get into work mode and get the wily woman out of his mind. He quickly realized that would be impossible, so instead he plotted as he grabbed a couple chairs and followed Ben across the grass.

They stacked the chairs against the gazebo and headed back to the truck for another load.

"Do you think Riley will freak if I ask one of her guests out?"

Ben stopped and leveled a look at him. "Are you referring to Ada attempting to kiss you for all the Eastport gossipers to see? And the ones that didn't can check it out on Chesnee's Snapchat. I guarantee Riley already knows."

Trip scrubbed his hand over his face. *I should shave before tonight.* "I really like her, man."

"That's obvious." Ben continued to the back of the truck and grabbed more chairs. "If Riley was freaking out about it, she'd be out here right now in your face, so I think you're okay."

As if simply saying her name had summoned her, Riley appeared on the front porch with two burly guys in coveralls. She gestured in their direction, talking animatedly with her hands. Then the workers descended the porch steps and climbed into the back of the truck.

By the time Trip and Ben had returned for another load, the other guys were dragging out huge pieces of white canvas that would eventually become a giant party tent for the gala on Saturday.

Riley waved and blew Ben a kiss, then went back inside. She wasn't freaking out. Maybe he was in the clear. Or maybe the grapevine hadn't reached Heron House yet.

Trip didn't have time to dwell on it, because it took the four of them and lots of yelling across the wide lawn to get the tent erected and secured for the event. By six, the truck was unloaded and rumbling down the driveway.

"You joining us for dinner, or is that date happening tonight?" Ben wiped sweat off his brow with his t-shirt.

"I'd like to take her to The Landing tomorrow night. Apparently, your girlfriend has arranged dance lessons for you tonight. So, dinner would be great. Can I help?"

Ben rolled his head back. "Dancing? Really?"

"It'll be fun."

He leveled another incredulous look Trip's way. "Since when are you into dancing?"

Avoiding the question, he slapped Ben on the back as they mounted the stairs. "Any excuse to hold a beautiful woman close, sign me up." He wasn't ready to share his dancing resume with his friend. *Gotta hold something back for the big reveal on Saturday.* "As if you'd ever tell Riley no to anything."

"I can't even deny it." Ben pulled open the screen door and headed for the master bedroom. "Meet me at the grill after you shower that stink off. And try to keep your towel on this time."

Trip, who was halfway up the stairs to the second floor practically got whiplash turning toward his friend. *How the hell did he know about that?*

Ben's laughter echoed down the hall as he disappeared into the kitchen.

***

They were just finishing dinner when the screen door slammed, and Chesnee called out, "We're here! Let's get this show started."

He dragged a less-than-enthusiastic Gina down the hall to the kitchen, where the four of them were finishing up a delicious meal of burgers and potato salad.

Riley took a swig of lemonade and rose from the table. "Great! You guys can go move the furniture in the parlor to make a dance floor and us gals will clean up the kitchen."

Trip still wanted to punch Chesnee in the mouth over the video incident. He had been hoping he wouldn't see him for a few days, long enough for the ire to subside and maybe some real kissing to happen.

Gina looked almost as thrilled as he felt. Trip wondered who had guilted her into this—Riley or Chesnee? She shuffled into the kitchen and Riley introduced her to Ada as they started gathering up plates.

Ada was still wearing that flowy white dress, but she had braided her hair, and it trailed down her back, like an arrow pointing straight at her ass. Trip had fond memories of that ass hovering over the bike seat from their morning ride into town. He must have been staring, because Chesnee grabbed his arm and jerked him down the hall.

"Dude, you need to get laid. What's it been? Two months? Hell, have you gotten any since you've been in Eastport?" At least his friend had the decency to lower his voice so the ladies couldn't hear.

"Pretty sure I'm not discussing my sex life with you." Trip had a theory that Chesnee was mostly talk when it came to his escapades, but he would likely be appalled at just how long it had been. Trip strained to remember. He had hooked up with some chick at the beach right after graduation. Or was it spring break? Whichever it was, it was less than memorable.

Chesnee rolled his eyes as he grabbed the end of one of the sofas. "So, Ada was just bluffing today, huh? About the naked time?"

Ben picked up a wingback and carried it to the back of the room. "No, she's definitely seen him naked."

Trip almost dropped his end of the couch. "Seriously, how do you know that?"

Shrugging, Ben moved aside so they could pass with the sofa. "Ada told Riley and Riley tells me everything." He shook his head. "Even things I really don't want to know."

They set the sofa at the far end of the room.

"I need more information." Chesnee looked between the men, his hands spread as if asking for more information.

Sighing, Trip checked to make sure none of the women had entered the parlor yet. "The first day Ada was here, I was running from the bathroom to the third floor in a towel and we bumped into each other. She accidentally grabbed the towel as she fell." He closed his eyes and briefly relived the moment. "I can't believe she told Riley. They barely know each other."

"You know how Ri is. Everyone's instant friend. And if you don't immediately share your innermost thoughts and feelings, she'll lure them out with a glass of fresh-squeezed lemonade." Ben grabbed a side table and set it upside down in a chair that had already been moved.

"It's damn good lemonade." Chesnee nodded, like it made all the sense in the world.

Trip couldn't argue the point, because he and Riley had become fast friends after they bonded over their fear of spiders, and he'd moved into the house soon after to help her with the renovation.

"Everyone got their dancing shoes on?" Riley stepped into the parlor and clapped her hands.

"Nobody told me I needed special shoes." Chesnee looked down at his flip flops and wiggled his toes.

Ada laughed. "We're not doing any crazy steps tonight, so you'll be fine. Just watch out that your partner doesn't step on your toes." She had swapped her sandals out for a pair of low, red heels with a strap—and damn were they hot.

Chesnee grabbed Gina and pulled her to his side. "Hear that? No stomping on my toes, Lucy."

Trip had never heard him call her that, and considering the daggers Gina threw his direction, she wasn't a fan of the nickname.

"I'll start the music!" Riley was way more bubbly than necessary, likely because of the tension between Chesnee and Gina.

"Told you so." He mouthed at Ada, giving a subtle head tilt in their direction. Talk about needing to release some sexual frustration...

Thomas Rhett blasted through the speakers, causing everyone to jump. Riley fumbled with her phone, trying to turn the volume down.

"Actually, Riley, just pause it for a bit. We'll start without music." Ada stepped in front of Trip and grabbed his hands. "Everyone start with a two-hand hold, keeping the arms loose and space between the dancers."

"Space, Chesnee." Gina pushed him backward as she practically growled the words.

"Okay, so, East Coast Swing is basically a single step combination with a couple turn variations. Guys, you're going to start with your left foot, and ladies, we'll start with our right. You'll move side, together, side one direction and then reverse and go the other direction."

Trip stepped to his left, slid his feet together and then took another step, with Ada following his actions.

"Great, now back the other direction, side, together, side. Excellent." She was a natural teacher, taking in everyone's movements as she demonstrated the steps. "That's a triple step. Next, you'll take your lead foot and step back, then rock forward on the other foot. That's the rock step." She released Trip's hands and stepped over to help Riley and Ben who were struggling with the rhythm.

Chesnee was spinning Gina around the room, clearly not interested in learning actual dance steps. But if the small smile on her face was any indication, Gina didn't mind too much.

"One and two, three and four, five, six. Yes! Great!" Ada counted off the steps as Riley and Ben got the hang of the movement. She smiled at Trip as she grabbed his hands again. "Now, let me show you how to move around the dance floor using these same steps."

Trip led as Ada described the two types of turns common in the dance, moving together like they had been partners for years. She continued to count off steps as they swirled around the parlor, her eyes wide with clear amazement. As she ducked under his arm, she leaned close. "You've done this before."

He smiled and pulled her back against him in a brief hold. "A time or two."

"Can we try it to music now?" Riley held her phone out. "I promise I've got the volume under control this time."

"Sure, just remember your beats."

This time, Thomas was singing at a normal decibel. Riley and Ben continued their counting, Chesnee and Gina reverted back to sixth-grade dance form and Trip pulled Ada in a little bit closer.

He could get used to the feel of her in his arms. She glided across the floor effortlessly, the lines of her neck and arms graceful and gorgeous. When the music switched to *Why Don't We Just Dance*, Trip forgot all his plans to hold back. He pulled her close, spun her around and performed moves he hadn't done in years.

By the time the song ended, they were the only two left dancing. Their friends stared dumbfounded as Trip dipped her in a final gesture. Applause rang out and Chesnee was hooting like a teenager at a rock concert.

"Who would have thought you could do that?"

Gina elbowed him in the ribs.

Chesnee gave her a wounded look. "What?"

"Where did you learn to dance like that?" Riley and Ben had taken a seat on one of the displaced sofas, and she was fanning herself.

Ada's cheeks flushed a pretty pink, and the hair around her face curled slightly. "Yeah, where did you learn to dance?" A teasing look lit up her eyes.

Trip shrugged. "I took a few lessons growing up."

Riley pushed off the couch and headed to the kitchen. "I'm getting lemonade for everyone." Before she left the room, she paused. "A few lessons, my butt."

Everyone laughed at Riley's remark, except for Trip. Suddenly, he was very overheated. "Let's get some fresh air." He pulled Ada out the front door.

The night air was cooler than the stuffy parlor and luckily no one else followed them outside. Light spilled through the leaded glass windows, casting colorful prisms around the darkened porch. Trip pulled her away from the prying eyes inside.

"I did not expect that, I gotta tell you." Ada stood against the railing, her smile evident despite the dark.

He stepped into her space, crowding her. "I didn't expect you." Without debating, he leaned down and captured that sweet smile.

Chapter Thirteen

Trip was full of surprises tonight. The man had moves. On the dance floor, and off it.

The kiss was better than nailing the perfect pirouette. His tongue explored her mouth with patience and care, like they had all the time in the world. His hands roamed her neck, back and arms, gliding over her skin like a gentle caress. Zaps of electricity jolted to her limbs, the soles of her feet lighting up with energy.

She didn't know what to do with her hands. She wanted to touch him everywhere, feel his skin against hers, explore every inch of the toned body she'd gotten a quick look at—but they were in public, basically, and Riley or any of the others could appear at any moment.

Trip's hand slid up her neck to her chin, which he cradled as he pulled his mouth away from hers and caught her eye. "You with me, darlin'?"

The nickname, or his breathy tone, or both, sent a shiver all the way down her body.

She nodded. "Yes. I mean, I want to be." She stared deep into his eyes, searching for understanding in their brilliant blue depths. "Sorry, I'm thinking too much."

His thumb stroked the line of her jaw, and the right side of his mouth quirked up. "Maybe you were thinking about our first meeting?"

Heat rushed to her cheeks, and she tried to avert her gaze, but he held her jaw firmly in place.

"No need for embarrassment. I haven't even seen you naked yet, and it's all I can think about."

Before she could respond, he took her mouth again, sending heat much farther south this time as he pulled her body taut against his. She didn't have to wonder about what she felt—she'd seen the merchandise in the flesh—and she was ready to sign on the dotted line.

"Trip? You out here?"

Ada pulled away, their lips releasing in a smacking sound that would be unmistakable. She dragged her hands over her face, mortified to be caught making out on the porch with a man she'd met a day ago.

"We'll be right in, Ri." Trip grabbed her hands and pulled them down. He lowered his voice and leaned in. "No embarrassment. Ever." He tucked a stray lock of hair behind her ear and gave her a chaste peck that straddled the corner of her mouth and her cheek. "I'll go in first, to give you a minute. But this is to be continued." He winked and walked back inside.

She could hear him explain to the others that they were cooling off outside and enjoying the night sky. The sarcastic nature of their replies was clear even from this distance. How was she supposed to finish the dance lessons now? This fling was turning out to be more complicated than she realized.

Suddenly, she heard her mother's voice from years ago over a long distance, telling her twelve-year-old daughter that if she wanted to be a professional dancer, then she had to put the work in and not allow anything to hold her back. Not fear, not a broken toe shoe, and certainly not her first period. "Better get used to it. You can't schedule your life around a little discomfort."

She'd learned from an early age not to rely on Charlotte. She wasn't even sure what made her call her mother about her unexpected introduction to womanhood. But when something was hard from then on out, she'd repeat the mantra. "Buck up. You have to go after what you want. No one is going to hand it to you."

So, she straightened, shoulders back, chin up—and walked back into the house. The others were gathered in the parlor, sipping Riley's famous fresh-squeezed lemonade and barely acknowledged her entrance. She slowly released the breath that had stuttered in her throat. Trip handed her a cool glass, his fingers lingering over hers for a moment longer than necessary. Their eyes locked, and it was like they were sharing a secret.

It was true in some regards. While their friends might have an inkling of what had happened on the porch, there was no way they knew about the heat between Trip and Ada. She had never experienced anything like it. Not with her first, not with the handful since then.

But reliving it was only going to make matters worse, so she swallowed her lemonade down, and then grabbed Ben to demonstrate the next dance she had planned to teach them.

If she touched Trip again, she'd combust—so she'd save that for when they were alone.

***

The dance lesson was over. Ben had swept Riley away to their hidden suite behind the kitchen, Chesnee and Gina had disappeared, and Trip was refreshing their lemonade.

"So, Chesnee and Gina. They've never?" She gestured subtly with her hands.

Trip chuckled and handed her a glass. "No one knows for sure. The most I've gotten out of him directly is that they briefly dated in high school and since then they've vacillated between best friends and frenemies."

The two hadn't paid much mind to her instruction, but sparks sizzled between the couple none-the-less. Gina insulted Chesnee's rhythm and Chesnee insulted Gina's form. But they locked gazes every chance they got, and Ada noticed Chesnee's hands straying from Gina's waist on more than one occasion. "Where do you think they went?" She felt a ripple of excitement from being adjacent to the town gossip. Much better than being the subject of town gossip.

Trip shrugged. "I'm not sure, but I was hoping you'd go for a walk with me."

More excitement zipped through her body. She smiled, set her glass down, and grabbed his outstretched hand.

He pulled her out onto the porch, where nighttime had fully taken over. There was a slight chill in the air and goosebumps spouted along her bare shoulders. She was overheated from the dancing, so the coolness was a welcome relief.

They descended the steps and stopped in front of the fountain, which was the primary noise that could be heard in the still night air. A few crickets far off and another, deeper chirping closer by.

"You hear that?" Trip leaned close to her ear, speaking quietly, his breath ghosting over her skin. Her goosebumps multiplied.

"Yes, what is it?"

"Frogs. They come to the fountain to breed. I don't know what kind they are, but they're tiny. Maybe the size of your thumb nail. See?" He shined his flashlight on the heron statue perched atop the fountain.

There, on one of the bird's copper wings, was a tiny green frog. Its throat expanded, revealing a vivid yellow pouch, as it chirped long and slow. Trip moved the light lower, where dozens of tiny frogs spotted the rim of the basin.

"That's amazing. Are they here all the time?"

"Just the last few weeks and only on clear nights."

They watched the frog for a few more minutes, then Trip tugged lightly on her hand, pulling away from the frog speed-dating, and extinguished his light.

They walked in silence for a while, his thumb occasionally stroking the back of her hand. Too many questions tumbled inside her mind, so she focused on the darkened landscape. The giant white tent they'd erected that afternoon looked eerie and stark against the green grass. Chairs and tables were stacked and leaning against the gazebo.

Thoughts of the gala, and particularly the auction, crowded into her mind, but she pushed them out and focused on the clear night sky. With no light pollution, hundreds of stars were visible, bunching here and there, making her wish she'd paid a little closer attention during that astronomy unit in high school.

"It really is beautiful here. I can see why you're reluctant to leave."

"Yeah, the place. The people. Nature. It's a triple whammy."

They skirted around the gazebo and headed up along the shoreline. In the darkness, it was hard to see the other side of the river, so the water looked endless. Reeds poked up along the banks and as they passed the house, they entered a wooded area full of live oaks.

He stopped between two of the trees and yanked on something. "Here's the hammocks I was telling you about."

As Ada's eyes adjusted to the darkness, she could make out several swags of fabric strung between the massive trees.

"Have a seat." Trip opened the cocoon of fabric and held it still while she hoisted herself inside, trying to keep her skirt from riding too high.

With his help, she swung her feet into the hammock and stretched out. "Wow." She could just make out the night sky through the gnarled branches and Spanish moss. The light from the moon filtered through the small leaves of the trees. It was surreal, like something out of a movie.

Trip hopped into the hammock beside her. "It's even better during the day. Primo nap spot."

"Has Riley figured out your hiding place yet?" Best break room ever.

His chuckle was low. "She's really laid back. Most of the time. I'm guessing she might get a little tense as the week progresses. She's worked really hard on this event."

"It'll be my first gala." Definitely not her first art auction. Her gut churned at the thought of her mother's work and the attention it would bring.

"It will be a breeze for you. You're a professional dancer."

Ada glanced in his direction, and he was sitting up in the hammock, facing her. She tried to mimic his position, but her skirt tangled around her legs, and she feared she'd flip right over and end up on the mossy ground. She settled for sticking one arm out, so she could see Trip better. "Yes, I've danced plenty, but usually as a performance, with months of practice." And a professional partner. But Trip was nearly as talented a dancer as some of her past partners.

"I seriously doubt you have anything to worry about. I've been to enough Eastport Beach events to assure you that within an hour everyone will be drunk enough that they won't be able to perform a box step. They'll think Ginger Rogers has come back from the dead."

"Ok, Fred. Can we talk about your dance moves?"

"Pffew."

She burst out laughing. "Pffew? Seriously?"

He shrugged. "My mother was a bored socialite. And my sister has two left feet."

"Did you compete?" Her voice rose on the last syllable because it was just so hard to believe. She tried once more to sit up in the hammock. Tried, and failed miserably. "Oof." She hit the ground, headfirst, white skirt falling over her and revealing her white thong to the heavens. And likely Trip.

He leapt out of the hammock—gracefully, of course— and rushed to her side. "Are you okay?"

Chapter Fourteen

Long, toned legs flailed as Ada tried to right herself. Guess they were even for falls today. Kneeling beside her, he gathered her skirt and covered as much as he could to preserve her modesty. They were also even for seeing each other's private bits.

She finally got into a seated position, smoothing out her skirt and the hair back from her face. Her cheeks had a beautiful rosy hue, but her eyes stayed fixed on her lap. "I'm fine, just a little mortified."

"Hey." He gently lifted her chin with his finger. "What'd I say about being embarrassed?"

A timid smile graced her lovely face.

"At least you have undergarments on. Not that I was looking." He winked and her smile widened. He trailed his fingers along her jawline and threaded them into her hair, drawing her head closer. "Look at it this way. We've both been swept off our feet today."

She wet her lips and heat barreled straight to his crotch, which was already on high alert from the thong sighting. He inched closer, until those kissable lips were only a breath away.

"We're already on the ground, so I think it's safe now." Then he closed the distance and continued the most-memorable make-out session he'd had in recent history. The one that had been cut off too quickly. She matched his vigor this time, pushing him back onto the soft ground beneath the live oak trees. They were far less likely to be interrupted out here.

She pulled back, panting, and ripped the elastic off the end of her braid. He'd messed it up and as her hair fell in a curtain between them, he had zero regrets. He grabbed at it, letting the loose strands slide between his fingers. She was practically straddling him, and he was considering just how safe they would be out here if things progressed like he wanted them to.

Ada leaned forward again, sucking his bottom lip into her mouth. There were far too many layers of clothing between them. He was getting ready to ask her back to his room when she sat up again, rubbing her hand across her swollen lips. Damn, she was stunning.

"You never answered my question." Her eyes twinkled in the twilight, and he couldn't for the life of him remember what she had asked. He just knew that he'd say yes to pretty much anything at this point.

He gripped her hips and aligned her heat with his throbbing member. "I have a question for you."

Her eyes went molten, she swiveled her hips, and he swore he blacked out for a moment. "Don't try to distract me."

His dick was a heat-seeking missile at this point and there was no way to cancel the launch code. "Uh, who's distracting who, here?" He didn't know his own name right now.

She walked her fingers up his chest, leaning farther down with every tap. Her breasts swelled against the top of her dress and all he could think about was tasting them. "I asked you if you danced in competitions growing up."

He wasn't ready to reveal the extent of his ballroom experience and who wanted to talk about dancing when they could be doing the horizontal mambo? He tightened his grip on her hips and flipped them over, taking control of this two-step. He answered with his mouth on hers, one hand sliding up her torso and finding a nipple just begging for attention. He tweaked it through the thin material of her dress—it was clear she wasn't wearing a bra and damn did that make him even harder.

Her moan shattered the quiet night, and he wanted to hear that sweet sound over and over again. He continued to ply her mouth as he searched for a way into the dress. There had to be a zipper or button somewhere.

Ada gasped.

"Yeah, babe, it's so good." He trailed his lips along her jawline.

"Trip, stop." She pushed against his chest.

He rolled off her, worried he had crossed some unspoken line. "What? Are you okay?"

She sat up, her hands covering her breasts even though he hadn't managed to undo her dress yet. "I heard something."

All he could hear was pounding in his head from the painful erection currently ruling over his body. He looked back toward the house, but everything was quiet, and no lights shone into the woods. "What was it?"

"I'm not sure. Like leaves rustling, maybe?"

He stood, helping her up off the ground, scanning the shore of the river, but it was pretty dark here under the trees. "It could be a waterbird, or a small mammal. We definitely have wildlife around here." He left the third option off the list because he didn't want to freak her out.

She pointed to a dark shape a few trees away. "Are there alligators here?" Her voice shook and she edged closer to him.

"Let's head back to the house." He pulled her along, increasing their pace as they wound between the trees, but not running because he didn't want her to panic.

"Trip, is it a gator?" Her voice rose to a pitch only the frogs could hear. So much for not panicking.

"Don't worry, they are more scared of us than we are of them."

"Then he must be freaking terrified," she shrieked, and started running, holding on to Trip's arm for dear life.

He didn't get a good look, so they could have been running from a log, but better safe than sorry. They reached the porch and Ada bounded up the stairs, grabbing for the screen door. She was inside before he could reassure her that it was probably only Stumpy, and that missing leg usually slowed him down. But the residents of Heron House knew from experience he could climb steps just fine, so Trip followed her inside and locked the front door for good measure.

Ada was bent over, hands on her knees, making gasping sounds.

Trip couldn't tell if she was laughing or crying. "Are you okay?"

She glanced up at him, a smile filling her face.

"It was probably just a log."

"Pretty sure logs don't snap at people."

"Snap? Who's snapping?" Chesnee came clomping down the stairs, inserting himself into their conversation.

"We may or may not have seen an alligator along the bank." Trip wondered if he'd come from Gina's room and what the story was there.

Ada straightened and crossed her arms over her chest. "We definitely saw a gator."

Chesnee waved his hand dismissively. "Eh, it was probably just Stumpy."

"Stumpy? The alligators have names?" She slid a step closer to Trip.

"Only the ones missing a foot." As usual, Chesnee was happy to step into story-telling mode.

Trip closed the distance between him and Ada and placed his arm around his shoulders. "There's just the one gator that's missing a foot. We call him Stumpy."

"Does he visit often?"

"Nah, mostly he keeps to himself." He stared Chesnee down, trying to send a message via ESP to downplay the whole alligator thing. He didn't want Ada afraid to go outside.

Chesnee shrugged. "I mean, we see him often enough that we named him."

Not helping, man. "Everything okay with Gina?"

"That's why I was looking for you. You got time for a quick beer?" His normally happy-go-lucky friend looked morose.

Trip looked at Ada, wishing they could rewind to their make-out session in the woods. Sans alligator.

She stepped out of his embrace and nodded. "I need to get to bed. You guys have a great night."

He grabbed her hand before she could mount the stairs. "I'll meet you in the kitchen, Chesnee."

"Sure, man. Good night, Ada. Thanks for the dance lesson." He ambled down the hall to the back of the house.

Trip jerked on Ada's hand and pulled her in close. "I really enjoyed our time together today."

They leaned their foreheads together, their breath mingling. "Me too."

"Would you like to have dinner with me tomorrow night?" It was likely foolish to pursue a woman that he might not see after this weekend, but he was having trouble talking himself out of it. She was intriguing and remarkable, and their chemistry was off the charts.

She licked her lips and nodded. "Yes, I would."

He captured her mouth, sealing her answer in so she couldn't take it back. Regretfully, he pulled back, his breath coming in short gasps. Kissing her was like an intimate dance. A lot of heat and close contact. "Good night."

"Night." She climbed the stairs, looking back at him multiple times, a shy smile lighting her face.

He stared after her until she disappeared from his sight. Damn, he was in deep.

Sighing, he strode down the hall to the kitchen, where Chesnee was waiting with two open beers. Trip pulled a chair out from the table and took a long swig from the bottle.

Chesnee hadn't touched his yet.

"What's going on with you? It's like someone stole your favorite toy."

His friend leaned back in his chair and stared at the ceiling. "Man, I usually don't kiss and tell, but she's got me all twisted up."

"You kissed Gina?"

He straightened in his chair, indignant. "Gina kissed me!"

Trip felt like he'd started a film in the middle and had zero clue what was happening in this scene. "And that's a bad thing?"

"No, it was fucking awesome." Chesnee raked his hand through his hair. "But then she was all, 'I can't do this again. It was just a moment of weakness.' And she threw me out." He took a swig of beer and raked his hand across his mouth. "I've got whiplash."

You're not the only one, buddy. "It sounds like she doesn't know what she wants."

Air whooshed out of his lungs. "That's always been the issue."

Trip itched to get more information about their past, but he'd never seen Chesnee this forlorn. "You two seemed pretty cozy during the dance lesson."

"Yeah, and then she took me upstairs and I thought, maybe, just maybe, she'd come to her senses. But it was too much to hope for. It always is." He stared into his beer, like the answers he sought could be found in its bubbly depths.

"Have you two ever, like, dated?" The whole town knew Chesnee carried a torch for her, but Trip wasn't sure if they'd ever been in a relationship. It was a touchy subject that his friend usually avoided.

"Let's talk about how you knew all that dancing shit?"

And apparently two sips of beer weren't going to get Chesnee talking about it tonight, either. Trip shrugged. *You don't like talking about your past with Gina, and I don't go around telling people I was a young ballroom dancing phenom.*

The two sat in a companionable silence for a bit, sipping their beers and avoiding their personal landmines.

"You close the deal with Ada yet?" Chesnee drained his beer and stared through the empty bottle.

"We have a dinner date tomorrow night." He didn't know what this thing with Ada was, but it wasn't a quick lay that he was willing to discuss over a beer. He stood and grabbed Chesnee's bottle and threw them both in the recycling bin.

"That doesn't answer my question."

Trip stepped into the doorway leading to the hall and turned back to look at his friend slouched against the kitchen table. "Watch out for Stumpy when you leave."

Chapter Fifteen

She woke up to something hard poking her in the back. For a moment, her dreams flashed back through her mind—wanton dreams about a certain naked dance partner. Sighing, she flailed her arm out, hoping she was wrong, and Trip really was lying beside her.

"Ow!" Her arm slapped against more hard objects, and she once again found herself regretting her life choices. She lay in the center of the large bed, surrounded by her mother's journals. Instead of bringing a hot man to bed, she'd stayed up late—again—trying to make sense of her mother's writings.

Nope. No more wasting time. She tumbled out of bed, determined to live in the present and not obsess over the past. Tonight, she would go to dinner with Trip, and if it seemed like he wanted more, she'd do gymnastics in this big bed with him instead of some dusty old indecipherable memories.

She rushed to get ready, remembering Trip's promise to feed her breakfast. She remembered other things too. Like his lips trailing along her jaw, his hands gripping her hips, and concrete proof of his attraction.

Her life was in limbo, so what did she have to lose? If she was going to float aimlessly through the next couple days, she might as well have a few mind-blowing orgasms along the way.

Obviously, she didn't know for certain that a Trip-induced orgasm would be mind-blowing, but she had felt and seen the tools at his disposal, and they were top-notch.

Her phone buzzed.

"Bethy, you are never going to believe where I am." Ada put the phone on speaker while she gathered up her mom's journals.

"Well, all I know is I woke up in Milan to a garbled message about alligators and erections. You should be grateful I waited this long to call you, but with the time difference, I figured you'd still be asleep." Her best friend had segued from ballet to modeling and was currently living a fashionista's dream.

Ada pulled the fluffy white comforter up and smoothed it out. "I'm in North Carolina."

"Okay, that tracks with the gators, but how does an erection come into the picture? I couldn't even get you to go out with that gorgeous Ralph Lauren model."

She scrunched her nose. "He looked like a Ken doll." She arranged several pillows against the headboard. "And had a similar personality."

"Yeah, yeah. Picky, picky. I don't date other models for the conversation." The truth was Elizabeth Golden didn't date at all. She had "brief and mutually satisfying encounters with the opposite sex."

That's why she was the perfect person to call about her current circumstance. She'd get no judgment from the self-described "Femme Fatale."

"I met someone."

"Someone with a penis, I presume."

Ada flung herself backward onto the freshly made bed. *An excellent penis.* "His name is Trip. He works at Heron House."

"A blueblood." She hummed.

"You know nothing about him."

Beth was always making snap judgments about the people they crossed paths with and reminding Ada of her naivety. She laughed. "Ade, honey, he's a third. Trip. Third. Only old money would dare to saddle their descendants with the same name for generations."

"What difference does that make? Maybe it means he has a strong family." Although he did hint that his family situation was difficult. She hated it when Beth was right.

"It's not like you're marrying the guy, right?" She snorted. "Please tell me you aren't marrying the guy."

"Gosh no! I was just considering a fling." It sounded silly saying it out loud.

Beth slow-clapped. "Finally! My sweet Ada is going to pop that stubborn little cherry."

She winced. That expression was so crass. "Beth, you know full well I've had sex."

"I'm talking about your casual sex cherry. The one most women in their twenties pass around from man to man freely. So glad you've entered the era of women's liberation."

From her history lessons, Ada remembered that happening in the sixties. "There's nothing wrong with wanting to have feelings for someone you sleep with." She wasn't even sure why she was arguing with her friend. She was planning to have casual sex, after all. Tonight, if possible.

"Get out of your head, Ade. Don't overthink it. Bang the rich dude with the rock-hard cock. Come more than once. I dare you." There was yelling in the background, mostly in broken English from what Ada could hear. "I've got to go, love. This photographer's got his panties in a wad. Kisses."

The call ended and Ada stared up at the ceiling, confused and a little aroused. Beth had always been the "advanced" girl of their friend group, losing her virginity at fourteen. Although she preferred to say that she didn't lose anything, instead she gained orgasmic enlightenment. Now she traveled all over the world, searching for enlightenment in each country she visited.

Kind of like Charlotte. Her journals read like a who's who of people she had slept with, except instead of listing their full name, net worth and career, she denoted if they had big ears, or a bushy mustache, or could crack a walnut with his ass cheeks.

Would sleeping with a man she'd just met make her like her mother?

Ugh, that's more than I'm willing to delve into this early in the morning.

She jumped off the bed and checked her face in the mirror before leaving her room. Regardless of what she decided, she wanted to look good for Trip. Keep her options open.

Makeup passing muster, she exited her room and bounded down the stairs. She heard voices in the kitchen and slowed down. She didn't want to appear too excited. But she couldn't wait to see him.

The smell of bacon wafted down the hall. Trip didn't forget his promise.

"Hey Ada!" Riley was seated on the counter next to the sink, Ben close by, both holding steaming mugs.

Ben nodded. "Morning. Can I get you a coffee?" He held his mug out slightly.

"No thanks." She tried to hide her disappointment. Trip was nowhere to be seen, and it wasn't a very big kitchen, so it was unlikely he was hiding. "I'd love some juice, if that's okay, Riley."

"Of course, help yourself. And Trip left something heating in the oven for you." She slid off the counter and rose up on her toes to give Ben a peck on the lips. "Hurry back. We can't leave those guys to their own devices for too long."

Ben set his mug in the sink and washed his hands. "I'll be less than an hour." He kissed Riley on the forehead and headed out the back door.

Ada finished juicing a couple oranges and opened the oven. There was a foil-wrapped packet on the top rack.

"That's one of Trip's legendary breakfast burritos. He won't tell me what the secret ingredient is. Damn, I'm going to miss him." She stared off into the distance.

If her love for Ben wasn't on full display, Ada would be a little jealous of Riley and Trip's easy-going relationship. "You guys are pretty close, huh?" She slid out a chair and sat at the table with her burrito and juice.

"Yeah, he's been awesome helping me out with this place. I can't even imagine finding a suitable replacement. Of course, most of the big projects have been completed, and I can handle the cleaning, so I may try to do it on my own for a while. Ben can do the yard, but Trip is so proud of the work he's done on the lawn. It was a patchy brown mess when I first got here and now it's golf-course perfection."

"Has he done landscaping before?" She realized how little she knew about him.

Riley wrinkled her nose in thought. "I don't think so. His family has money, and they don't love the idea of Trip working with his hands. I think they expected him to get a real job after law school. Ha! He went from the law to lawn care." She laughed at her own joke.

Beth was getting more right by the minute.

Ada bit into the fat burrito. "Ohmygosh," she mumbled through fluffy eggs, crispy bacon and some spice she couldn't put her finger on.

Riley nodded. "I know. So good."

"Is it cumin?" She took another bite, working the food around her mouth, trying to ferret out the flavor.

"Dunno. He's crazy secretive about it." She sat in the chair opposite Ada and leaned forward. "But, you know, he's really into you. Maybe you could get it out of him. And while you're at it, find out why his eggs are so fluffy."

Ada swallowed the bite, unable to determine the mystery spice. "You think he likes me?"

Riley narrowed her eyes. "From my experience, kissing on the porch indicates interest."

Her cheeks heated. "Yeah, I guess you're right. I'm not used to a lot of attention from attractive men."

"You're kidding, right?"

"No. I mean, I dated one guy when I was eighteen, but that was kind of a disaster. Since then, there've been a couple more, but nothing that turned into anything serious."

"Are you wanting something serious?"

Ada shrugged. "I don't know. I mean, my life is a shambles right now. Nothing is going the way I planned."

Riley smiled. "Sometimes the best things happen when we don't have a plan. Look at me and Ben."

"You guys are so cute together. How long have you been dating?"

"Just a couple months, but we've been serious from the get-go. We just fit, you know? I never expected it."

Ada sighed. "I'm trying to just go with it and not get too bogged down analyzing every little thing." She popped the last bite of burrito in her mouth.

Riley stood and rinsed out her mug. "Well, you don't have to worry about Trip. He's solid." She wiped her hands on a towel. "Chesnee, on the other hand, has to be watched like a hawk. I better get outside and monitor them until Ben gets back from the office. You want to meet up later? I was hoping you'd help me go through my uncle's paperwork."

"Absolutely." She was itching to find out more about Archie and Charlotte's relationship. "Just let me know when you're done wrangling the guys." She was also itching to wrangle one of those guys herself later that night.

Chapter Sixteen

"I think there's enough lights." Chesnee stood, hands on hips, appraising their work so far.

Trip rolled his eyes. "We've done two trees. Pretty sure Riley wants all the trees in this area done. You got other plans?" He pulled the ladder over to the next tree and grabbed another box of the string lights.

His friend looked back toward the house. "No, no plans."

Gina appeared on the porch, spoke briefly to Riley and Ada and then climbed in her car and drove away. "Has she mentioned the kiss?"

Chesnee startled and searched the yard until his eyes lit on Ben, who was over by the gazebo. "Dude, Ben could have heard you." He took the end of the strand from Trip and unfurled it as he walked backward.

"Ben, of all people, knows you've got it bad for Gina." He wound the strand through the gnarled branches of the live oak.

"I don't have anything bad for Gina. We're friends."

"Uh-huh. Sure." Ben appeared behind Chesnee, who jumped a mile in the air. "And Riley said not to upset Gina at the gala. She needs happy guests."

Chesnee shot Trip a look then puffed up his chest before turning to his boss. "Why would I upset Gina?" He laughed but it came out as a croak. "We're great. Awesome. Good friends." He pulled his shirt away from his chest like it was strangling him. "Anyone else getting hungry?"

"I made up some sandwiches for us and Riley's got lemonade." Trip wound the last bit of the light strand through the branches and descended the ladder.

"Oh, great. Yeah. I was going to offer to go into town, but sandwiches are great."

Ben slapped Chesnee on the back. "I haven't seen you this nervous since you interviewed to be my assistant. Did something happen after the dance lesson last night?"

Trip laughed as he walked toward the house, taking his time so he could hear how Chesnee got out of this mess.

The last thing he caught was his friend changing the subject by talking about a law brief the two had been working on.

Good luck, buddy. You're not pulling the wool over anyone's eyes.

He neared the house, and his attention zeroed in on his date for the evening. Ada and Riley were in matching rockers, a small table between them, a pile of books teetering on top.

"Ladies." He climbed the steps as he checked out Ada's long, lean legs. Today she wore crisp white shorts and a minty green tank top. And if those peaks in her shirt were any indication, no bra. Their date couldn't come soon enough.

"You keeping Chesnee on track?" Riley looked up from the papers spread in her lap.

"Barely. He's struggling even more than usual today." He chuckled, kind of loving the way Gina was getting in his normally confident—who was he kidding? cocky—friend's head.

Ada sat quietly as Riley drilled him about decorating the yard and setting up the chairs and tables. Trip watched her out of the corner of his eye, noting that she peeked up from the leather-bound tome she was holding every few seconds.

"Don't worry, Ri. Ben's cracking the whip so you don't have to." He winked at Ada, who gave a silent chuckle.

Riley wrinkled her nose. "I just want everything to be perfect for the gala."

"It will be. I'm grabbing lunch for the guys. You ladies interested in turkey clubs?"

Ada set the book aside. "That sounds great. I'll help you." She rose from the chair but looked back at Riley. "That okay?"

"Of course." She waved her hand dismissively. "We need a break from these dusty journals. I'll go down and check on Ben and Chesnee for myself. Take your time with the sandwiches." Her eyes twinkled as she grinned.

Trip grabbed Ada by the waist and pulled her close. "Tell Chesnee to gnaw on a tree branch in the meantime."

They all laughed, and Riley bounded down the stairs. Once she was farther away, Trip dipped his head and nuzzled the spot between Ada's shoulder and neck. "Hmm, you smell heavenly."

She giggled and pulled away. "And I'm super ticklish."

"You should not have told me that."

Her eyes grew wide, and she darted into the house.

As Trip followed her inside, he wondered just how long his friends would be willing to wait for lunch.

***

Trip had Ada plastered against the refrigerator when his phone rang. He ignored it, of course.

As determined as he was to keep kissing those luscious lips, someone was equally determined to reach him, so on the fifth call, Ada pushed away from him and insisted he answer. He growled and yanked the phone out of his pocket. He could have been shoveling a load of fertilizer and wouldn't have wanted to stop to speak to his mother. But it was pure torture to have to answer the phone with Ada mere feet away, her mouth swollen from their passion. Before he could pick up, the call disconnected. Then immediately started ringing again.

Chesnee strode into the kitchen. "How are those sandwiches coming?" He looked at the flushed Ada and the frustrated Trip and was opening his mouth, no doubt to say something snarky, when Trip glared at him and pointed an aggressive finger. His friend wisely zipped his lips, so Trip used that same finger to answer his phone. He mouthed an apology to Ada as he slipped out of the kitchen and into the study for a bit of privacy.

"Hello?" He didn't even bother to hide his irritation from his mother. Not that she would notice.

"Oh, good, Carlton. I was worried you might be busy."

So worried you called me six times in a row? "What is it, Mother?"

"You'll never guess who I ran into at the club this morning." As usual, she was either completely oblivious to his annoyance or chose to ignore it.

"Princess Diana," he deadpanned.

"Oh ho," she chuckled, and if she was laughing at one of Trip's "jokes," she really wanted something he was going to hate. "Try again."

He couldn't care less which stuffed shirt she ran into at her precious country club. "Mother, I'm in the middle of making lunch for the work crew. Can we speed this guessing game along?"

"Jenny Jolly!"

He threw his head back and it thunked against the wall. "That's nice." If Satan's mistress in a tennis skirt could be considered nice.

"She's single again. Can you believe it?"

As one of a line of poor, miserable bastards that had the unfortunate curse of dating her, yes. Yes, he could believe it. He hummed to keep from saying bad words out loud.

"I was telling her about your little party and by some miracle she's free this weekend!"

No, no, no. "Mother, we are completely full up. You got the last room, and the gala is completely sold out." The last thing he needed was that plastic Barbie in pearls to show up at Riley's grand reopening.

"She could always bunk with you, honey." The one time his mother, Miss Prim and Proper, decided to loosen her strict no sleeping together until marriage rule, and it was for JJ? He gagged a little in his mouth.

"No, she can't, Mother. I'm seeing someone and she's my date for the gala." He hadn't asked Ada yet, but with the way things were progressing, it seemed likely they would go together.

Karina Westinghouse gasped. "Well, I swear. How was I supposed to know that when you never tell me anything about your life? Who is this girl? And more importantly, who is her family?"

Trip pinched the bridge of his nose. How was he related to this woman? "It's a fairly new relationship."

"Oh, so it's not serious, then. Maybe you could find Jenny a hotel nearby?"

"It is serious." He knew he was talking out of his ass, but he had to shut down this notion of her bringing his ex along. "It would be embarrassing for Jennifer to be here while I'm with my new girlfriend." If anything could penetrate his mother's thick skull, it was etiquette.

She sighed, clearly not happy, but also unable to argue. "Okay, well I expect to meet this girl tomorrow when I arrive. And if it doesn't seem like it will work out, maybe Jenny can still make it in time for the party."

Trip counted to five, using the time to stuff his rage deep in his chest so it wouldn't come bursting out in a tirade of profanity. "Mother, Ada is lovely, but your opinion on the matter has no bearing on whether or not we are together."

"You are so much like your father. In all the repugnant ways." She disconnected the call without a proper salutation. Miss Manners would be appalled.

Now he just had to convince Ada not only to go to the gala with him, but to pretend they were more serious than they were. No big deal. Right?

Chapter Seventeen

Trip was tense when he returned to the kitchen. He gathered the sandwiches and arranged them on a platter while Ada poured lemonade into five glasses. Chesnee rambled on about some crazy tennis match he'd watched the day before, but she was pretty sure the guy could talk to a wall.

She tried to catch Trip's eye, to make sure everything was okay, but he avoided looking directly at her. What could have changed between their intense make-out session and whoever was persistently trying to reach him? Could it be a woman? Surely Riley would have mentioned if he was dating someone. They hadn't really talked about other people, but who would pursue someone if they were involved with someone else? Certainly not anyone she wanted to date.

But was she really considering *dating* Trip? If this was meant to be a fling, she had no right to be jealous if he had another woman in his life. In a few days, they'd both go back to their normal—whatever that looked like now that hers had imploded—lives.

"Chesnee, can you grab the grapes from the fridge?" Trip hoisted the tray full of sandwiches and headed toward the front door.

Ada tried to lift the drink tray, but it was heavy and awkward. "Hey, Chesnee, can we switch? I'll grab the fruit, and you can get the lemonade?"

"Sure." He handed the bowl of grapes to her and scooped up the drinks like they didn't weigh a thing. "So, then they called the line judge over and the dude threw his racket at her head." He laughed. "It was wild."

"Sounds like it." She hadn't been following the story, but he seemed happy to have an audience.

When they stepped out onto the porch, Riley and Ben were there and everyone dug into the lunch Trip had prepared. Lunch meat and veggies were piled high on fluffy buns and the sandwich had a tangy kick to it.

"Hmm. What is that sauce? It's so good." She slid next to where he stood leaning on the porch railing, hoping to get back to the comfortable vibe they'd shared earlier.

Riley piped up from the swing where she sat with Ben. "Yeah, Trip, maybe you'll tell Ada about your secret sauce."

Trip gave a half smile from behind his sandwich.

"Ignore him, Ada." Chesnee popped a grape between his teeth. "He's always doing this. Showing off his cooking skills and then being all hush hush about the recipe like it's a state secret. You're not a chef, dude." He bit into his sandwich and before he swallowed the bite, he mumbled, "It's a fucking great sandwich, though."

That seemed to break the last bit of frost off Trip's demeanor, and during the rest of lunch the five of them joked around and talked about what else needed to be done before the gala.

Before the guys went back down the lawn to finish hanging lights and lanterns in the trees, Trip gave her a quick kiss on the cheek and whispered in her ear, "Six-thirty, okay?"

She nodded, smiling, happy he was also looking forward to their date.

***

About an hour later, Ada was stretched out on a blanket Riley had laid on the porch floor, surrounded by journals for the second time that day. Only this time, they were Archie's.

"I think I found something!" She'd been scanning pages, searching for any mention of her mother's name and finally "Charlotte" had jumped off a page about halfway through a tome labeled "Residents."

Riley scooted closer, moving books out of the way so she could see the entry.

Received application for residence from young artist Charlotte Maddox. Painter. Shows innate skill and vision. Notes the need for a change in scenery and mentorship. NYC gallery show. Current mentor? Represented? Mid-April?

The entry was scrawled in Archie's distinctive script in blue ballpoint. Beside it, a large red checkmark had been drawn, likely indicating that he had approved the application.

"I don't think I've seen this before." Riley stuck her finger in the page and flipped the book closed to look at the cover. "Yeah, I haven't gotten to the Residents pile." She opened the book again. "It looks like he could tell she had talent before she even arrived."

Ada rolled to her side to see Riley better. It almost felt like a slumber party, which her mother had never allowed—because children made a mess, and it wasn't just their home, it was her studio space, and she couldn't risk someone messing with her pieces. Ada sighed. One more thing that wasn't normal about her childhood. "Mom was twenty-four or twenty-five when she met Paul and she had her first gallery show pretty soon after that." That instant success had created the monster that was THE Charlotte Maddox. "She sold out that first show."

"Wow. She was a really big deal." Riley mimicked Ada's position and propped her head on her hand.

"She liked to think so." Ada hated how bitter she sounded. Her mother was alone and confused with a debilitating disease and no one could do a damn thing about it, so why did she feel so guilty?

"It must have been hard to live with someone who was so famous, especially in New York."

Ada nodded. "She thrived off the attention, for sure."

Riley looked truly engaged in their conversation and for some reason Ada felt like she could open up to her.

"She didn't plan to have a child, and she refused to change her lifestyle once I came along."

"So, no mother-of-the-year award?" Riley scrunched up her nose.

Ada laughed. "More like once a year, someone had to remind her she had a child."

"How are you so well-adjusted?"

"Paul and Elaine." She smiled, thinking back to the dinner she'd had at their house right before she came down here. "They treated me like I was their kid a lot of the time. Elaine took me to musicals and clothes shopping and all the other things a mother's supposed to do. And Paul always had my back."

"Thank goodness she found a manager that cared so much. I'm sure a lot of them are just in it for the money."

Ada rolled over and stared at the bead board ceiling. "I wouldn't have survived without them. Sometimes, when my mother was traveling and I was staying with them, I would pretend they were my real parents. It was like I was floating on a cloud. Then she'd come home and pop my fluffy bubble and remind me I was a nuisance."

"I'm sure she didn't think that."

"It wasn't all bad. I got to meet a lot of other artists who were fun and really sweet to me. Some of them would even come to my recitals. Everyone always encouraged me to dance."

"Even Charlotte?"

Ada turned her head to look at Riley. "She liked being able to show me off. I was good at something, so that reflected well on her."

"Do you think it would have been different if you'd known your father?" Riley zeroed in on her exact issue.

"Definitely. How different would things have been if I had one parent who was present? Physically and emotionally." When other teenagers were dreaming of boys, Ada was dreaming of meeting her father. "There're so many things I missed out on. And will continue to.""Like your dad walking you down the aisle?"

She let out a whoosh of air and whispered, "Yeah."

They laid there in companionable silence until a car pulled into the driveway.

They sat up at the same time and watched as Gina climbed out of the driver's seat.

Ada leaned close to Riley. "So, what's the deal with Gina and Chesnee?"

***

She was drying her hair when her phone rang. She dashed into the bedroom and swiped the screen. "Hey, Randi."

"Whatcha, doing? How's North Carolina?"

"Well, I'm getting ready for a date, so I'd say it's pretty good."

Miranda squealed. "You've been there, what? Like three days? That's got to be a record."

Ada perched on the edge of the bed facing a painting of the NYC skyline. Her mother had done some variation of the skyline many times over. In this one, the sky was dark and dotted with hundreds, maybe thousands of stars. The Empire State Building was lit in its traditional red, white and blue and there were fireworks over the East River. "It's been a wild couple of days. I've given ballroom lessons, rode a bicycle for the first time in years and made out with a man I barely know."

"Wild? It sounds awesome! Tell me about the guy. Is he a good kisser?"

Good didn't begin to describe Trip's prowess in the kissing department. She was hoping those talents extended to the bedroom. "He's good at everything he does. Including dancing."

"Oh yeah? Picked it right up?"

"More like he competed as a kid."

"Shut up!"

Ada went back into the bathroom, balanced the phone on the sink, and started applying her makeup. "He hasn't gone into any detail, but I think he's had years of training. His form is perfection, and he knows all the moves." Not just on the dance floor.

Randi whooped. "Yeah, he does! Where's he taking you tonight?"

"All I know is dinner, but Eastport Beach is small, so I'm guessing someplace downtown."

"Is he local?"

She sighed. "Actually, he's leaving after the gala. Back to Virginia."

Her friend gasped. "He lives here?"

"Not exactly sure where, we haven't gotten that far."

"Too busy locking lips to get deets. No shade from me."

Maybe she could pry a little tonight. If he lived close enough, maybe this didn't have to be a quick fling. "Have you talked to Susan? How is she doing? I was thinking when I come back, I could start the class back up on my own dime. If she'd let me use the studio."

"The girls would love that. I ran into a couple of them with their moms at the mall. Elsie burst into tears when she saw me and asked when they could come back to class."

"Those poor girls. Elsie is a wild child, but I think I can get through to her in time." I missed the girls and I'd only been teaching them for a couple weeks. I had half a mind to go to D.C. and march into that senator's office and read him the riot act. Or better yet, take a couple of the girls with me and see if he had a heart in his cold, dead chest. "That Westinghouse guy has no soul."

"He's probably on some power trip and decided the money would be better spent lining his friends' pockets." Miranda scoffed. "About Susan."

Ada felt the other shoe getting ready to drop. "Oh no, what now?"

"She's going to have to have a full hip replacement, and she'll need help getting around afterward, so she's moving in with her sister. In Boca."

"Florida? When will she be back?"

"She's closing permanently. She's already got an offer on the building. We're officially unemployed."

Ada dropped her makeup brush in the sink. "Oh my gosh. What are we going to do? I just signed a lease a month ago. And you were going to buy that townhouse."

Randi groaned. "Yeah, I had to pull out of escrow. I've contacted all the other dance studios around here and none of them need teachers."

"You'd think with Susie B's closing it would mean they'd get more students."

"Yeah, but apparently that doesn't translate to more teachers. They're happy to pad their class size."

She squeezed her eyes shut, trying not to cry and mess up her freshly applied makeup. "It's always about the bottom line. Not about people."

"You know how fiercely competitive the dance world is, Ada. There's not a lot of humanity in the sport."

It was why she hadn't considered competing in ballroom. It was cutthroat and sapped all the joy out of the dancing. "This sucks."

"For sure. And I hate that I've pooped all over your happy date night. Let's talk about something else. How's this guy's ass? If he's a dancer, it's got to be tight, right?"

Ada laughed. Randi was the queen of shock value. They'd barely had time to get to know each other and now it seemed their friendship was doomed. "I'm going to hate not seeing you every day."

"Same girl. Now, about the ass?"

Chapter Eighteen

"You taking her to The Landing?" Ben heaved another load of debris onto the pile. They'd have a raging bonfire later tonight.

"I know I've only been here for the summer, but is there another nice restaurant I've missed?" Trip grabbed the empty wheelbarrow and headed back to the area where they were clearing brush.

Ben laughed. "Nope, you haven't missed a thing. It's where I took Riley for our first date and likely every other couple in this town."

The Landing was cozy, had great seafood, and boasted an incredible view of the water. "For being small, Eastport has great food."

"Yeah, too bad everything else closes by 7 p.m."

Trip rammed the shovel under the pile of branches and leaves. "The Landing it is, then." His phone vibrated in his pocket. Robert. He hadn't seen him since their graduation from law school. "Hey, give me a few, Ben." He walked down toward the water and answered the call. "What's up, Bobby?"

"Mr. Westinghouse Sr. needs you in his office on Monday."

So, this was a business call. Satan himself was summoning him. He hadn't even gotten back home, and it was already starting.

"The last time I saw you, you were shitfaced after drinking an entire bottle of Fireball. No 'how you doing? Seen any good movies?'" He still couldn't believe his friend had gone to the dark side and was working for his grandfather.

"Is there a time that works better for you?" He sounded like a fucking robot.

"When hell freezes over?"

"Yes, sir, 3 p.m. will be fine. We'll see you then. Let me know if you need your parking validated." The robot ended the call and Trip felt like he'd entered another dimension.

He yelled at the phone. "I cleaned your barf off my shoes, asshole."

He shoved his phone in his pocket to keep from chucking it in the river. He wasn't even back in Virginia and his blood pressure was through the roof. Those people—his family—drove him completely insane. Why couldn't he have been born into a normal family? Growing up, all his friends called him rich, privileged, lucky. What he wouldn't have given to have parents who actually enjoyed their children and didn't just see them as pawns in a political game. He would have given up all the trappings of "having money" to just be able to camp out on the beach with his friends and go crabbing.

No, he had a reputation to uphold. One that wasn't even his own. He couldn't make his grandfather look bad. He couldn't just be a kid.

Well, he wasn't a kid anymore and he was tired of playing their game.

Before he lost the nerve, he shot off a text to Robot Robert.

Cancel my meeting. Something's come up.

Riley said he could stay as long as he wanted. Her and Ben had become his best friends. And tonight, he had a hot date with a girl he really liked. So much that he dreaded having to introduce her to his family.

Hopefully she liked him enough to overlook genetics.

***

Trip stood on the porch, his leg twitching and his heart racing. He was fucking nervous.

Now that he'd made the decision to buck his family obligations, this date had taken on new possibilities. It was no longer a fling with someone he wouldn't see again. There was a chance this could be something. A chance he could be with someone who wasn't after his family name and the clout it carried.

Ada appeared in the doorway, wearing a simple black sundress, accentuating her smooth, pale skin.

He exhaled and it came out like a whistle.

Her cheeks reddened and she ducked her head.

Did this woman not realize how stunning she was? He opened the screen door and extended his hand. She slipped her fingers into his, slotting together in the perfect fit. He stared at their hands, transfixed by the contrast of her delicate fingers and his rough, tanned ones.

He realized he hadn't said any words yet, so he dragged his gaze away from their intertwined hands and focused on her lovely face. "You look amazing."

"You clean up well." She winked and stepped through the doorway onto the porch.

She'd seen him after clearing brush, mowing the lawn and jumping into the river to cool off.

"And fully dressed, no less." She ran her fingers across his chest and tugged lightly on the collar of his shirt.

A zing of delight raced through his body. This woman was spectacular. "Eastport Beach is a laid-back town, but they still expect shirt and shoes at dinner."

"I guess your pirate doesn't get to eat, then."

He laughed, and relief washed over him. He could feel his blood pressure lowering, his muscles loosening. Ada was good for him. She made him feel normal. "Pretty sure Captain Percy doesn't even own a shirt."

"He'd be a pretty lousy naked pirate if he did."

Trip settled his other hand on her waist and pulled her closer. Her lips called to him, luring him into her orbit. He didn't even try to resist.

Ada looped her arms around his neck, meeting him with a matching fervor.

"Bravo." Chesnee's obnoxious voice sliced through their passion, and Trip reluctantly pulled back. His friend proceeded to slow-clap. "He's remaining standing, folks. Great job." Chesnee was dressed in white tennis shorts and a dark blue t-shirt, which barely looked wrinkled.

"Did you lose the match so quickly you didn't have time to sweat?" Trip tucked Ada into his side, placing a protective arm around her waist.

"Or I won so handily that I didn't need to exert myself?" He brushed his hand against his shirt.

The front door opened, and Gina came out. She was dressed in a short skirt and a nice top and had her red hair styled in a spiky 'do. "Hey, Ada, nice dress. Don't let Trip cheap out on you. Order an appetizer and dessert." She pushed her palm against Chesnee's chest and propelled him down the steps. "Glad you decided to dress up for me, Chessman."

Chesnee had a goofy grin on his face as he opened his passenger door for Gina, and she slid into the seat. "Don't worry, I've got pants in the car. I just figured you'd prefer to stare at my legs on the drive down." He shut the door to his convertible with a flourish.

"As if." Gina flipped the visor down and slid the mirror open. She pulled a scarf from her purse and tied it around her hair.

Chesnee rounded the car, and then hopped over the closed door, landing in the driver's seat. "Don't wait up for us, kids!" He revved the car and took off down the driveway, Gina's scarlet scarf waving in the wind.

"What the heck just happened?" Trip turned to Ada, but she looked as confused as he was.

"Riley said they aren't dating. But that seemed awfully 'date-like.'"

"Yeah, it did. Gina actually seemed happy to see him, which is weird. Usually, she's just mildly annoyed by him."

The door opened again. This porch was starting to feel like Grand Central Station and the other guests weren't arriving until tomorrow. "Are you two not gone yet?" Riley had a blanket under her arm and a bottle of wine in a basket.

"Are you trying to get rid of us?" Trip could see Ben coming down the hall, wineglasses in one hand and a charcuterie board in the other. Seemed everyone had a date night planned this evening.

"No, of course not." Riley opened the door for Ben. "Ada, you look lovely."

"Thanks, you too."

Riley was a little dressed up, which was odd, because normally she wore shorts or jeans and retro band t-shirts.

"Any idea where Chesnee and Gina went?" Maybe someone had cast a strange love spell over Heron House.

Ben placed the glasses in Riley's basket. "They're going to a concert in Myrtle Beach. Chesnee bought the tickets like a year ago. It's one of her favorite bands, so I guess she's willing to put up with him for a couple hours."

"That tracks." Trip addressed Ada. "Gina loves live music. She's always going to concerts and festivals to listen to bands."

"She loves musicians." Riley snickered. "Too bad Chesnee can't carry a tune in a bucket."

Ben laughed. "If you ever have the opportunity to see him do karaoke, it will be the best night of your life. I highly recommend it."

"I'll keep that in mind." Ada smiled up at Trip. "How about you? We know you can dance, but can you sing?"

"We better get to dinner before there aren't any tables left."

Everyone except Trip laughed.

"You two have a great time. Since it's our last night before more guests arrive, we're going to sleep on the boat." Ben nodded toward the dock the next lot over where his sailboat was moored.

Now all the romantic picnic implements made sense. "I'll lock up the house for you." This couldn't have worked out better if Trip had planned it himself. He and Ada would have the place to themselves after dinner. Hell, maybe they should skip dinner and grab their own bottle of wine.

"Thanks!" Riley skittered down the stairs with Ben close on her heels.

"Well," Ada dragged the word out, "it looks like Wednesday is date night in Eastport Beach."

Trip fought against his baser nature—the one that wanted to throw her over his shoulder and take her upstairs—and decided to keep the nice-dinner-out plan. There was always *after* dinner.

He pulled her down the steps. "I guess so, and since they roll Main Street up at nine o'clock sharp, we better get going."

***

Ada had called it, because it appeared every couple in Eastport was at The Landing. The hostess said there was a thirty-minute wait and sent them to the bar.

Before their drinks arrived, they were surrounded by locals.

"You're the dancer!"

"I heard you gave Riley and Ben lessons."

"I heard Chesnee broke Gina's toe."

Ada looked shellshocked, so when Nic slid her Fuzzy Navel across the bar, she grabbed for it like it was a rope ladder and she was hanging off a cliff.

"Guys, you're overwhelming her." Trip stood and tried to push back the crowd that had formed.

"Is it true Trip can dance? I've heard tall people make better dancers."

"No, Irma, tall people are at a disadvantage because their legs are harder to control."

Trip tried to hide his snicker behind his glass of Shark Attack lager, but Ada caught it and leaned in close. "Maybe that's why you fell down when I kissed you." She whispered it, but there was no such thing as a secret in Eastport Beach. Especially on a slow news day.

"Are you talking about in front of the Law Office? I heard he cracked his head open."

"You must be some kisser to knock a guy out."

This was quickly spiraling out of control and more people were coming in the front door by the minute. He grabbed Ada's hand and pulled her off the stool and through the throng of people. As he passed the hostess, he told her they'd be on the boardwalk.

The night air was refreshing after the intensity of the crowd in the bar, and the breeze off the ocean was a blessing to his heated skin. He blamed it on a combination of his date's hot factor, Sharkey's potent beer, and maybe just a smidge of embarrassment that the entire town had likely seen Chesnee's video of Trip falling on his ass in a flowerbed.

"So, the locals seem friendly." Ada smiled broadly as she took another swig of her fruity cocktail.

He chuckled and pulled her closer. "If nosy as hell equals friendly, then they should win a prize." He placed a kiss just below her ear.

She twitched, whether from the kiss or from the breeze off the water, he wasn't sure.

"You cold?" He was a dolt—he didn't even have a jacket to offer her. September in Eastport Beach was still warm, but down here by the water it was always on the chilly side, especially at night. For good measure, he wrapped his arm around her shoulders.

She snuggled into his embrace. "Nope, you just gave me goosebumps."

"Good ones, I hope. Not the creepy kind?"

"Nothing creepy about the way you make me feel."

Hell, yeah.

"Trip! We've got a table for you!" the hostess hollered over the sound of the waves and the chatter from the patrons seated on the deck.

To be continued. He kissed her again, on the temple this time, then slid his hand down her arm to twine his fingers in hers. It felt so natural to hold her hand. They fit like puzzle pieces, but really satisfying ones, like when you spend all winter working on a 1000-piece puzzle of skiers on a snowy hill and over half the pieces are white, then finally, when your mom threatens to clear it off the table because it's spring and she can't stand the look of snow for one more minute, you place that last piece and for sixty seconds, you just revel in your accomplishment.

Hopefully his sister wouldn't show up and with great pleasure sweep it into the floor just to watch it fall apart.

"Justine will be your server. Enjoy your meal." The hostess went back to her stand where a line of people had formed.

"I swear it's not usually this busy. It feels like the entire town is here. And a handful of tourists."

Ada opened her menu. "Well, it's probably a testament to how good it is."

Trip laughed. "It's good, but it's also the only restaurant open past seven p.m."

Her mouth formed a little "o" as she lifted her drink. "And the only bar?"

He nodded. "Until Sharkey gets the brewery open that is." He lifted his glass, swirling the amber liquid around. "Shark Bite Brewing Company is local, although right now he just does festivals and such, but he bought the land behind Heron House and is going to open a brewery."

"Like where we saw the gator?"

"A little farther up the river, but basically."

"I'm not sure drunk people and gators mix." She set her empty glass down.

He waved off her concern. "Stumpy won't want to have anything to do with a bunch of noisy drunks. It'll be fine."

"He might have to change the name to Gator Bite Brewing Company."

Trip chuckled. "I'll make the suggestion next time I see him."

"Hey guys, sorry it took so long. I think everybody in Eastport Beach is here tonight." Justine seemed out of breath as she stepped up to the table.

"We were just saying that. Can you think of anything special going on?"

She shook her head, then took a pad out of her pocket. "I know people are excited about the gala, but I don't know what that has to do with running me ragged tonight." She patted her apron, then her head, finally locating a pencil in her bun. She rolled her eyes. "Sorry, the baby had me up most the night."

Ada's face brightened. "You have a new baby?"

"Yeah." Justine pulled her phone out of her pocket and flashed the lock screen. "Orion. He's three months old." She slid the phone back into her apron. "And I can attest that newborn brain is even worse than pregnancy brain, so I've got to write everything down these days."

Ada asked a few questions, then they ordered, and Justine took off for another table that had been sat nearby.

"Do you want to have kids someday?" Trip felt like he was having an out-of-body experience, because normally he would never ask that question on a first date, hell, maybe not even a fifth or sixth date, but for some reason, with Ada he really wanted to know.

If she was shocked by the question, she didn't let on, but she was thoughtful as she considered her answer. "I think so. I would just want to make sure I was in a place in my life that I could really focus on them, make sure they knew how important they were to me."

He nodded, realizing he understood exactly what she meant. "That makes a lot of sense." He hadn't had the strongest role models for parenting, so he never even considered the possibility of having children. But he appreciated her thoughtful consideration, and it made him realize the matter wasn't completely settled in his mind.

"I've never known my father." Ada practically whispered the statement but shared this very personal detail nonetheless.

"And now your mother is sick. I'm sorry, Ada." He placed his hand over hers and squeezed.

She gave him a little half-smile. "Yeah, I feel like now I may never get answers."

"Have you considered genealogy?" Today he'd made the decision to defy his family's wishes, and here she was searching for hers.

She shrugged. "Maybe. It's part of the reason I came here. My mother did her residency at Heron House the summer before I was born."

"So, you think she met your father here?"

"Maybe."

"Archie?" That would be a wild connection. "You'd get Riley as a cousin." He grinned. He'd be thrilled to call Riley family. Then something else occurred to him. Would Riley lose Heron House if there was another heir?

Ada fidgeted with her napkin. "I mean, it's definitely crossed my mind, but honestly, I hope it's not him."

"Why do you say that?" At least she wasn't down here on some inheritance hunt.

"Because my mother has never been the least bit nurturing, and now, she barely knows who I am. It'd be nice to find out that my father is still alive. That I could have a relationship with him."

Trip wondered if the man who left Ada's mother to raise her alone would even care to be found. It gutted him to think of her getting her hopes up and then finding out she wasn't wanted—by either of her parents.

Chapter Nineteen

She couldn't believe she'd told Trip about not knowing her father. On their first date, no less. Between that and discussing children, the conversation had gotten heavy real fast. She was failing at this fling thing.

Luckily, the food had arrived, and they'd spent the meal talking about the work he'd done around Heron House and the quaint town he'd grown to love.

"You know, living in a New York City apartment building is a bit like living in a small town. You've got crazy neighbors, people who feel like family, and that one odd woman who decorates for Christmas in August."

"It must have been fun to grow up around so many different people. Our closest neighbor was miles away. My sister and I were raised by a series of nannies and even when our parents were around, they were too busy arguing to pay us any attention."

She would have given up her favorite stuffed bunny to have a sibling, or a nanny, for that matter. Another person so she didn't feel so alone all the time. "My neighbor looked after me sometimes, but even when my mom was home, she was so focused on her art, she couldn't have told you what clothes I was wearing that day. She never looked up while she was painting."

"I guess it goes to show you, there's no guarantees in life. I had two parents, and you only had one—but they were all narcissistic assholes—no offense to your mother—"

"Are you kidding? It's like you've met her." Ada laughed.

"And I'd say we turned out okay."

"I can't refute the asshole part of your statement, but I currently have no plans for my future, a lease I won't be able to afford without a job, and my only skill is knowing the steps to about a hundred dances."

Trip leaned back in his chair, appraising her. Her body lit up everywhere his gaze roamed.

"Teaching dance is a very useful skill, which could easily translate into a job. But have you ever considered modeling?"

"Is that a pickup line? Because I already said yes to the date." A model. Ha! If he saw Bethy, he'd nix that idea real quick.

He chuckled. "Not a line but let me tell you about this rudderless ship." He gestured to himself. "I have a law degree, and I detest the law. My family expects me to work in the family business, and I'd rather shovel manure for a living—which, come to think of it, is kind of what they do. I'm currently mowing the grass and performing odd jobs for a roof over my head."

"So, this is a competition of who's got the least prospects?"

"I mean, I don't want to brag or anything."

Justine arrived at their table holding a fresh drink for each of them.

Trip accepted the beer with a confused look. "We didn't order more drinks, Justine."

She nodded toward the crowd. "Courtesy of the looky-loos at the bar."

Ada shifted in her chair so she could see the bar area, where a dozen or more people waved at them.

"Which ones?" Trip asked.

Justine rolled her eyes. "All of them. They heard you gave some ballroom dance lessons at Heron House last night and they want to know if you'll have another lesson before the gala."

"See, I told you your dance skills were useful." Trip sat back in his seat, smugness written all over his face.

"We struggled for room with three couples, I doubt we could fit everyone in."

A blonde woman at the next table leaned out of her seat. "I already spoke to Lance Huffman. You can use the Eastport Gallery space tomorrow night." She reached her hand out to Ada. "I'm Piper. Eastport Beach's finest realtor."

Justine smirked. "Pipe, you're our only realtor."

Ada looked to Trip to gauge his reaction.

"You know the space we saw? Hardwoods, tin ceiling, mosaics?"

A chill of excitement shot through her body. "Will you help me?"

"Of course." His grin matched hers.

She turned to Justine. "I guess we're in."

The waitress stuck her tray under her arm and cupped her hands around her mouth. "Tomorrow night in the old Eastport Gallery space, ballroom dance lessons will be provided by Ada and Trip, donations highly encouraged." She looked at the two of them. "What time?"

Ada shrugged. "Seven?"

"Seven o'clock," she bellowed. "Shirt and shoes required." She dropped her voice and leaned closer to Ada. "In this town, you always have to specify."

***

"You didn't have to agree to the dance lessons. The residents of this town can be a little pushy." Trip held the door open for Ada. Behind them, the entire restaurant seemed to bid them farewell.

"Are you kidding? I can't wait to see that space." She sucked in the cool evening air and reveled in the feel. "I mean, it's a little creepy that they planned it all out, but I love to teach." Between the impending lesson and a lovely evening with a great guy, she was happier than she'd been in a long time.

"Hold on, I'll be right back." Trip slipped back into the restaurant and headed back toward their table.

She wondered if he had forgotten to leave a tip.

Instead, she watched him lean down and speak to the realtor, who dug through her purse for a minute.

An older couple approached the door to The Landing, the man opening it for his lady. But she stopped short when she saw Ada. "You're the dancer!"

Ada laughed. "Yes."

"We can't wait for our dance lesson tomorrow night! I've got a new dress for the gala and the only dance this one knows is the hustle." She jerked her thumb in the direction of the gentleman holding the door.

News sure did travel fast in this town.

"Mr. Jessup, Mrs. Jessup, lovely evening." Trip came out the door and tipped an imaginary hat at the couple. He grabbed Ada's arm and pulled her toward the street.

"We'll see you tomorrow, Trip."

Ada let him lead her away from The Landing, happy to have a bit of alone time with her date. "They're coming to the lesson tomorrow."

"I imagine the whole town will show up. We may need to hire security." They passed his car and kept on walking.

"Do I need to be worried?"

"Nah, as long as there's no alcohol, it should be manageable."

Eastport Beach was shaping up to be the most interesting town she'd ever visited. Once again, she admired the architecture of the older buildings lining Main Street. She couldn't wait to dance in that cool old building.

They passed the coffee house and came to a stop in front of the building with the brown paper over the windows.

"Do you think they'll mind if we take the paper off the windows?"

"Piper said we could do whatever we needed to as long as it wasn't permanent." He held up a shiny brass key.

She tapped her feet in excitement. "We can go in now?"

"Sure can." He turned the key in the door and then stepped aside. "Ladies first."

It was dark inside, but a door-shaped light spread across the floor from the streetlamps outside. Trip turned his flashlight on and walked to the back of the space. He tried a couple switches until locating the one that bathed the room in bright lights.

Ada spun around, taking in the white walls, the wood floors and the tin ceiling. It was easy to envision mirrors along one wall, a barre, and the room filled with the laughter of children. The alcoves at the front could feature a shoe display, or leotards, or advertisements for upcoming shows. The whole place screamed with possibility.

Music filled the room, and Trip grabbed her, pulled her into a waltz hold and swept them around the room.

She gladly followed Trip's lead, even though she couldn't tell his intentions. He was doing a combo of steps she'd never experienced, which either meant he was extremely advanced, or couldn't remember a full dance from his competition days. Either way, she didn't care. It felt nice to be held by a confident man, with his gaze focused on her face and their bodies molded together.

She couldn't remember the last time she had danced for the pure joy of it. That's what dancing with Trip was—joyful. She didn't want it to end.

"Playing music on my phone is okay for right now, but I'm going to see if we can borrow the sound equipment from the church."

"It might be nice to have a few chairs too, in case someone needs to rest." She spun out from his embrace, gripping his hand as he pulled her back in. She hadn't felt this carefree since she was a kid learning the grand jeté.

Once she was firmly in his embrace, he leaned down and kissed her nose. "And a cooler with some water. We don't want anyone to get overheated."

He was extraordinary. She wasn't the least bit nervous about throwing together this impromptu dance lesson for the whole town. Not with Trip by her side, knowing exactly what needed to be done.

"Thank you."

He dipped her. "For what?"

"For dinner. For this. For everything."

He pulled her back up and ended the dance with a real kiss.

***

The ride back to Heron House was tense, but electric. Trip kept his large hand firmly planted on Ada's thigh, the heat from it fanning the excitement coursing through her body. They didn't speak, but after the intense make-out session at the temporary dance studio, it was clear where this night was heading.

Ada refused to talk herself out of spending the night with Trip, even though it was completely out of character for her. But in the past few weeks, her life had been turned on its head and she was relying on her gut instinct for once. All the careful plans she'd made had gone up in smoke the day she got the phone call about her mother's accident.

Planning hadn't gotten her anywhere.

She wanted Trip and he clearly wanted her. There were no plans or responsibilities to use as an excuse to chicken out. She was a grown-ass woman. She wasn't a naive young girl any longer. Trip wasn't taking advantage of her. She would go willingly to his bed.

He pulled the car to a stop beside the fountain. He turned the ignition off and faced her. His thumb stroked the inside of her leg. "You, okay?"

The question surprised her, so she paused to take stock of the situation. The moon was high in the sky, highlighting the lawn and the house in a soft glow, but the interior of the car was fairly dark.

Sure, her heart was beating a mile a minute, but she was excited, not nervous. So excited that her leg was jiggling. Ninety percent excited. Right?

"How about we take a walk?"

She let out a whoosh of air. How could he see that she was twenty percent nervous? "That sounds nice."

He gave her leg a squeeze before getting out of the car.

Pull it together, Ada. This is normal. People date, they have sex. It's not a dirty little secret like the first time. Trip is nothing like him.

She startled when Trip opened her door. Maybe she should have had that second drink to calm her nerves. He reached his hand out and pulled her up, but instead of shutting the car door right away, he boxed her in against the window.

He didn't say anything for long moments, just staring into her eyes. His hand came up to brush her hair out of her face, then he trailed his fingers down her cheek to her neck. Leaning closer, he kissed the corner of her mouth, then the other side, finally placing a light peck square on her lips. "I really like you, Ada. But I would never want to pressure you." His words were a whisper, caressing her worried heart.

She brought her hands up to his face. "I really like you too." Peace filled her body as she leaned in and kissed him deeply. Her nervous energy was quickly replaced with a burning desire. She kissed along his jawline. "And I don't feel pressured."

"Good." He drew her lips back to his for a quick, but intense kiss. Then he grabbed her hand, and they headed toward the gazebo. "It's so peaceful out here at night. There's no city lights or noise, just the water, the stars in the sky, and the occasional bird that hasn't gone to bed yet."

"Don't forget about Stumpy." Ada was kidding but did a quick scan near the water for log/alligator shaped objects just in case.

Trip chuckled and squeezed her hand. "Luckily Stumpy mostly minds his own business."

They reached the gazebo and sat on the bench staring out at the water. She moved close to him, and he stretched his arm over her shoulders. It felt like this was their special place, even though all they'd done that first night was hold hands—and share a bit about their family difficulties.

After they had gone into a bit more detail tonight, she felt even closer to him. Like he was someone who understood the way she grew up. Like maybe they would be a good match, because they had similar backgrounds.

His hand traced circles around her shoulder, lighting up her skin and making the other arm jealous for attention. She leaned her head back, looking up at him. He grinned, then lowered his mouth to hers, taking his time, exploring her body with his hands.

He made her feel treasured, adored, like she was worth the time he spent with her. Things she hadn't felt before. Her mind wandered back to her conversation with Bethy, about Ada having casual sex for the first time. She felt safe with Trip. Then she remembered the other thing Bethy had said.

As he trailed kisses down her neck, she whispered, "Trip's a nickname, right? Like you're something something the third?"

He froze, his lips pressed in the sensitive spot behind her ear. "Yeah." After a few seconds, he nipped at her earlobe.

"So, what's the something something?"

She pulled away from his mouth, wanting to read his expression, because clearly, he didn't care for this line of questioning.

"What? Is it like Ernesto or something? Is your middle name Muriel?" She wondered if he'd get the *Friends* reference, but he didn't laugh.

He raked a hand through his hair. "It's Carlton Wingate Westinghouse III."

It came out as a whisper, but she wasn't sure why he seemed to hate it. "Carlton, that's not awful. But maybe your dad goes by that?" Something was nagging at the back of her mind, but she couldn't place it.

He shook his head, but his posture had gone rigid, and he'd pulled farther back from her. "My dad goes by Win." He audibly swallowed. "My grandfather goes by Carlton."

Carlton Westinghouse. Why is that familiar? Carlton Westinghouse. Senator Westinghouse. No!

She tried to school her face as the realization hit, but she obviously failed, because Trip reached for her, a worried expression on his face.

"I'm nothing like my grandfather. Or my father, for that matter."

He's going back to Virginia to work in the family business. He's going into politics. Would he play God with people's lives like his grandfather? She needed to get away. There wasn't enough oxygen in this gazebo. In this riverside oasis.

She started to get up, but Trip's face crushed her. Would she want someone to judge her because she was Charlotte Maddox's daughter?

"Please, Ada, don't hold my family against me. It's why I don't want to go back to Virginia. I don't want to have anything to do with that life."

She needed time to think this through, to piece together her feelings, because it felt like her happiness bubble had been pumping up all evening and it had just popped. But if she decided she could live with this, she didn't want Trip to hate her for acting poorly. So, she drew on her experience of pushing down unwelcome emotions before a performance. She stuffed her hatred of Senator Westinghouse and his awful policies in a box and locked them up tight until she could be alone with her thoughts. "Of course, I understand. Obviously, you aren't them. You love Eastport Beach, and mowing the lawn, and making lasagna." She reached out and patted his knee.

He grabbed her hand like it was a lifeline. His shoulders sagged in relief. "I wasn't trying to keep it from you, I just don't feel like Carlton III. I feel like Trip.

Especially here. Especially with you." He turned her hand over and kissed her palm.

"I get it." She forced a smile. Intellectually she understood, but emotionally, she felt someone had just squirted silly string all over the Zen Garden she'd spent years raking.

"Speaking of my family, I need to ask you a favor." If he had been tense when she asked his name, now he looked like he was facing the Inquisition. "I told my mother I had a date for the gala because she was threatening to bring my ex along. I told her we were serious."

It took Ada a full minute to realize that he meant her. *He told his mother he was in a serious relationship with me. Before I even knew his real name. This is too much.* She pulled her hand out of his and practically leapt off the bench, backing toward the stairs. "I'm sorry, Trip, but I don't feel comfortable lying to your family. I don't think this is a good idea."

He may have said something, but all she could hear was the pounding in her head as she ran across the lawn under the moonlight, praying the entire way that the front door was unlocked and she wouldn't have to wait for him to open it. Because right now, she never wanted to see Carlton Wingate Westinghouse III again.

Chapter Twenty

Trip got up early to tackle the massive checklist Riley had before guests started arriving. He knew the morning would be busy, so he'd made a breakfast casserole last night after his disastrous end of the date with Ada.

Cooking usually calmed him down, but he had barely slept. He never should have withheld his identity from Ada. Trip knew from experience that people either hated his grandfather or thought they could get something out of a relationship with Trip because of his powerful family. He preferred to stay anonymous for as long as possible, but this time it had truly bitten him in the ass.

On top of that, even though it was obvious she wasn't thrilled to hear he was a Westinghouse, he'd asked her to pretend to be his girlfriend. Which was doubly ridiculous, because he *wanted* her to be his girlfriend. She was unlike any woman he'd ever met. Sweet, but a little cynical. Smart and real. Stunningly beautiful. She understood a life of growing up in the shadow of a famous person. Of being mostly left to fend for herself despite having money. Understanding that money only went so far.

But he'd blown it. And she hadn't even come down for breakfast. In fact, as he went from room to room on the second floor, getting everything ready for the new guests, he hadn't seen her at all. She had either left super early or was hiding out in her room because she couldn't stand the idea of seeing him.

He'd checked off most of Riley's to-dos, so he headed to the kitchen, where his casserole was still warm in the oven. He secured aluminum foil over the top and slid it on the bottom shelf of the fridge. Ben would probably snack on it tonight.

He was checking ingredients for lunch when the text from his mother came through.

Not saying she'd be there in five minutes, but "we'll be there in five minutes". *Who is we?* She likely had a driver, but she never included the help in her pronouns.

He closed the refrigerator door, his appetite scuttling away like the mouse Ansel refused to kill.

Had his parents decided to ride down together after all? He had trouble picturing them in the same car for almost six hours.

His sister was doing a semester abroad, so it was highly unlikely she'd show up to a small gala on the coast of North Carolina.

His mother had promised she wouldn't bring his ex—but her track record on keeping promises wasn't noteworthy.

For that matter, why was Karina Westinghouse so set on attending this event?

And what was he going to tell her about his lack of the girlfriend he'd sworn he had?

He considered throwing back a Heineken to take the edge off, but his mother would smell it on his breath and definitely not approve of alcohol before noon. Except for mimosas. She always made an exception for mimosas.

There was no time to juice oranges, so he plodded to the front door to get it over with.

A black town car pulled to the base of the porch steps and the driver rounded the car to open the rear door. A slender, dark-haired man exited the car, then helped Karina out. He wore a white dress shirt with far too many buttons undone and a narrow blue scarf. Trip had spent enough time in Europe to spot an Italian. Although the smooth chest was throwing him for a loop.

The real question was why his mother was arriving at his place of work with an Italian man that couldn't be a day over thirty-five?

"Carlton, darling!"

The man assisted her up the steps in a way that reeked of familiarity. All the hairs on Trip's arms stood up and started running for the hills. His mother had a way of creating drama at the most inopportune times. He almost wished she had brought Jenny instead.

Grabbing her son's face, Karina kissed him on both cheeks—yet another European touch that didn't belong in coastal Carolina. "Honey, you look wonderful. So tan! I guess you've been hitting the beach every day."

He didn't bother to tell her that his tan was from working outside all summer, getting the landscaping ready for the big event. "Hello, Mother. It's nice to see you." He tried not to grit his teeth, but the whole affair was painful.

The driver carried several bags up the steps and Trip stepped forward to take them from the older gentleman.

"Oh, honey, let the bellhop get those. We need to catch up."

"Mother, this isn't The Plaza, this is a small retreat center. I'm the bellhop, and the landscaper, and anything else Riley needs me to be."

Her brow creased momentarily, but she quickly realized it and smoothed her expression. Wrinkle removal was expensive, after all. "I don't know what's worse—partying all summer or working below your station."

Trip scanned the property to make sure no one was nearby to hear his mother's elitist comments. "Mother, there is no shame in doing manual labor. I'm proud of the work I've done here. If you're just going to insult me and my friends, you can get back in that car and go home to Virginia."

Her eyes widened at his impertinence. "What has gotten into you?"

"Who's your friend, Mother? I hope he has a room reserved elsewhere, because we are full up." If she was going to be a boor, so would he.

The man straightened, puffing out his hairless chest. He barely came up to Trip's shoulders, and there were clearly lifts in his shoes.

"This is Maurico Donovan, we're on the Arts Council together, so of course, I told him he just had to come along. He's retired from the Italiano Supremo Ballet Company." She beamed at the man, who preened under her attention.

Trip fought back an audible gag. "Nice to meet you, Maurice. I'm Trip. Your best bet is the Comfort Inn over in Bluffville."

"I'm sure you can find room for my friend, Carlton." Karina tilted her head in that I'm-serious-son way.

"We have six guest rooms. Riley was nice enough to save one for you, but there is no extra space."

Karina was going to have to visit Dr. Creston if she kept scowling like that.

"Carlton, I'm sure you can work something out."

Just then, the screen door banged open, and Ada stepped onto the porch. Seeing them, she froze, her eyes widening and her breaths coming in shallow gasps.

"Ada, is everything okay?" He forgot about sparring with his mother and stepped closer to make sure she was alright.

Her eyes darted from his mother to the smarmy Italian to Trip.

"This is my mother and her friend, Maurice." He practically growled the word friend, trying to hold back the bile that rose in his throat.

"Ada"—the Italian slid his arm around Karina's waist—"it's lovely to see you."

Trip was torn between punching the guy out and comforting Ada, who looked like her favorite pet had just died.

Their eyes met and something unspoken passed between them. Unfortunately, it was a one-sided conversation, because Trip was stunned when she leaned forward and kissed him lightly on the lips. "Everything is fantastic, babe. I was just coming to find you for lunch. I didn't think your mother was arriving until later." She turned to Karina and held out her hand. "Trip has told me so many wonderful things about you. I'm Ada, his girlfriend."

His mother looked as shocked as he felt. He could have sworn Ada said she would not pose as his girlfriend to get his mother off his back. Just last night.

After they shook hands, Ada slid her arm around Trip's waist and leaned into him. "Maurico, it's lovely to see you also."

Clearly, they knew each other. And from the way Ada was vibrating against him, he was guessing they weren't best buds reuniting.

"Are you staying here, Ada?" Karina narrowed her eyes at the younger woman.

"Yes, that's how we met." She looked up at Trip, smiling, but she was trying to talk with her eyes again. "And we've been inseparable ever since." She pinched his side. "Right, babe?"

Trip's brain was short-circuiting from too much input.

"Well, there's our solution, then. Ada can let Maurico have her room and she can stay with you, Carlton."

Ada's hand tightened on his waist as her smile tightened on her face.

As much as he'd like to get Ada into his bed, he didn't want her forced into it. And after last night, she probably didn't want to spend any alone time with him. "Ada is a paying guest here at Heron House. We aren't going to kick her out of her room and make her stay in my sterile staff quarters."

"Well, if you're really a couple, I would think you'd want to stay together." A challenge gleamed in Karina's eye.

"Karina, Bellissima, please, I'll go. Is fine." Maurico picked up a leather valise.

She put a hand on his arm to stop him. "Maurico, don't be silly. My son will go get your room ready right now."

Ada leaned close to Trip's ear. "It's fine, let him have my room."

"Are you sure? I don't want you to feel uncomfortable." He gripped her shoulders lightly, stroking her arm with his thumb. Her skin felt like velvet.

"Too late." Ada threw a glance at Maurico before turning and opening the screen door.

He was fairly certain no one else heard the muttered words, because his mother looked triumphant, and Maurico set down his luggage.

"You can wait in the parlor while I get the rooms ready, Mother." Trip grabbed the bags and headed inside. They could find their own way for all he cared.

Chapter Twenty-One

Ada was flinging her clothes into her bag, stomping around the room, when Trip knocked on the open door.

"Can you explain to me what happened down there?" Trip set a brown leather suitcase on the floor under the window. "Last night you said you wouldn't lie to my mother."

That was before Maurico Donovan appeared on the porch. In North Carolina. At the exact same place she was staying. "When I saw how your mother was treating you, I felt sorry for you." She shrugged, trying to appear casual.

He narrowed his eyes. "Not that I don't appreciate the gesture—but you missed most of my mother's passive aggressive attempt to control the universe. How do you know that Maurice guy anyway? You basically stopped breathing when you saw him."

Why did he have to be so perceptive? She hoped a partial truth would keep him from asking too many more questions. "We used to perform together. A long time ago."

She could practically see the gears grinding in Trip's head. She needed something to gunk up those gears and make them grind to a halt.

"I was just surprised to see him is all." She crossed the room and took Trip's hand. "This will be fine. I mean, we enjoy each other's company, right?"

He wound his fingers between hers and pulled her closer. "Well, yeah. I don't have a problem spending more time with you. I just don't want you to feel pressured to..." He licked his lips nervously.

"Trip, there's a big difference between sleeping together and *sleeping together*." Her heart rate kicked up and she leaned a little closer. "I'm sure you will be a perfect gentleman."

"I'm certainly going to try." His gaze dropped to her mouth. "But I'm far from a saint."

As close as they were, the kiss still took her by surprise. It was tender, Trip applying gentle pressure to her lips, teasing them with his tongue, asking to enter but not banging on the door. And damn if she didn't let him in.

She was breathless when he pulled back.

"Listen, about last night—"

"Trip, it's fine. Don't worry about it. I was just surprised." Right now, it was more important to save face in front of her ex than to worry about Trip's relation to the bastard who canceled the funding for her program. She'd sort that out later.

"Carlton! Where are you, dear?"

His whole body went rigid at the sound of his mother's voice. "I'm really sorry about my mother. She thinks the universe revolves around her. You can stay in my room, and I'll figure something out."

Karina Westinghouse and Maurico appeared in the open doorway.

Ada's body echoed Trip's discomfort.

"Mother, your room is at the top of the stairs. Your friend's room will be ready in about an hour." He shooed them out of the room.

"Oh my, this is the Maddox suite. Is that Charlotte Maddox? I met her once at a gallery opening in New York. What a talented painter." Trip's mother poked her head back in the room, taking in the paintings on the wall.

Ada stared Trip down, hoping he wouldn't spill the beans.

It didn't matter, because Maurico shook that can up and opened it wide. "Ada is Charlotte's daughter, Karina."

"Oh!" Mrs. Westinghouse's entire demeanor changed in an instant. Suddenly, Ada was deemed "interesting" and "acceptable." She swept back into the room. "Darling, your mother is one of the most talented painters of our time. You must tell me all about growing up with such an artistic genius."

Ada guessed she'd become "Darling" because Trip's mother hadn't absorbed her name back when she was nobody. But she noticed the woman didn't offer the suite back to its rightful occupant. "It was interesting, that's for sure."

She clutched her pearls (literally). "I can only imagine! Do you paint, dear?"

"Ada's a dancer, Mom."

"Oh, yes, of course. That's how you two know each other, right?" She gripped Maurico's arm.

Her ex preened like a horny peacock. "Yes, Ada danced with my company. I was a mentor of sorts to her."

The ick from that statement shot through her body and threatened to escape her in a violent fashion.

Trip must have seen something on her face, because he grabbed her and her half-packed suitcase and pushed past her mother and the scum of the ballet world. "I'll be back in a few minutes. I'm just going to take Ada's stuff up to my room." He propelled her up a narrow staircase, like they were escaping a fire-breathing dragon.

Except Ada felt like she was the dragon, and she'd love to singe every hair on that pompous prick's head. How had she ever been attracted to him? The foolishness of youth, she supposed. Another shudder raced through her body.

Trip pushed open a door and threw her bag on the bed. He turned and grasped her shoulders. "Let me get my mother and that Italian dick settled and then we need to talk about this"—he gestured between them—"arrangement." He placed a gentle kiss on her cheek and left.

The room was sparse—a double bed, a chest in front of the window, a bag of golf clubs in one corner, and a wardrobe. Certainly not the room of a power-hungry rising political star. That's why Ada was having such a hard time reconciling who she thought Trip was with who he revealed himself to be last night. He'd grown up wealthy, but she saw evidence of his hard work all around her. His family wielded great influence, but he had fallen in love with the simple people in this small town.

I'm doing exactly what people do to me when they find out who my mother is. I'm judging him based on his parents and grandparents' decisions and lifestyles. She sank down onto the bed, burying her face in her hands. *Hypocrite.*

She'd finally met a man who intrigued her, who had awoken desire in her, who was sweet and kind and funny. His name didn't change any of those things. *Damn, I'm a fool.*

"Ada, is everything okay?" Gina appeared in the doorway to Trip's room.

She lifted her head, shaking off the shame she was experiencing. "Yeah, I'm fine. Trip's mom brought an unexpected guest, so we're playing musical beds." She laughed, but it sounded screechy and unnatural.

"Are you staying in here?"

"That's the plan for now. Trip said he'd figure something out."

Gina leaned against the doorframe. "I'm guessing it won't be a hardship based on how cozy the two of you have been."

Ha! Ada wanted to say "back at you" about Gina and Chesnee, but she held her tongue. "Actually, we sort of told his mother that we're dating."

"Are you?"

She shrugged. "TBD."

"But you like him?"

"How was the concert last night?" Ada stood, facing Gina.

The other woman lost her confident pose and the spark in her eye. "It was fine. I mean the music was great, but you know."

"No, please enlighten me."

Gina was wearing black leggings and a simple white tee, but she made the outfit look edgy with her spiked red hair and dark eye makeup. Those soulful green eyes darted to the floor. "It's hard spending that long with Chesnee. I mean, I love the guy"—she threw up a hand in the universal stop gesture—"not like that! Anyway, if we spend more than a couple hours together, I can see the wheels turning in his head, thinking there's something more between us."

"And there isn't?" Ada raised her eyebrows.

Gina stood up straight, one foot back, almost like she was setting her mark for a race. She looked ready to bolt. "No. There can't be."

Ada decided not to point out the difference. "You're worried you're leading him on?"

"Yeah. But I really wanted to see that band."

Both women laughed and the mood lightened.

Gina tugged on her earlobe. "Trip's a good guy. If you're not into him, don't..." A noise from the stairwell grabbed her attention.

"I won't."

Trip appeared, looking weary.

"Hey, Trip. I heard your mom arrived."

Gina flicked her eyes back to Ada briefly and Ada recognized the girl code immediately. Keep the conversation to yourself.

"Yeah. Yippee." He pushed past the two women and collapsed on the bed. "Anyone have a Valium?"

Ada's shock must have been written across her face, because he rushed to amend his question.

"For my mother."

Gina laughed. "I can't wait to meet her, but I've got to get to work."

"Lucky." Trip raked his hands over his face and blew out a sigh.

"Bye, Gina. Maybe we can talk more later." Ada tipped a hand up in a wave.

Eyes narrowed, Gina backed toward the stairs. "Maybe." She waved before turning and clomping down the narrow staircase.

"I'd ask what you ladies talked about, but I imagine it comes with a strict code of confidentiality, so I won't bother." He looked uncomfortable, stretched sideways across a bed far too small for his statue.

"That bed is barely big enough for you, how are we supposed to both sleep in it?"

He peeked one eye open. "I can think of one way." His tone had gone from exhausted to salacious in two point three seconds.

Ada cracked a smile. "Har har."

Trip opened both eyes and sat up, reaching his hand out.

She took it and he pulled her down to sit beside him on the bed.

"Again, I'm sorry about my mother. She struggles to act like a normal human."

"Trust me, I get it. Charlotte Maddox has always believed she was queen of whatever universe she lived in."

He was lightly tracing circles on her thigh, and it was starting to affect other parts of her body. Namely the sexy bits.

"I'm going to check with Riley and Ben and see if I can stay on the boat."

"Are they not staying there?" That's where they had been headed last night when the two couples parted ways on the porch.

"I'm pretty sure that was just for last night. Riley wants to be up before the guests to make juice and cinnamon rolls." He shook his head and sighed. Ada snickered. "Maybe you should make something."

"Oh, I plan to, although my mother will probably have a heart attack when she finds out I can cook."

"Oh, is this a new thing?" She found herself leaning closer to him, drawn by his natural charm.

His hand was venturing farther up her leg as they spoke. "We weren't allowed in the kitchen growing up. I doubt my mother could manage to boil water. As soon as I got out of the house, I started taking cooking classes. I love experimenting with recipes and trying new dishes."

"Everything I've had so far has been delicious." *Including those lips.* She leaned closer, focused on his face.

"Ada, I think we should talk about this dating thing." He inched closer to her, so close their breaths mingled in the air.

"What about it?" She brushed her lips lightly over his and he groaned.

Gripping her chin, he pushed her back far enough that he could meet her eyes. "We need to make sure we're on the same page."

She licked her lips, and he sighed.

"Fuck it." His mouth crashed against hers and within moments, their bodies were tangled up on the bed.

"We should have kept the big bed and made Maurico sleep up here. It's more his size anyway."

Trip guffawed and then took her mouth again.

He had just yanked her shirt over her head when his phone rang.

Chapter Twenty-Two

He ignored the phone and kissed along Ada's collarbone. Her skin was like creamy whipped butter—soft, fair, and delicious. He pulled one of her bra straps off her shoulder and explored the area with his mouth. Ada's breaths came in soft huffs, her hands pressing him closer and her legs crossing over his, holding him in place. *Fine with me, I'm not going anywhere.*

When the phone rang for the third time, Ada pulled away from him. "Do you need to get that?" She panted, her skin flushed.

He'd never seen anything more beautiful. "Fuck, no." The only person he cared to talk to was underneath him and despite the niggling thought at the back of his mind, he was fully committed to seeing this through. He'd been imagining this since the moment she collided with his naked body in the hallway.

She pawed at the hem of his shirt, pulling it up and over his head. Her nails raked lightly down his chest, sending signals straight to his cock.

But the phone relented. It beeped with a voicemail. "Let me just make sure the house isn't burning down." He yanked the device out of his pocket, wishing they'd never been invented, because it was way too easy for his family to reach out. The voicemail was from his dad and his smart phone helpfully wrote the message out for him to see.

Win: Lunch? I'm on my way to pick you up.

He groaned, and not because Ada's hands had made their way to the waistband of his pants. Because this was worse than the house being on fire. This was a fucking missile heading in their direction and he was the only one who could save this little world he'd built here.

Ada lay beneath him, her tongue peeking out between her lips, her hair spread out on the mattress below her.

"Fuck, Ada." He leaned down and captured her mouth. Teased that tongue. And he deserved a medal for pulling away from her warmth. "I've got to go prevent World War III. Can we please, I beg you, come back here later? Right to this very moment?"

The smile slowly spread across her face. "Sure, whatever you need to do."

She was a fucking unicorn.

He stole another quick kiss, then stood, adjusting his pants that suddenly felt two sizes too small. As he headed for the stairs, he dialed his father. "Hey, I'm out, so I'll just meet you. Don't come to Heron House. I'll text you an address."

He hung up without a goodbye, because his father never bothered. The door to the Maddox suite was closed—he'd have to deal with that later. At the other end of the hall, his mother's door stood open, and her bags lay on the bed. She'd likely be appalled when she returned and no one had unpacked her luggage. *This isn't the fucking Four Seasons.*

Trip shot a text to his dad with the address of the country club in Bluffville. He didn't want to risk running into his mother and her "companion," wherever they had disappeared to. He flew down the stairs and out the front door, relieved that his mother's car and driver were still in the driveway. Hopefully they'd stick close to the house and not take their unrealistic expectations into Eastport Beach.

As soon as he was heading down River Road, he dialed Ben to offer a brief explanation of the current shit show. Ben promised he'd fill Riley in on the new sleeping arrangements and told him to have fun with his dad.

Yeah, that wasn't even a remote possibility.

***

The Bluffville Country Club was about thirty minutes from Eastport Beach, but it felt worlds away. It resembled a grand Southern plantation, and he was honestly surprised they hadn't been canceled for that yet. He'd spent a fair amount of time there, because it was the only gold course for thirty miles. It was basically a smaller, less politically correct version of the club he'd grown up going to.

By the time he parked and approached the entrance, his father had pulled under the portico and was likely waiting for the valet.

Trip slapped the roof of the car and leaned in the driver's side window. "They only have valet when there's a special event."

Win Westinghouse's face registered shock at the notion of parking his own car. "It's like we're in a third world country."

He laughed and pointed toward the lot. He assumed his dad was mostly joking. At least this parent had a decent sense of humor, if not an ounce of morality. Trip was shocked that his dad's "assistant" wasn't with him. Amber accompanied him on most of his trips, because one never knew when one might need someone to take a memo.

Trip watched his dad park and walk back toward him. It was amazing how alike they looked and yet how completely different they were. His father enjoyed all the trappings of their politically connected family. Thousand-dollar-a-plate charity dinners, hobnobbing with the rich and famous, vacationing on luxury yachts. Kissing the ring of the great Carlton Wingate Westinghouse Senior. Trip intended to end that cycle. He might be saddled with the name, but he didn't have to follow in their footsteps.

"You've got a nice tan going, son." Win slapped him on the back. "Wish I had time to lie around on the beach."

Trip mentally rolled his eyes. He'd been to the beach one time this summer—and only because Chesnee had dragged him there for a volleyball tournament. "Just a lot of working outside." They walked into the lobby of the club.

His dad surveyed the room, scoping out the decor as well as the members. "Quaint." He checked his watch. "What do you recommend? No seafood, I've got a meeting later."

Who the hell was he meeting with in North Carolina? They were two hours from Raleigh. "The filet is decent, but the chicken piccata is excellent."

They approached the hostess, who greeted Trip by name and sat them at a table overlooking the golf course.

Win watched the young woman walk away. "So, you're familiar with the hostess? She's cute, but a little on the young side."

Hello Pot, it's me, Kettle. But that was beside the point, because he wasn't "familiar" with Abby. "Chesnee and I eat here after golf every week." Then he made a split-second decision. "Besides, I'm seeing someone."

His father's eyebrows shot up. "Really? Is it anyone I would know?"

Trip had to assume he'd at least heard of Charlotte Maddox, but he didn't want to define Ada by her famous mother. He certainly didn't want to be defined by his well-known family. "No, I met her here. But she does live in Virginia."

"So, it's serious?" Win scanned the dining room, likely searching for someone to bring him a scotch.

"Enough." Then he decided to tell him the other thing. "Actually—"

"Waiter!" His father waved at the young man that was pouring water at another table.

He approached the table like a scared deer who really wanted that corn cob. "Yes, sir? Would you like some water?"

"God, no. Scotch. Top shelf. Neat." He waved his hand dismissively.

"I'll let your waiter know."

Win shook his head. "Everyone's always trying to pawn the work off on someone else."

Says the man that shows up to an office maybe twice a week and spends the rest of his time "networking."

Trip didn't bother trying to set him straight. It was a lost cause. "No Amber this trip?

A strange expression briefly crossed his father's face. One he couldn't quite place. "I had to let her go."

Well, blow me over with a leaf. "Wow, that's surprising."

"The campaign. Optics." He huffed. "Speaking of your grandfather..."

Do we have to?

"He told me you cancelled a meeting for next week."

Or Robert snitched. "That's what I was going to tell you—"

A different waiter appeared with Win's drink, which clearly had ice cubes in it.

Trip prayed he wouldn't make a scene.

"Do they not know what neat means in the Deep South?" He wagged his finger at the poor, unsuspecting server. "No ice, son. Try again."

The young man took the offending drink back with an apology and retreated.

Wow, his dad had chilled considerably. Normally, he'd have someone's head on a platter. He was probably worried about bad press just before the campaign launch. "This is hardly the Deep South, Dad."

Win flipped through the menu. "I guess I could have said the boonies."

Thank God for small favors. "I'm going to stay in Eastport Beach a bit longer."

His father looked up from the menu fast enough to get whiplash. "That wasn't our agreement."

"I know, but I love it here and I'd like to see where things go with Ada."

"I thought the girl lived in Virginia."

"She does, but she's staying here for a while." He actually didn't know Ada's plans, but he figured that argument would pass muster more than him wanting to stay at Heron House and keep working.

His father closed the menu and stared across the table. "You can't just cancel meetings with your grandfather, and you certainly can't void our agreement on a whim. I need your support on this campaign. It's why I paid to put you through law school and play around all summer."

"I've been working all summer. I haven't taken a dime from you or Mom."

"That's beside the point." The waiter arrived with the scotch neat. "Thank God." Win knocked the drink back and slammed the glass on the table. "Another one. And we'll both have the filet medium rare."

Trip was done being told what to do. He was a twenty-six-year-old man. "No, I want the chicken piccata with a side salad, please."

Win's nose twitched and his cheeks burned red. Trip wasn't sure if it was the drink or his impertinence. So much for having chilled. "Carlton, we all do things in this life that we don't want to. I married your mother. I've worked for my father for years. I brok—fired a perfectly good assistant."

"Well, I'm going to do things differently. I'll marry who I see fit, I'll work where I want to work, and I'll stay out of D.C." He didn't know where this streak of courage came from. Maybe Ada's kisses were magical.

The waiter returned with a second scotch and then realized Trip didn't have a drink at all. "Anything for you, sir?"

He considered something to take the edge off, but one of them had to stay level-headed. "Just water, thanks."

Win was staring out at the golf course, waiting for the help to leave the table. "How's the course?"

Okay, so we're playing it that way? "The front nine is pretty standard, but the back has a few tricks up its sleeve."

"You have time to play this weekend?"

He should play nice with his father, smooth things over. But what little time he had free he wanted to spend with Ada. "No, there's a lot to be done before the gala. I'm actually neglecting my work right now." He'd left without preparing the Maddox suite for the little Italian wiener. He was letting Riley down and that's the last thing he wanted.

"I've got meetings back-to-back. Probably for the best." His dad sipped his drink this time, continuing to stare out the window.

They spent the meal trading golf stories like two strangers who'd met in a bar. When they were walking out to their cars, his dad hit him with a doozy. "If I were you, I'd make that meeting on Monday. Your grandfather doesn't tolerate dissension."

Chapter Twenty-Three

Trip texted that he had to run an errand for Riley, but he'd be back within the hour, so Ada grabbed another pile of Archie's journals. She was holed up in Riley's study hoping to avoid running into Maurico.

As she flipped through the pages of a tome marked "Photag," her mind wandered back to making out with Trip. It was so outside her normal behavior, but he had a way of making her feel completely at ease, even with her shirt off and his mouth heading south. She was still on the fence about the entire situation, but somehow, she didn't have any doubts about sleeping with him.

And man was she ready to get back to it.

She set the journal aside, realizing that she wasn't paying enough attention to her task to prove useful. Maybe Riley had something else she needed help with. Something physical that would redirect her sexual energy until she and Trip could sneak away again. And toss their phones in the river.

Straightening the desk, she piled the journals she had gone through on one side and those needing to be tackled on the other. As she tidied the pile, she noticed an envelope sticking out of one of the books. She plucked that one out of the stack and opened it to where the envelope was holding a place.

The page contained a list of names, Charlotte Maddox among them. There were six of them, but none of the others seemed familiar. She would google them later. Turning the envelope over, she gasped. In her mother's flowy handwriting was Archie's name and the address for Heron House. The return address read a New York City address Ada didn't recognize. She collapsed back into the chair, her foot tapping the floor. She'd been searching for information about her mother for days, and now that she finally held something in her hands, she was too nervous to open it.

She examined the envelope closer, tracing the seams of the paper, studying the loops of her mother's Os. When Charlotte wrote her name with a pen, as opposed to a paint brush, she added a little flourish to her Os. Ada had noticed it before, but for the first time, she realized it was only in her name. Heron House didn't have the fancy script. Or North Carolina.

Ada wondered if it was something her mother had decided intentionally or if it was just a natural thing that happened when she wrote her name.

This intense internal debate about her mother's handwriting was just a procrastination tactic. She needed to buck up and open the damn envelope.

In the end, fate intervened, because the last time she spun the envelope in her hands, something fell out of it and fluttered to the floor. A photograph, maybe? She pushed the chair back and got down on her hands and knees. The photo had slid all the way under the desk and now lay face down out of her reach.

Just then, Riley's feet appeared, red flip flops on display. She stooped down and grabbed the picture. "Who's the baby?"

Ada rushed to stand up, hitting her head on the underside of the desk. "Ow!" She rubbed the spot, then backed up and slowly rose to standing. Did she hear Riley correctly? Baby?

Riley stood in front of the desk, her eyes wide and her mouth hanging open. She slowly turned the picture around so Ada could see what was written on the back.

Ada Grace Maddox

"I need to sit down." Ada grabbed for the chair, but it pushed farther away on its wheels. She planted her hands on the desk so she wouldn't fall over.

Riley rushed around the desk and helped Ada into the chair. "Where did you find this?"

Ada pointed numbly at the envelope and the open journal.

Tracing her finger down the page, Riley counted. "I bet this is a list of guests. Six guests, six rooms." She picked up the envelope and examined it. "The postmark is too faded to read."

If Ada had to guess, it was likely the year she was born. "Why would my mother send your uncle a baby picture of me?" She picked up the photograph Riley had laid on the desk. It was the type the hospital took of all newborns, wearing the pink and blue striped hat that all babies get saddled with on their first day in the world. "How many of these do you suppose the hospital gives out?" Maybe it was like school pictures where you could buy a sheet of six wallet-sized pictures. Or maybe they only give you one and Charlotte chose to send it to Archie.

Most of her friends growing up had baby books—newborn pictures, first lock of hair, funny anecdotes. Ada had once asked her mother if she had any pictures of her as a baby. Charlotte simply tapped her head. *I remember it all vividly. I could paint it tomorrow.*

The ballerina painting mocked her from across the room. It was the only time Ada knew of that her mother had painted her. Now all those memories were locked in Charlotte's brain, and no one had a key.

Ada stared at her newborn self. Her hair was darker than now, sticking up in wispy spikes, her head was dented on one side, and she did not look like she was enjoying her coming into the world party. No wonder, with Charlotte as the hostess.

"Oh good! I've found you." Trip's mother rushed into the room like she owned the place.

Ada grabbed the first book she could find and stuffed the picture inside. She certainly didn't want to reveal her childhood drama to this woman.

"Riley, did you tell her the good news?"

"Not yet." Riley leaned closer to Ada and dropped her voice. "I apologize in advance."

Karina Westinghouse pressed forward. "Riley was telling us about how the whole town is meeting up tonight for dance lessons. Maurico has agreed to help you lead the lessons! I had to give him a little nudge, but he'd do most anything for me." She patted her overly styled hair.

Hell would have to freeze over before I dance with that man again. "That's not necessary, Mrs. Westinghouse. Trip is going to help me with the lessons."

She waved her hand dismissively. "Oh, poo. Carlton hasn't danced in years. I doubt he even remembers the steps."

Ada was tempted to tell the nosy socialite just how many moves her son still possessed, but she decided to stick to dancing. "Actually, Trip dances incredibly well. We taught Riley and Ben the other night and he was an absolute pro." She bumped Riley's hip, hoping the desk would hide her movement.

"Yes!" Riley perked up. "Trip and Ada are an excellent team. They could enter a dance competition tomorrow."

Reel it back in, Riley. "Please thank Maurico for me, but his services are not required." Just saying his name left a bitter taste in her mouth. Trip couldn't get back fast enough.

Karina's face revealed her disapproval. For a society lady, she wasn't very good at hiding her emotions. Ada imagined most people didn't dare tell her no. *Well, lady. No, nope, hell no!*

"Mrs. Westinghouse," Riley said, rounding the desk, "have you tried my lemonade yet? It's fresh squeezed."

Trip's mother definitely wanted to stay and argue with Ada, but like a proper guest, she allowed herself to be led out of the study. Before they reached the French doors, though, she stopped in her tracks and pointed at Charlotte's painting. "My goodness, this is so striking. Who is the artist?"

Riley glanced over her shoulder and made eye contact with Ada, who shook her head. "We're still searching for provenance, so I can't be sure—"

"It's a Charlotte Maddox!" Apparently, the older woman had had work done on her eyesight as well, if she could read the signature from that distance. She spun on Ada, her finger outstretched. "Is it you?"

Ada nodded begrudgingly.

Returning her attention to the portrait, Karina tsked. "She certainly was a talented painter to capture something so mundane so beautifully."

In that moment, Ada realized why Trip had issues with his mother. She was positively vile.

***

"Do you think either of us stand a chance of being a good parent?" Ada pushed the dust mop across the floor.

Trip was atop a ladder, changing light bulbs in the track lighting. "You mean because of our terrible examples?"

She hadn't told him what his mother said, so the question probably seemed out of the blue, but it was amazing how he got what she was thinking. "Yeah."

"I take it my mother said something awful while I was gone?" He climbed down the ladder and crossed the floor toward her.

"She's so critical—not just of you, but of everyone. How did you manage to turn out so normal?" She balanced the mop against the front door of the former art gallery.

He leaned against the wall, looking debonair in his khakis and polo. "I could say the same of you." He grabbed her waist and pulled her closer. "And yes, I think we could be better parents. We know what not to do." He kissed her cheek, then below her ear, then buried his face in the crook of her neck. "Are you ready to start trying now?"

"Trip!" She giggled as his warm breath sent shivers down her body. "We met four days ago and neither of us has a plan past this weekend. I'd hardly say we're ready to start a family. I'm not even sure I like you yet." It was a blatant lie, but she loved getting a rise out of him.

He pulled his head out of her neck and stared at her in shock. "When I got back to the house, you practically leapt into my arms. Was that just a show for my mother?"

She laughed, unable to keep up the ruse. "No, I was happy you were back so I could get away from her." And Maurico, but she left that part out. "I forgot to tell you—she tried to force me to do the lessons tonight with Maurico. Said you wouldn't remember how to dance."

"Just goes to show how little she knows about me." He pushed off the wall, keeping Ada in the circle of his arms and waltzing her around the room. "Besides, that prick is too short. You'd have to lead."

She snickered. She'd been taller than Maurico even when she was a teenager. "I doubt he knows ballroom. He was strictly a ballerino, he had no interest in other disciplines."

"You said you performed together? How long ago was that? While he's far too young to be associating with my mother, he also seems quite a bit older than you."

Ada faltered, missing her count.

Trip slowed to a stop, continuing to hold her. "Ada, what is it? That guy gives me the creeps, so what is it? Did he come on to you when you were dancing together?"

She was out of breath, and they'd only danced for a few minutes. "What time are you picking up the sound equipment? I need to finish the floors." She tried to break the hold, but Trip remained firm.

"Hey, you can tell me anything." He removed his hand from her shoulder and stroked the side of her face.

The last thing she wanted was to tell Trip the whole sordid tale—about how naive she was and how Maurico tricked her into believing she was special. She had left the company after that, and it haunted her to this day. Would she still be dancing professionally if she had resisted his advances? "Maybe later?" She held Trip's gaze, willing herself not to cry, not to give away just how hard it was to see her mentor again.

He appraised her for a moment, then crushed her into his chest, enveloping her in his embrace. Smoothing his hand down her hair, he placed a kiss on her temple. "Whenever you're ready."

Trip was a good man and nothing like his hoity-toity family. And there was nothing fake about her feelings for him.

Chapter Twenty-Four

He could only imagine what his mother may have said to Ada, and he was livid about it. At this point, his parents were in a race to see who could be more awful. And there was definitely more to the story with this Maurice fellow. She wasn't ready to share, but he would do whatever was needed to keep the smarmy bastard away from her.

Pastor Cedric White was waiting for Trip beside the door to fellowship hall. He'd become friendly with the minister while delivering load after load of donations from Heron House earlier this summer. "Trip, great to see you!" He slapped a massive hand on Trip's back. "When are we gonna shoot some hoops again?"

"I think you embarrassed me enough the last time."

"Man, I thought with your height you'd be a baller."

Trip shrugged. "You know what they say about white men..."

The older man's laugh was deep and booming. He'd been a college basketball phenom until he blew his knee out junior year. That's when he'd found his true calling. Which apparently was ministering to a town full of mostly white people.

"Thanks for meeting me here. And letting us borrow the sound equipment."

"Happy to help. Besides, I'm coming tonight to collect on the free lessons. I don't want to be the only guy without rhythm at the gala."

"I doubt that. I've seen you bust a move during Friday Night at the Pier."

"That's different. The gala is fancy. You gotta count steps and stuff." He mimed spinning around the room.

Trip appreciated how normal the minister was, never judging people and always speaking in an accessible and authentic manner. "Sharkey will be set up there and you know Eastporters will imbibe. By the end of the night, we'll be lucky if people can stand upright, let alone do the East Coast Swing."

"That's a good point. I might need to have a later service on Sunday, so people have a little recovery time before they come repent." He chuckled at his own joke.

The two of them piled the sound equipment onto an AV, cart chit chatting more about the gala and who was expected to attend.

"I'm telling you, this is the social event of the year for little ol' Eastport Beach. Riley and Ben opening Heron House back up is already revitalizing our community. I have big hopes for what's to come." Cedric tucked a mic into the space between a receiver and a turntable.

"We're not doing karaoke, Pastor. We don't need a mic."

The minister gave Trip a stern look. "I told you to call me Cedric. And I'd take the mic. No telling how many people are going to show up tonight. You may need a little crowd control."

"You volunteering?" Trip was mostly kidding.

"You know I'll help any way I can, son. Do you need help getting it across the street?"

Trip pushed the cart to the door. "Nah, I can manage. See you tonight." He waved as he exited the fellowship hall. He crossed the parking lot and nudged the cart up on the sidewalk.

"You ripping off the church?" Chesnee appeared out of nowhere, startling Trip. "The jumpiness makes you look extra guilty."

"You're hilarious. How was your date with Gina last night?"

His friend helped hold the equipment on the cart as they pushed it down the street. "It wasn't a date, man. Just treated my friend to a concert. Where she proceeded to moon over the guitarist the entire show, by the way."

"You don't sound bitter at all."

Chesnee grunted. "What about you? I heard the entire town joined you and Ada. A whole village of cock-blockers."

"I did that all by myself," Trip mumbled.

Of course, Chesnee heard. Nothing got by the town gossip. "What stupid thing did you do this time?"

"This time? It's not like I have a pattern of striking out with girls I like." Trip didn't usually have trouble meeting women, if he was so inclined. Lately, he just hadn't cared. Until he met Ada.

"Yeah, yeah. Anyway, what did you do?"

"She asked me what Trip was short for."

Chesnee nodded. "And she doesn't like entitled rich boys with a political future?"

"Hey!"

He laughed. "I'm kidding. You're nothing like your family—or we wouldn't be friends. But she obviously recognized the name."

"Yeah. She didn't give me specifics, but right up until that point things were...progressing. And then suddenly it was like I'd sprouted boils all over my body."

Chesnee tapped the sound equipment. "But the dance class is still on tonight?"

"Dude, it's the weirdest thing. Last night I asked her to act like we were kind of serious so my mom would get off my back and Ada was like 'no way.' Then my mother shows up today—with some freaking Italian ballet dancer, no less—and suddenly Ada is acting like we're in love and she can't get enough of me."

"Just in front of your mom?"

"No, I'm getting crazy mixed signals. We almost, you know, up in my bedroom earlier and then when we got down here this afternoon she asked about kids."

Chesnee stopped. "Your kids would be freakishly tall."

Trip glared at his friend. "Not the point. She's got some history with this other dancer, but she won't open up about it."

"The one your mom is with? And aren't your parents still married?"

"Never stopped my dad." *But it's still gross.* He preferred to think of his mother as asexual.

Chesnee looked like he'd just stepped in dog doo. "So, your mom brought a boy toy with her and he's possibly an ex of Ada's? Kinky."

"Seriously, Ches. I really like her. I'm not going back to Virginia."

His friend threw up his hands and shook his head. "You're defying the great and powerful Senator Westinghouse?"

"Yeah?" Trip wanted to say it with more confidence, but instead it sounded like a mouse had asked a question.

"You realize you're basically cutting off the money train?"

"I haven't taken money from them all summer. Riley said I could stay as long as I want, and I like working at Heron House."

Chesnee slapped him on the shoulder. "It'll be nice to have you around. Although I will miss the Aspen chalet."

Trip rolled his eyes. "We went one time."

"Yeah, but snow bunnies, man. It was epic."

The door opened across the street and Ada stepped out onto the sidewalk. "Do you two need help?"

Chesnee waved. "Hey, Ada. We're just shootin' the shit, if you know what I mean." He lowered his voice. "Are your mother and Signore Tutu coming tonight? Because I don't want to miss any of the action."

"They better not show up. I gave her driver directions to the club, so hopefully we'll be pest free for the evening. Oh, and my dad popped into town today too."

"If your sister shows up, it'll be a full-on family reunion. And she better save me a dance." He wiggled his eyebrows.

Trip sighed. "Bro code means you can't sleep with my sister."

Chesnee gripped his chest like he was in pain.

"You are so dramatic. And Lisa's in Europe, so I didn't think I have to worry about her making an appearance."

A bell clanged and Captain Percy appeared on his bike. Trip watched Ada watch the Naked Pirate as he rode by. Seriously, this town was awesome.

"I'll see you later, Ches. I think Maude may keep the Mermaid open late tonight, so if you want to go gawk at Gina, we'll probably be over there after the lesson."

"Gina said she was working late, but I figured she was just fibbing, so she didn't have to see my ugly mug two nights in a row."

Trip laughed. "I mean, it's valid."

Chesnee shrugged and headed back toward Ben's office. It was the middle of the workday after all.

Trip started to push the cart across the street, and Ada met him halfway.

"Does Captain Percy wear clothes when the weather gets colder?"

"I'm not sure, I've only been here since June." It had only been a few months, but this place felt far more like home than the town in Virginia where he'd grown up.

She covered her mouth as she gasped. "You don't think he'll come to the gala, do you?"

Trip laughed. "I doubt he has a tux for the parrot."

"Was Chesnee talking to you about his date last night?"

"He swore it wasn't a date."

"Gina said the same." She hooked her arm in his and leaned against him. "Do you think they agree on a narrative or is it more like a collective delusion?"

Trip maneuvered the cart onto the sidewalk, then pulled Ada close once more. "It's like a juicy Telenovela that I can't wait to watch the next installment of. Glad I'm staying so I can see how it all comes out."

"You're staying in Eastport Beach?"

He moved his hands down to her waist. "Yeah, I told my dad and my grandfather's assistant. I'm hoping I can get away without telling my mother until she's back in Virginia."

"You'll stay at Heron House?"

He nodded. "Riley said I can stay as long as I like. It's not a career, but it will keep me afloat until I figure the rest out." He couldn't believe how free he felt—just from saying it out loud.

She stepped closer to him and wrapped her arms around his neck. "I'm proud of you, standing up to your family."

"Chesnee thinks I'm an idiot for turning my back on the gravy train. But it doesn't even feel right to take their money. I can't get on board with their greed and power-hungry motives."

"It's brave, walking away from the stability of family money."

"It's worth it to be able to look myself in the mirror every morning."

Ada rose on her tiptoes and kissed him.

"Ah, young love." Edna Windsor's gang of seasoned women were exiting Murray's. "Remember when we used to make out in public, Roz?"

The tallest lady of the bunch grabbed her chest. "I've never kissed a woman in my life. And I certainly wouldn't have chosen you."

Edna patted her pink hair. "I meant kissing our fellas, but you don't have to insult me. I'm a catch."

"Ladies, we're far too old be questioning our sexuality. Let's leave these young people to their PDFs." Midge Myers, who ran the monthly Uno tournament at Heron House, waved her hands at her friends.

"It's PDA, Midge." Edna rolled her eyes. "PDFs are like alien stuff."

Ada buried her head in his chest, vibrating with laughter. It took everything Trip had not to join her. He had to work with these ladies on a regular basis, so he had to be respectful.

The foursome waved goodbye and continued down the street, one of them insisting that Edna meant UFOs.

"Those ladies need their own reality show. They're hilarious." Ada let go of Trip and pushed open the door to their temporary studio.

Trip pushed the cart over the threshold and into the space. "You should be there for Uno night. It gets pretty cutthroat. The claws come out when the draw four is in play."

"Do you play with them?"

"God, no. I keep them hydrated and try to keep the hair pulling to a minimum. Honestly, they're worse than Manny's poker game. The guys come once a week, and luckily the Uno is only once a month."

"Maybe you should talk to Riley about hazard pay."

"You have no idea."

Chapter Twenty-Five

They'd spent most of the afternoon getting the space ready for lessons. "Are you sure I'm not keeping you from work at Heron House? I didn't realize it would take this long to set up."

Trip grabbed a cold bottle of water from the cooler they'd put in the front alcove. "Nah, Riley considers this gala adjacent, so I'm off the hook." He unscrewed the cap and took a swig. "Besides, she's in full matchmaking mode, so she thinks we should spend lots of time together." He stalked toward her, arms outstretched.

"Did you tell her about the new sleeping arrangements?" She sidestepped and ducked under his arm, playing a fun little game of keep away.

"Yeah, about that," he said as he lunged toward her. "I can sleep on the boat tonight, but her sister is coming in tomorrow and she'll be sleeping on the boat for the rest of the weekend."

"Well, we haven't made things official yet, but I'd prefer if you didn't sleep with another woman this soon into our relationship." She darted away from him on tiptoes and spun in a tight pirouette.

He stopped and watched her spinning. "Very funny. Considering her husband will be with her, it'd be pretty tight quarters."

Ada stopped spinning and stepped closer to him. "You're welcome to share tight quarters with me instead." She licked her lips.

Trip's focus remained on her mouth as he grabbed her waist and pulled her in. "It's a small bed. There probably won't be any extra space for pajamas."

She threw her head back, laughing.

Trip took advantage of the position and kissed up the line of her neck. "You smell like strawberries." He grabbed a handful of her hair and gave it a sniff.

"I used the fancy shampoo Riley had in the bathroom."

"I love strawberries."

She worked her hands up under his shirt, wanting to feel his skin. "Well, tomorrow Maurico will probably smell like them, so you can sniff his hair."

Trip nipped at her neck with a growl. "I have a master key, so I'll make sure to switch the shampoo out for something a little more manly. He won't be used to it, but maybe he can fool a few people."

Ada wished she'd been as quick to figure Maurico out as Trip obviously was.

"Hey, you okay?" He stopped kissing her and pulled back. "Ada?"

She tried to snap out of her trip down Regrettable Decisions Lane. "Yeah, I'm fine. I was just thinking it would have been nice to have the suite with the private bathroom."

He closed one eye like he was thinking really hard. "You did, until my mother flew in on her broomstick."

"No, silly." She pushed against his chest lightly. "I meant I wish *we* had the private bathroom. With its nice big tub."

He leaned his forehead against hers. "Now I really hate the little prick."

Her phone rang, so she gave Trip a quick peck on the lips and ran over to grab it from her bag. "Hey Paul, one sec." She covered the phone. "I'm going to take this outside. Be right back."

She pushed open the door and stepped into the sunshine of late afternoon. "Sorry, how are you?"

"I'm good, I got your message, but your voice sounded a little off. Is everything okay there?" Paul could read her so well. She'd rarely hid anything from him. Except what she needed to ask him about right now.

She'd left the message right after Karina Westinghouse barged in on her discovery of her newborn picture in an envelope addressed to Archie Kirkwood. It was a miracle she could speak at all.

But then Trip had shown up and they'd come downtown to get the temporary studio ready, and the kissing, teasing and touching had soothed her nerves.

"Everything is great. I'm kind of seeing someone I met down here, so that's been fun. He actually danced when he was younger, so we've been casually giving ballroom lessons to people who are attending the gala."

"People? What kind of people?"

She laughed. "Well, a bunch of locals kind of begged for a quick lesson, so we're doing that tonight." Dancing and romance, what more could a girl ask for? Try knowing who her father was.

"Just be careful, Ada. You haven't known this guy for long." He'd always been protective of her. Paul had actually grilled her very first date—which was just riding the subway together to a school dance. But he'd given him the third degree.

"I know, I will." She bit her lip and forced herself to broach the subject she'd called about in the first place. "Do you have any pictures of me when I was a baby? Like did my mom ever give you one?"

The line was silent for a full thirty seconds. "It's possible I have some around here. I don't honestly remember. What brought this on?"

"I found a newborn picture of me in Archie's stuff. Archie's the guy who ran—"

"I know who Archie is. He and your mother were close back then. It doesn't surprise me that she sent him something."

He had said he'd been to Heron House. Now he was admitting he knew Archie. "Do you think they were, like, together?" It was so awkward to talk to him about this. I'd never spoken to him about who my father might be, because he'd done such a good job filling in that I didn't want him to think it wasn't enough.

Paul sighed. "Your mother was a complicated woman who loved freely. It's possible."

According to my mother's journals, it could be Archie, or the bartender at a hotel she stayed at, or the taxi driver who'd taken her to the airport, or the monk she met in Tibet. "I guess I wish she'd been a little less complicated."

"I know, sweetie." He paused, then went on. "I'll tell you what. I'll ask Elaine to go through our albums and see what pictures we might have. You were a beautiful baby, Ada."

"I looked like someone bashed my head in with a hammer."

Paul laughed. "They used the forceps on you, so you were dented for a couple weeks. Your mother always had you in a hat because she was mortified that her child's head wasn't symmetrical."

She'd never heard any of this before.

He continued. "Then one day she showed up to drop you off for a couple hours, you were maybe five months by then, and you didn't have a hat on. All that hat wearing had worn your hair off, so you were as bald as a billiard ball, but a perfectly round one. Seriously, Ada, the cutest little baby."

It was surreal learning all of this. *How is it that I'm hearing about my first year of life from my mother's manager? This was not normal.* She was not normal. "I've got to go, but thanks for looking for the pictures." All of a sudden, she couldn't get off the phone fast enough. All this information was too much and not enough at the same time. Blood pounded in her temples.

"Love you, kiddo."

"You too." She ended the call and leaned against a light pole because suddenly she couldn't support her weight.

She closed her eyes, so it was a shock when arms reached around her. She jumped.

"Ada, what's wrong?" Trip's voice was laced with concern.

The last thing she wanted to do was burden him with her silly family drama. He was dealing with his own crap. She was an adult; it's not like she was a little kid who'd suddenly become an orphan. She'd felt like an orphan most of her life. What was different now? Why was this so important? "I'm fine, really. Maybe a little dehydrated."

Trip led her back inside and gave her a cold bottle of water, then closed and patted the lid of the cooler. "Sit."

She didn't argue, happy to get off her feet since she felt lightheaded. She sipped the water, careful not to shock her system with the chilled liquid. Trip paced the room, giving her space, but clearly wanting to know what the phone call was about, because he looked over at her every half-rotation. He'd shared a little of his family stuff, so maybe she should reciprocate. Despite everything, she felt safe with him. "Trip."

He'd paced to the back of the room but now raced toward her and kneeled in front of the cooler.

"I found a picture today in Archie's papers."

"What was it a picture of?"

"Me. As a newborn. You know those sad little ones the hospital used to give out before everything went digital?"

He shifted back on his heels and hummed. "That bolsters the hypothesis that Archie was your dad."

Ada nodded, feeling conflicted. "It's almost as if the closer I get to this, the less I want to know the truth." She wrapped her arms around herself. "I guess I'm scared I'll discover that I don't have either parent anymore."

Trip put his warm hands on her knees. "If you don't know, then you still have hope."

She bit her lip, trying to stem the flow of tears. She'd been more emotional on this trip than ever in her whole life. This place was really having an impact on her. Could it be because she had a connection to this place? A genetic one? "My mother never kept photo albums, so it's the first time I've seen a baby picture of myself."

"And then Archie has one. But what was the phone call about? You were fine before that."

"It was my mother's manager, Paul. He and his wife took care of me a lot when my mother was"—she made air quotes with her fingers—"unavailable. I would pretend they were my real family."

"Hey, I get that. I still keep in touch with one of my nannies."

"So, I asked Paul if he had any baby pictures of me."

He nodded. "Like maybe she sent a bunch of them around to her friends, even though she didn't keep any for herself. That you know of."

"Charlotte was always mysterious, like it was part of this persona she had. So, it's possible she has stuff stashed somewhere. But I've cleared out her loft, so who knows?"

"Did Paul have a picture?"

"He's going to ask Elaine to look through their albums. You know, like a normal person who documents their children growing up. They had two boys that were grown by the time I came along."

"Okay, so we'll put Operation Newborn Ada on hold until you hear back and focus on Operation Teach Eastport How to Dance." He grinned and reached up to wipe away a tear she didn't realize had escaped.

He really was a good guy. "Thanks. Sorry I'm such a mess."

"You are not a mess, darlin'. You are a strong woman who grew up under difficult circumstances. You're the furthest thing from a mess."

She leaned forward and kissed him, feeling peace settle somewhere around her heart.

Chapter Twenty-Six

It was only sixty-thirty, and a crowd was gathering outside the temporary dance studio. Trip couldn't see where the mass of people ended. "We're going to need some help with crowd control. Are you up to doing several lessons, or should I send half these people home?"

"We can do a couple rotations, I guess." Ada stood on her tiptoes looking over his shoulder. "Maybe six couples at a time."

Pulling his phone out, he shot off a text to Chesnee. "I can't believe this many people want to learn how to dance. I've been to plenty of festivals here and no one cared about how poorly they danced."

Ada's cheeks were flushed a pretty pink and she was bouncing on her toes. "Do you think they'd be willing to pay to learn? Not tonight, obviously, but maybe, I don't know, at a dance school?"

"You want to open a school? Here?" The thought of Ada sticking around for a while made his heart skip a beat.

She shrugged and looked down at the floor.

"Hey"—he dropped his voice as he tilted her chin up—"what did I say? No embarrassment. It's a great idea. Look at all these people clamoring to get in."

"Free lessons are one thing. I don't know if anyone would be interested enough to enroll in a class."

The space they were in would be perfect. He could envision little girls lined along the wall, adorned in pink tutus, and Ada demonstrating ballet moves. "You could offer a variety of classes. For all ages. It really could work. You could even do something at night where you teach a lesson and then have open dance."

"Like a different dance each week. East Coast Swing one week, then the tango, or the waltz."

Her excitement was contagious. Maybe he could help her. "I can ask Piper how much the rent is if you want. It wouldn't take much work to turn it into a real studio." They'd just cleaned up a little and it was already a great space.

"It's probably just a pipe dream. I'd have to find someone to sublet my place in Virginia. I'd have to find a place here. It's silly."

"It's not silly at all."

Chesnee banged on the door.

Trip grabbed Ada's hand and squeezed it. "To be continued, okay?"

She nodded, but he could practically see her brain spinning ideas around.

"Dude, let me in. The natives are crazy out here!" Chesnee's voice was muffled from the other side of the door. The crowd was pressing him closer to the glass.

"Maybe we should start early since so many people are already here."

Trip nodded. "I'll see if I can let the first six couples in without a stampede." If he failed, his friend would likely be trampled. He unlocked the door and cracked it open. "Eastporters!" He tried to project his voice. "If you can't act appropriately, there will be no lessons. Back up and act like you have some manners."

"Yeah, chill out!" Chesnee croaked from his spot smooshed against the glass door.

There was rumbling in the crowd, but people started backing up. Trip was a little concerned about how they would act at the gala if they couldn't even behave themselves here. He grabbed Chesnee's shirt and yanked him inside. "I needed backup, not a damsel in distress to rescue."

"Hey!" His dramatic friend gripped his lapels. "Those people are animals. I think we need to start uninviting people to the gala. You get a couple of Sharkey's ciders in them and all hell's going to break loose."

"You read my mind." He had to figure out a way to get this group under control and fast. "Ada, is there any paper in that office back there?"

"Yeah, I think so. What are you thinking?"

"Let's do slips with numbers one through eighteen. Each couple can draw a number for their turn. We'll do six couples for thirty minutes and then switch."

"Three sessions seems reasonable." She disappeared into the back.

Chesnee plucked the microphone off the cart. *Ah crap, he was the last person who needed a microphone.* He started humming and singing under his breath.

"Is that *Total Eclipse of the Heart*?"

"Yeah, the band last night did a cover of it. Brought down the house. Can't get it out of my head."

There were worse songs to sing on a loop. "See if you can find something to put the numbers in."

Chesnee saluted and went into the back. Trip grabbed the microphone—it would come in handy after all. He adjusted a few knobs on the receiver and tested it.

"You can sing too?" Ada sounded exasperated.

He'd just sung the opening line of a Luke Combs song. He shrugged. "I've done a little karaoke in the past."

She stepped closer and slid her arms around his waist. "I bet girls threw their panties at you."

"What kind of karaoke bars have you been going to?"

She laughed. "The ones with drunk guys who couldn't carry a tune in a locked briefcase with the secret service standing guard."

He threw his head back with a guffaw. "That's oddly specific."

Her eyes sparkled and her smile threatened to knock him on his ass—again.

"If you two are done canoodling, I found a vessel for the numbers." Chesnee waved a ridiculously large mug over his head. It was shaped like a mermaid tail with sparkly purple glitter scales.

"Is that from your personal collection?" Trip teased.

Chesnee clutched it to his chest. "No, but I'm totally stealing it." He shoved it between Trip and Ada, leaving a trail of sparkle down the front of his shirt.

Ada dropped the handful of folded papers into the mug.

Trip cracked the door open again and tapped the microphone to gain the crowd's attention. "Listen up! Obviously, there are more people here than we expected so we're going to implement a lottery system. Each couple will draw a number and we're going to have three sessions with six couples each. I'm sorry if we won't get to everyone."

People started pushing and shoving to get to the front.

"If you're unruly, I won't let you draw a number." He pointed at Edna, who was elbowing her way past one of the Murray boys. She slapped her hands to her sides and tried to look demure. "Okay everyone, make a path. Chesnee is coming around with his magic mug. And he's starting in the back."

Chesnee shook his head. "I'm not going out there."

Trip covered the mic with his hand. "Half of them are senior citizens and the other half are reasonable people. Go on, spread your sparkle around."

He grunted but plowed through the throng of people. "Be nice or no number for you." It was a sad imitation of the soup nazi from *Seinfeld*.

Groans and cheers could be heard as people unfolded their numbers. But Trip was going to keep them on their toes. Once all the numbers were gone, he tapped the mic again. "Numbers thirteen through eighteen will go first. You can head inside."

Spiked red hair appeared as Gina hoisted herself up on a short wall that lined this part of Main Street. She cupped her hands around her mouth. "The Mermaid is open until ten tonight, so while you're waiting for your turn to dance, come in and spend a little money. Maude made a slew of pies."

Everyone cheered because Maude's pies were almost as legendary as Ida Mae's fudge. The couples that weren't dancing first filed into The Spicy Mermaid and Chesnee was left alone on the sidewalk holding his mermaid mug and staring at Gina as she corralled people into the diner.

"Ches, since you'll be over there keeping an eye on"—Trip coughed into his hand—"things, send the next group over in thirty minutes, okay?"

"Sure thing, boss." His gaze remained glued to a retreating Gina.

His friend had it so bad and Trip couldn't even say anything, because he felt the same way about Ada that Eastporters felt about Maude's pies.

Chapter Twenty-Seven

The last couple thanked Ada and Trip and walked out the door. Ada slid down the wall, hitting the floor with a thump. She kicked her shoes off and wiggled her toes. "Man, that was exhausting. So many questions!"

"So many people that can't count to four." Trip sat in front of her and grabbed one of her feet.

Ada nearly moaned out loud. "I was going to say you don't have to do that, but please don't stop."

Trip applied the perfect amount of pressure to her insole, giving her a bit of relief from the hours she'd spent in heels.

"You'd think someone could design a shoe that looks good and doesn't kill your feet."

"I'm guessing they exist—for the right price." He pressed his thumbs into her heel.

The moan slipped past her lips, and she wasn't even sorry.

He switched to her other foot and started the process over again. "You think this feels good, just wait until we get some alone time."

Her pulse kicked up and she licked her lips. "Technically we're alone."

"Technically, half the town is next door at the diner and would have their faces pressed against the glass." He rubbed his knuckles up the sole of her foot.

"Mmm, yeah, and I promised Gina we'd get pie after." Ada loved pie, but she imagined Trip would taste just as good—especially with a little whipped cream on top.

He gave her foot one final squeeze, then hopped up. "Come on, we've got to roll this sound equipment back to the church and then we'll find something delicious to eat." His lecherous look had Ada doubting he meant pie.

They were wrapping up cords and gathering their things when someone knocked on the door.

"Sorry, man, the lessons are over." He waved at the older gentleman who'd knocked.

The man gripped the handle and pushed the door open.

It was Eastport Beach, so neither of them had thought to lock the door. Ada got a little chill and wondered if it had been a foolish mistake.

"Sorry, son, I can't hear well." He looked harmless enough. Gray tufts of hair framed his face, he sported a scruffy white beard, and it appeared he hadn't stood upright in a decade.

He probably wasn't an axe murderer.

"I said the lessons are over," Trip repeated, stepping in front of Ada.

"Oh, no, I'm not lookin' to learn anything. Old dog and all that. I'm looking for Ada Maddox. Riley from Heron House sent me down here."

Well, if Riley sent him, he must be okay. "I'm Ada." She put her hand on Trip's arm and stepped closer to the man.

He squinted behind his wire-rimmed glasses. "Oh yes, I see it now. You've got your mother's nose."

"You knew my mother?"

"Oh, yes. We studied together at Heron House one summer. Before you came along. Your mother was quite the looker. All us fellas were jockeying for her attention." He chuckled. "And talented, woo! She could paint anything with two hands tied behind her back." He looked around the mostly empty space. "Is there somewhere I can sit down? I'm afraid my knees aren't keeping up with the rest of me."

Ada was overjoyed to meet someone who had known Charlotte during her stay in Eastport Beach. Maybe this man would know if Archie had been sweet on her as well. "How do you feel about pie?"

"It's un-American to not like pie." He held his hand over his heart.

She giggled. "I agree." Turning to Trip, she grabbed his hand. "Can you return the sound equipment while Mister—I'm sorry, I don't know your name."

"My father was Mister. I'm just Barry."

Trip looked wary but nodded. "Yeah, I'll take care of it. You guys go next door, and I'll meet you there."

"Thanks." She stood on her toes and gave him a quick peck on the cheek.

Barry hooted. "She's a charmer, just like Charlotte."

Except I don't spread my charm all around. "What kind of pie should I order for you?"

Trip shook his head. "Doesn't matter. Maude can't make a bad pie. We'll be lucky if there's any left."

Ada threaded her arm through Barry's and led him to The Spicy Mermaid. "Are you a painter, as well?"

"Oh no, I was into mosaics. Tile work." He held up a gnarled hand. "It destroyed my hands, unfortunately."

"That's so interesting! Did you do building projects?"

She held open the door to the diner and followed Barry inside.

Gina was behind the counter. "Just sit anywhere."

They grabbed a booth near the door and Gina brought over two ice waters. "Did you dump Trip for a more sophisticated gentleman?" She winked at Barry, who preened with the attention.

Ada laughed. "He'll be here in a few minutes. This is Barry. He knew my mother."

"Ah, are you an artist too, Barry?"

"At one time. I spent two sabbaticals at Heron House. It always inspired me and got the juices flowing again when I was in a rut."

"Barry did mosaics."

Gina oohed. "I used to rent an apartment with a gorgeous tile backsplash. It was definitely a work of art."

"It's a dying art, unfortunately. It's all white subway tile now. Pooh!"

"I agree wholeheartedly. Now, what kind of pie do you want? I think we have lemon meringue, strawberry rhubarb and coconut cream left."

Ada's stomach growled. She shouldn't have skipped dinner. "What do you think, Barry? Shall we do one of each?"

"It'd be a waste not to."

Gina tipped an imaginary hat and disappeared into the kitchen. The diner was about half full, mostly locals who'd been at the dance lessons. They were sipping coffee, eating pie and likely gossiping about the new stranger in town.

"You were telling me about your work, Barry."

"Yes, of course." He straightened his glasses. "At the height of my career, I did commissioned projects, including a grand ballroom in Spain. Over a thousand square feet. I tiled a sauna for Sly Stallone, a garden path for Regis, and a meditation room for Madonna. And in between big jobs, I made trivets and serving trays that I sold at farmer's markets. It was a crazy life with tons of travel and many interesting people along the way. Including your mother."

"I'm not sure if you've heard, but Charlotte had to be admitted to a memory-care facility. She doesn't remember much anymore."

"Oh dear." He reached his arthritic hand across the table. "My body has betrayed me, but I can't imagine my mind going. I'm so sorry."

Ada gripped his hand briefly. "Thank you. It's been a difficult time. There's so much she never told me, including about her time here in Eastport Beach."

The door chimed and Trip slid in the booth beside her just as Gina appeared with the pies. "Sorry, I got caught up talking to Cedric." He squeezed Ada's thigh under the table. "Everything good here?"

"Yes, Barry was just telling me about all the famous people he's done commissions for."

Gina set four pieces of pie in the middle of the table. "I found one more piece of apple in the back." She winked at Barry, whose cheeks blushed a deep red. She gave them each a small plate and silverware. "Now, no fighting over the pie. I cut each piece into three slices." She turned to leave, then spun back toward the table, jerking a can of whipped cream from her apron. "Almost forgot." She left the can on the table and headed back behind the counter.

That's when Ada noticed Chesnee seated on a stool at the end of a long bar, nursing an ice water. He watched Gina go about her work, occasionally glancing down at his phone. He was loyal, she'd give him that.

Trip took charge of pie distribution and Ada manned the whipped cream. Soon, everyone's plates were overflowing with pie.

"I may end up in a sugar coma, but what a way to go." Barry dug into the lemon meringue.

Ada tried the rhubarb first. It was the perfect combination of sweet and tart with the flakiest crust she'd ever eaten. "Maude knows what she's doing."

"Yeah, she sells whole pies once or twice a year and people drive all the way from Raleigh."

"Move over Marie Callender." Barry had polished off the lemon and was starting on the coconut cream.

They spent the next few minutes in companionable silence, interrupted only by occasional moans over how good the pie was. Gina stopped by the table with a glass of water for Trip and he asked if there was any left to take to Ben and Riley. She said she'd already put a few slices back for them.

By the time Ada got to her last sliver of pie, she was feeling dizzy from all the sugar. "Too bad the kitchen isn't open. I could go for a greasy burger to even out this sugar overload."

"We can run into Bluffville and grab fast food if you want. I should have brought us something to eat."

"Trip, it's not your responsibility to feed me." Although she likely would have starved this week without him.

He tucked her hair behind her ear. "I like taking care of you."

She felt the tips of her ears heat up. And Barry was watching their exchange like it was the latest episode of his afternoon soap opera.

"How long have you kids been seeing each other?" Barry had slaughtered his pies and was using his finger to get the last bit of whipped cream off his plate.

Ada's cheeks joined her ears in the race to be the reddest. "We met on Monday."

He clapped his hands together, but it wasn't so much a clap as a bump, since he couldn't straighten his fingers all the way. "Nice job, son. Way to lock her down fast. Anyone ever manage to lock your mother down, Ada?"

"No, sir." Not even her daughter.

"Charlotte was a creative genius. Sometimes that means they can't get out of their own head long enough to connect with another person on an emotional level. If I remember correctly, her and Archie were close. They were both like that. Too many ideas battling to get out of their minds."

But close how? "Barry, would you say they were romantically involved?"

He shrugged. "Now, I wouldn't know that. All I know is I struck out—not that I blame her. I was never much of a looker, and I was a good deal older than her, but I couldn't resist throwing my hat in the ring. She was just that alluring."

The only thing Ada could definitively say at this point was that Barry wasn't her father. But at least her stomach was full of pie.

Chapter Twenty-Eight

When they arrived back at Heron House, all the lights downstairs were blazing, and Riley was manning the turntable. She had eclectic musical tastes all on her own, but when she'd found her uncle's record stash this summer, her range grew even wider. Currently, there was a big band tune blaring in the parlor and several people milled around the room, including his mother and her "companion." The house was full of visitors for the first time since Riley took over, and Trip was happy to see her relaxed and enjoying herself. She'd worked so hard to get to this point.

Barry had beat them back to the house and Trip could see him through the leaded glass windows speaking to Ben. Before they ascended the steps, Trip grabbed Ada's hand and pulled her back. "Do we really want to get dragged into a social event with a bunch of senior citizens?"

Her eyes sparkled in the twilight. "I'd hardly call Riley and Ben senior citizens."

"That's her record. Archie's stuff was way more current."

She laughed. "You mean you don't want to twirl your mother around the parlor and prove your dancing chops?"

"Not even a little." He pulled his phone out and shot a text to Ben. "Come on." He pulled her around the fountain and across the yard, fleeing a possible encounter with his mother.

Ada didn't have any issues keeping up with him, despite the fact that she was in heels and had spent the better part of the evening dancing in those shoes. Her laughter was musical, lilting along the night air, mixing with the sounds of crickets and frogs. "Where are we going?"

He glanced over his shoulder and heat shot to his crotch.

Her hair fanned out behind her as she ran, her cheeks pink with the mild exertion—or anticipation—he couldn't be sure. But she was beautiful, and he wasn't waiting one more minute to be alone with her. "You'll see."

She didn't question him further or nag him for details. She willingly followed him, allowing him to lead—just as she had on the dance floor. Jenny had always needed to be in control. To dictate where they would go and what they would do, and oftentimes, she'd rope his mother into the process, running events and such by her to make sure they were deemed politically expedient. God, he hated that.

He slowed down as they reached the tree line that separated Ben's property from Riley's—although he figured the two would merge eventually. He tucked Ada close into his side, making sure they navigated safely around trees and brush.

"This isn't Stumpy's hangout, is it?" She warily eyed the river, which could be seen through the trees.

He chuckled and yanked her toward him, hooking his arm under her legs and sweeping her off her feet. "I'll protect you from the disabled alligator."

She didn't fight him, just looped her arms around his neck and leaned against his chest. "Not many men could pick me up."

He scoffed. "What are you talking about? You barely weigh anything." She had the slender body of a dancer for sure.

"It's my height. I've been told I can't have roles with lifts because I'm too tall."

"That's ridiculous. If they found a real man, he'd be able to lift you—unlike Luigi back at the house."

She snickered and whispered into his neck. "Guess I found a real man."

"Hell, yeah, you did."

They emerged from the darkness of the woods and the moon lit up the river that snaked in front of them. A long dock jutted into the water and Ben's sailboat was moored to it.

"Does Ben ever take this out?"

"Not that I've seen. Mostly he was living on it before he hooked up with Riley and moved into Heron House. He planned to build a house here, but his first wife passed away and he never finished the build." He set Ada down on the wooden slats that made up the dock.

"That's so sad. He's awfully young to be a widower."

Trip wrapped his arm around her waist, wanting to keep her close. There probably wouldn't be any alligators, but it never hurt to be vigilant. "Chesnee said Ben had resigned himself to just growing old alone, but then Riley showed up and he was a goner."

"They seem really sweet together. He's supportive of her without being overbearing."

"Yeah, total ship goals." He'd never imagined he could have that—because he didn't want to subject a woman he loved to his family and their expectations. But if he was pushing back—maybe even completely rebelling—maybe there was hope. Maybe he could be with someone like Ada. He faced her, tracing his finger down the side of her face, reveling in how beautiful she was in the moonlight. "I know we've flirted around this all week, Ada, but I'd like your permission to take you onboard this boat and have my way with you."

Her eyes grew wide and round, and she bit back a smile. "I'd like that very much, as long as I can have my way with you as well."

"I wouldn't have it any other way." He closed the distance between them, capturing her mouth and pressing the evidence of his excitement against her. He wanted her to know the effect she had on him. He'd been half hard all week, his dreams fixated on getting this woman in a bed. Any bed would do—including one below deck.

Her hands roamed his body, sneaking under his shirt and smoothing over his abdomen. Pride surged through him—he worked hard to keep his body toned. He moved down to nibble on the sensitive skin behind her ear. She responded with mewling noises and dug her fingers into the meat of his back. Maybe she'd been thinking about this all week too.

"Inside." He reluctantly pulled his mouth away from her sweet skin, wanting to get her on the boat where he could get that dress off and have access to all of her. It was fairly private down here on Ben's dock, but he wasn't taking any chances of some new guest wandering around. She sighed and released her hold on him.

He helped her step from the dock onto the boat. Water gently lapped against the sides as the boat rocked just from them climbing onboard. *Just wait until we really get it rocking.* He led her below deck, which was a bit cramped for two tall people. Luckily for them, they were planning on spending most of their time horizontal.

On the table in the galley was a bucket of ice with a bottle of champagne. Two plastic flutes sat nearby.

"Ooo, champagne! When did you have time to set this up?"

Riley. The little matchmaker. He'd have to thank her later. "Would you like a glass?"

"Just one, I've still only had pie to eat tonight."

He'd been so anxious to get her alone, he'd forgotten to feed her. On a hunch, he opened the small refrigerator. Inside was a plate loaded with fruit and cheese.

He was going to have to make Riley a few more casseroles for her freezer as a thank you.

Ada beamed. "You really did think of everything." She popped a cube of cheese into her mouth as he worked to open the bottle.

The cork sprung from the bottle, hitting the low ceiling and falling back to the table. He captured the flow with one of the plastic flutes. Both glasses full, he offered up a toast. "To finally being alone."

She clinked her plastic cup against his and giggled. "To being alone. On a boat, no less." She took a sip and licked the bubbles off her lip.

Trip's body heated up just from that little tongue peeking out. He'd waited long enough. They could eat after. He took the flute out of her hand and set it on the table. He locked his gaze on her face, stalking toward her with exactly one thought on his mind. Naked. Turnabout was fair play, after all. "My turn."

She backed up with each step he took, her eyes wide like a Disney princess, only she was prettier than any of the princesses in those movies his sister had been obsessed with. Finally, she bumped into the bed and sat down with a plop. "Oh my. I bet you dance the tango like a pro."

"We're going to dance all night, darlin'."

Chapter Twenty-Nine

T he man radiated heat and lust. She could practically hear the music in her head. Her chest heaved and her dress felt tight all of a sudden. She might spontaneously combust.

Trip reached behind his head and grabbed his shirt, ripping it off in that sexy way she'd only seen in the movies.

Do boats have air conditioning?

His skin stretched tight over muscles and sinew. It glistened in the limited light, like maybe he was as hot as she was.

He stepped close to her and yanked her off the bed. Reaching behind her, he slid the zipper on her dress down like he'd been studying it all night, waiting for this moment. His fingers brushed her shoulders as he opened it from the back and glided it down her body.

Everywhere his fingers touched turned into molten lava. Ada had never felt anything like this, and they'd barely started. Would she be able to handle a whole night with this magnetic man?

This fling thing had sounded so simple. But then she'd gotten to know him and like him. In spite of who his grandfather was and what he did. The pull between them—it was impossible to resist. Even if they were just pretending for his mother's sake.

But his mother wasn't here now. And by the look on his face, as he took in the sight of her wearing only a tiny pair of lace undies, he wasn't pretending at all.

She didn't know what to call it anymore.

Then he touched her, and she knew.

Electric.

"Trip." His name came out on a breath, because she couldn't speak as his hand raked across her flesh. His mouth followed the same path as his hands, exploring, tasting, teasing. She dug her nails into his back, wanting to mark him, wanting to hold him here so he couldn't get away. "Don't stop."

He looked up from where he'd been circling her nipple with his tongue. "I can't stop, Ada. I'll never get enough of you." His head lowered back to her chest, his exploration continuing while she squirmed underneath him.

It was an exquisite form of torture. It was not enough and too much all at once. Somehow, he was kissing her abdomen, and she could feel a tingling in her toes, like that time she got acupuncture, and they stuck needles in her arm, but she felt a jolt on her leg. Another thing she didn't understand, but felt confident it was working. What Trip was doing was definitely working.

He reached those lacy undies and traced his tongue over the fabric, mere inches from a place no man had ever kissed her before. She wondered what it would feel like, if it would be better than penetration—as her friends had told her. Maurico had never been too concerned about whether she had a good time. Sex with him had felt good, but not great. There hadn't been any screaming or earth-shattering moments.

The handful of others hadn't ranked much higher, although a couple had asked if she'd come. It seemed rude to say no.

"Ooo!" She jerked her pelvis up off the bed, nearly taking Trip out in the process. She'd been lost in her head, so when his tongue ran along the crotch of her underwear it took her completely by surprise.

With her hips off the bed, he seized the opportunity to remove the lacy barrier. He slid them down her legs and as he removed them, he placed a kiss on the inside of her ankle. And then one a bit higher up, and so forth, until he was back between her thighs.

She was paying attention this time. Completely focused on his breath and how it felt on her sensitive skin.

He looked up and locked eyes with her.

Her chest was heaving, her breaths coming in short, frenzied puffs.

"You with me?" He squeezed her thigh, rubbing his thumb in soothing circles.

She nodded, the anticipation overwhelming, the ability to speak having completely escaped her.

"Good. I'm going to make you come so hard you'll see spots."

Sweet baby Jesus. She gulped. No one had ever made a promise like that to her.

His eyes didn't leave hers as his tongue flicked out and made its first contact with her most sensitive flesh.

She squealed and squirmed underneath him. It felt so different than fingers, a penis, a vibrator. Foreign.

He turned his head and kissed the inside of her thigh. Then he reached his hand up and took hers, twining their fingers together.

It was like an anchor. Her breathing slowed, she unclenched her muscles, and released the anxiety that had coiled in her chest.

When he licked her again, she felt heat from his breath and the most delicious jolt of pleasure raced through her abdomen. Soon, she was squirming again, not to get away, but to get closer, to get more. It was unreal how all her bones felt like gelatin. How she couldn't get enough of this thing she'd never known before. The ultimate pleasure.

She plowed her free hand through his hair, wantonly pushing him down, oblivious to anything else but reaching that peak she could feel coming.

When he grabbed her ass cheek, she exploded, like a light bulb hitting the ground and shattering into the finest dust. She screamed his name, nearly broke the fingers of the hand she was holding, and squeezed his head between her legs like Riley's high-powered juicer.

And he was right. There were definitely spots swimming before her eyes.

Chapter Thirty

Watching Ada come was magical. It was like he'd taken her to Disney World and told her she could eat all the funnel cakes, ride all the rides and have afternoon tea with Minnie Mouse. After she rode out her orgasm on his face, she collapsed back, like a limp fettuccine noodle. Her pale skin was flushed a beautiful pink, her hair fanned out around her head like a halo and her chest rising and falling with each breath. She was stunning.

He was hard as a rock, between her taste, her moans of pleasure and the mere sight of her. But he could tell she needed a few minutes to recover. He'd made a bold promise, but from the looks of it, he might have just succeeded.

He kissed his way back down her leg and stood, watching as her body twitched and she murmured indistinguishable words. He yanked his zipper down, freeing his aching cock. All week he'd been dreaming about being with

Ada, and the reality was so much more than he'd imagined. He couldn't get inside her fast enough.

With enough restraint to earn a freaking medal, he shed his pants and climbed onto the bed beside her, pulling her into his arms. They had all night. His dick would just have to wait.

After a few minutes of cuddling, Ada opened her eyes and looked up at him. Her lashes were thick and long, and her eyes practically twinkled. A sly smile and flushed cheeks signaled embarrassment, and he'd warned her about that.

He kissed her forehead. "I don't ever want you to hold back with me. You coming undone like that—it was sexy as hell." He took her hand and placed it on his still-erect member. "See what you did to me?"

She gripped him hard, and it nearly took his breath. "That was my first time…" She cut her eyes away from him. "You know…"

Knowing that he was the first man to taste her, to bring her that kind of ecstasy—he felt giddy with the honor. He tipped her chin up and attacked her mouth. He couldn't get enough of her supple lips and soft tongue. He couldn't get enough of her. Pulling back just enough to take a breath and see her eyes, he whispered, "Can you taste yourself on my tongue? How incredible you are?" He kissed her again, swallowing her sharp moan.

She stroked him, bringing him closer to the edge. He had to get inside her now, before he exploded. Regretfully, he left the warmth of her hand to dig in his pants pocket. Pulling the single condom out, he mentally cursed. Of course, one time with Ada wouldn't be enough. He should have been more prepared.

He was looming over her, taking in every gorgeous inch, yanking on his cock, getting ready to make her scream again, when it occurred to him that maybe she meant her first time, first time. He crawled back up the bed and cradled her face in his hand.

"Darlin', when you said first time…"

She shook her head, but she was smiling now. "I just meant oral. I've had sex before, just probably not good sex."

The fact that she had any question about that told Trip he needed to take this slow and make sure she woke up tomorrow with zero doubts. "Well, hold on, Ada, because this is going to be better than good. This is going to be life changing."

"It already is." That pretty flush crept up her cheeks again.

Oh, there was so much he wanted to show her. Fuck. Only one condom.

Then again, Ben and Riley came down to the boat to have alone time, so maybe... He reached over and opened the drawer in the small built-in nightstand.

Jackpot! Someone had been down to Myrtle Beach and hit the Costco. He'd forever be in Riley and Ben's debt—but who was he kidding, he already was.

Knowing he had backup, Trip wasted no time rolling the condom down his shaft. He positioned himself between Ada's legs, giving her a minute to adjust to his weight on her. He kissed her long and slow, one of his hands gripping her hair, the other teasing her nipples. His cock twitched against her, ready to get in on the action.

When she reached down and positioned his dick at her entrance, he felt like he'd won the freaking lottery. When he felt the tightness and warmth of Ada, he felt like the king of the world. This would be a major challenge for him. She felt too damn good. And Chesnee had been right—it'd been too damn long.

He was glad he hadn't been with anyone recently. It made this time with Ada that much more special. In fact, he couldn't remember the last time he was with a girl he truly liked. Someone he could see himself with long term.

Ada was stiff at first, her muscles clamping down on him like a damn vise. Which wasn't helping in the making-it-last department. He sank in a little farther and her shoulders hunched up. He wasn't even fully seated, and he felt like that champagne bottle out there.

"Darlin', I need you to relax." He kissed her lightly on the nose, then the mouth, then each nipple. He circled his tongue around her areolas. Her shoulders dropped and her legs opened wider. He pushed forward, keeping his attention on her breasts—because it was working and they were spectacular.

"Trip." Her voice shook. "I think you're too big."

He was almost fully seated, but she was still clenching. "Just a little farther." He wasn't huge by any measure, so whoever had come before must have been puny. Which tracked with her impression of the sex she'd had. He bent forward and sucked one of her tits into his mouth.

Ada gasped and released her grip, allowing him to gain the extra inch or so.

It was fucking perfect. "See? We fit just right." He stayed still for a minute, to let her get used to him. While he waited, he sucked her other tit into his mouth.

"Holy hell." Ada gripped his back, her nails digging into his flesh.

He looked up from his encampment around her chest, gauging her expression. She was still a little bleary-eyed from the first orgasm and now she was watching him like he might take a bite out of her at any moment. *It was a possibility.* "You ready for me to start moving?"

She licked her lips, and his dick twitched inside her. Her eyebrows winged up in surprise.

He laughed and kissed her again. He was content to stay here as long as was necessary. Couldn't think of another place he'd rather be, as a matter of fact.

While they were kissing, Ada's hips started moving. She was working herself on his cock, and it was hot as hell. *Fuck, it was going to be hard to hold on. Alabama—Montgomery. Alaska—Juneau. Arizona—Phoenix.*

She was sucking on his neck and thrusting up to meet him. It was like the bottom half of his body was operating completely independent from his brain. *Arkansas—Little Rock.* It was no use. She was murmuring his name over and over again. They were moving together in a frenzy, to the point that he could hear waves lapping against the boat.

"Oh my gosh, oh my gosh, oh my gosh!" Ada's body tensed up and she drew his name out into about twelve syllables.

Her pussy clenched his cock over and over again, like the most suffocating and delicious pressure ever. He drove into her two more times and came like a rocket ship, completely forgetting the capital of California and his first name.

Chapter Thirty-One

Ada was right. She hadn't had capital S-E-X before. She'd had "sex." Trip had officially ruined her. Not only was she going to expect an orgasm from here on out, she was going to expect a mind-numbing, screeching, out-of-body orgasm.

The morning light filtered through the small windows above the bed, dancing an elegant waltz across Trip's naked body. They were still tangled up together, as they had been most of the night. There had been patches of sleep, but mostly lots of pleasure and a little bit of talking. But Ada didn't feel tired, she felt invigorated. A real orgasm was better than any energy drink you could buy at the 7-Eleven. Four was like someone had pumped straight adrenaline into her veins.

She traced the line of his muscle down his arm, keeping her touch light, but his eyelashes fluttered. It wasn't her intention to wake him up for another round, but she wasn't opposed to it. And the stiffness poking her in the side suggested he would be on board as well.

Her fingers wandered to his chest, where she traced the small tattoo she had discovered last night. Even though she'd seen him with his shirt off multiple times, it wasn't noticeable until you got close. It was simple and elegant. One word, written in cursive. *Push.*

She wanted to ask him about it, but they'd been distracted most of the night.

His eyes slowly opened and when they lit on hers, a huge smile spread across his face. He leaned closer, pressing a soft kiss against her temple. "Waking up next to you is like the best dream I've ever had." He reached for her hand and twined their fingers together.

Ada felt such peace. They'd had a night full of passion and pleasure, but this proved it was more than that, it was something deep and meaningful.

Yup, she wasn't a fling kind of girl. Or at least not with Trip.

He was coming close to her again when his phone pealed from the kitchen area. They'd come below deck and basically dropped everything once they had a little privacy.

The ringing phone didn't stop him. He grabbed the back of her head and angled it before meeting her lips. Kissing Trip was like the series of pirouettes in Swan Lake—fast, elegant and they made you a little dizzy.

He pulled her closer, sinking into the kiss and ignoring when his phone rang again. The third time, he growled into her mouth and clutched her tighter.

She tried to tell him it was okay to answer, but he was plastered to her mouth.

Finally, he pulled back, panting, and licked his lips. "Hold that thought. Let me just make sure nothing's on fire."

He climbed out of the bed and walked into the galley.

Trip looked damn good naked, she already knew that. But Trip naked from behind—holy hell. Someone needed to make a bronze out of that image.

He picked up his phone and his whole body tensed. He spun around.

The front was really good too.

"It's nine. I can't believe I slept that late. Riley is losing her shit." He grabbed his pants off the floor and tried to pull them on while texting.

Now Ada was turned on and laughing. "I'm sorry I made you late. Is there something I can do to help? I don't have any plans today."

He dropped the phone on the bed and buttoned his pants. Crawling up the bed toward her, he looked like a hungry tiger on the prowl. "Last night was worth every bad word Riley probably left on my voicemail."

He kissed her again, stealing her breath.

When she could get a gulp of air, she laughed. "Riley doesn't say bad words. She says stuff like 'fiddle my diddle'."

Trip threw his head back and roared. "She does say ridiculous stuff, but no one has ever said 'fiddle my diddle'."

Ada shrugged. "I guess I should copyright it then. The memes will go viral, and I'll be famous."

He gave her a quick peck, then backed off the bed. "Okay, internet sensation. Get dressed. We've got orders to obey from our tiny dictator."

As she pulled her dress over her head, she realized she'd be walking back into Heron House in the same clothes she wore yesterday. Pre-spectacular-orgasms Ada would have been mortified, but post-four-minding-blowing-orgasms Ada intended to walk in with her head held high. And she really hoped Trip's mother and Maurico were around to witness it.

***

The house had been empty when they arrived, which was weird because it was fully booked, and the gala was tomorrow. They quickly changed clothes and grabbed a pastry off the counter. They were in a pink bakery box, so Ada assumed Riley had ordered them in. Maybe someone had told her about her cinnamon rolls.

She could tell Trip felt guilty about not getting up early and making a proper breakfast, it was the first morning with a full house, after all. They wolfed down their baked goods and went in search of Riley and Ben.

They'd walked across the front lawn on their way back from the boat, so they started looking in the back. Ada eyed the river as they passed it, keeping a close watch out for anything scaly.

As they came out of the thick patch of trees, they found the residents of the house huddled near the riverbank. Ada hadn't walked this far before. There was a large clearing and one of those containers off a cargo ship. She squeezed Trip's arm and pointed.

"This is the land that Sharkey bought for his brewery. That container will be a bar eventually."

They approached the crowd of people, but no one seemed to notice they had arrived.

Luckily, they were both tall, so they could easily see what had caused all the residents of Heron House to come gawk. On the riverbank lay a huge alligator—easily eight feet long—tangled in a fishing net. There was a float attached to the net, which made him look like he had a tumor on top of his head. And his front right foot was missing.

"I take it this is the infamous Stumpy."

Trip nodded. "Yup. Obviously, he gets himself into messes like this regularly, hence the stump."

"So, is everyone just going to gawk at him, or are we going to help him?"

Everyone turned to look at Ada as she pointed out the obvious. There were murmurs in the small crowd, then Riley appeared in front of the group and pointed up at Trip. "I've been calling you!"

"I know, I know. Sorry. The boat is really comfortable."

"Carlton, whatever were you doing on a boat?" Mrs. Westinghouse was fully made up, dressed like she was attending an afternoon tea with the royal family.

Ada was beyond tempted to correct her. The question was *who* was he doing on a boat? *It was me! Me! I'm the lucky one!* In her mind, she was jumping around doing cartwheels. In reality, she bit her lip to keep from speaking.

Riley narrowed her eyes at him. "Well, this is your punishment." She pointed at Stumpy, who had the decency to look pathetic tangled up in the net.

"One thing you ladies aren't accounting for are his very sharp teeth. And the fact that he's bigger than me."

"My son can't possibly approach an alligator. He's a Westinghouse."

Ada saw the switch flip in Trip at his mother's suggestion.

He stepped forward, grabbing Ben and pulling him closer to the reptile. "Back up people. We need room to work."

Ben was shaking his head emphatically. "I'm not part of this 'we.' Riley would murder me if I died the day before her gala."

Just then a large, bearded man appeared. He pushed through the small crowd and consulted with Trip and the very reluctant Ben. The three men huddled together—hands gesturing, heads shaking 'no,' and hushed expletives escaping.

Finally, they did some hand over hand football cheer thing and faced the group of onlookers.

Trip slapped his arms around both men. "We have a plan. We only ask that our significant others not witness our deaths or maiming. So, everyone head back to the house. Gina, you can stay to call 911 if things get dicey."

If Trip and Ben seriously thought they were getting rid of Ada and Riley, they were sorely mistaken.

Chapter Thirty-Two

With a lot of coaxing, most of the guests headed back to the house. He'd been pretty sure Ada and Riley wouldn't budge, but he was grateful to see his mother walk away. The last thing he wanted to do was prove her right.

Sharkey had a plan. It wasn't a perfect plan, but Trip was guessing there was no guidebook for this situation.

Gina was filming the disaster with her phone, so at least it would be documented for future generations. If they made it out alive and with their reproductive organs intact, because none of them currently had future generations.

Sharkey took one step closer to Stumpy, and the gator snapped his jaws in warning.

"At least the float is limiting his bite radius," Riley helpfully said from the sidelines.

"Pretty sure he could still take someone's hand off." Ben stayed a healthy distance back from the massive reptile.

"You gotta admit, it'd be a little ironic if the alligator missing a leg took off someone's appendage."

Wow, this crowd is super helpful. "You're just filming, Gina. Not directing." He dropped his voice and leaned close to Sharkey, because he was the idea guy. "I don't think he understands that we're trying to help him."

The brewer assessed the gator, then undid his belt buckle.

Is he going to try to intimidate the creature with his manhood? Trip hadn't ever seen his friend naked, but he was a big dude, so one just assumed he was...

Sharkey whipped his belt out of his shorts and before anyone knew what he was doing—including Stumpy, thank goodness—he'd wrapped his leather belt around the alligator's snout and cinched it tight. He pulled a massive knife out of his waistband and held it out.

Trip put his hands up and shook his head. "The plan was for you to cut the net off."

Sharkey grunted, because that was his normal mode of communication. He was a man of very few words. "You wanna hold the belt?"

Cutting the net off it is, then. He stepped forward and grabbed the knife, surprised by its heft. *How did its weight not pull the man's shorts down? Especially once he took his belt off?* Again, he assumed it was the size of his manhood holding those shorts up.

Trip swung around toward Ben, who jumped backward.

"Hey, watch it. I'm not losing a limb to you or an alligator today."

"You're supposed to hold the tail."

Ben grumbled and moved to the back of the animal.

Trip closed the distance between himself and certain death. He slid the blade under the net. *Here goes nothing.* He yanked up and a small portion tore.

Someone on the bank clapped. He assumed it was Ada, but he didn't dare turn his back on Stumpy to check.

The net had dug into the gator's skin in several places, so Trip had to pull the net away and wedge the knife in some of the tighter areas.

"What's his skin feel like?" Riley shouted.

"You want to come down here and feel it for yourself?"

"No, I'm good."

Yeah, that's what I thought. He worked his way around Stumpy's midsection, dreading the part closer to his head and those jaws of steel.

While he was working, he heard Riley tell Ada the story of Stumpy going after her ex-husband during the hurricane earlier in the summer. Trip hadn't been there to witness it himself, but the story had become legendary around Eastport Beach.

For the most part, Stumpy laid still, possibly understanding that the men were trying to help him. Every once in a while, he'd growl, and his whole body would vibrate with the movement. The first time it happened, Ben and Trip both jumped up and away, but Sharkey just growled back at the gator, keeping the belt cinched tight. The man was a beast. Props.

Finally, Trip had most of the net off, but the part that was left was wrapped tightly around the alligator's head. Stumpy was getting antsy and now that his back end was free, he wasn't being still any longer.

"Ben, hold him still."

His friend glared at him. "How do you suggest I do that?"

"Ben told me he wrestled gators every day of the week except Sundays," Riley yelled from the safety of the bank.

"So, you're an expert." Trip waved the knife at him.

Ben grumbled a bit, then flung his body over the back half of the alligator. Stumpy was so surprised he squeaked, Riley whooped, and Trip dropped the knife.

"Get on with it!" Ben snapped.

There was a commotion up on the berm and Trip thought he heard someone suggest landscape mode. Chesnee was going to be so sorry he missed this.

Trip secured the knife once more and worked it under the net circling Stumpy's neck. There was a wound that suggested he'd been tangled up in this net for a long time. "I'm sorry, buddy." He patted the rough scales lining the animal's back. Raising his voice, he yelled up to their spectators. "He has a pretty bad gash. Should we put Neosporin on it?"

Riley yelled back. "How about some liquid bandage? Since he'll obviously get it wet?"

Trip shrugged and turned to Sharkey. "What do you think?"

Sharkey rolled his eyes.

"Whatever you're going to do, get it done. Some of us are currently laying on top of an alligator!" Ben ground out.

"On it!" Riley yelled back. "And don't you even think about getting hurt while I'm gone!"

"Don't worry, I'm still rolling," Gina assured Riley.

"Not the point, Gina," Riley shouted as she ran toward the house.

Trip sliced through the netting that was wrapped around the float. "Anyone want a souvenir?" He held the blue float up in the air.

"Sharkey could hang it in his bar," Gina said. "It would be a great conversation starter."

Trip looked to Sharkey who grunted again.

He tossed the float up on the bank.

Sharkey's grunts were like *Aloha*. They could mean, yes, no, maybe and fuck off.

By the time Riley returned with the first aid kit, Trip had managed to cut most of the net away. She scurried down the hill toward the three—well, quartet.

"What do you think you're doing?" Ben shouted.

She stopped, hands on her hips in immediate defiance. "I'm helping this poor defenseless animal."

"A) this animal weighs more than all of us put together, so he is far from defenseless. And B) you better get back up on that berm or I'm going to be wrestling you to the ground next."

Trip had seen this particular battle of wills play out many times over the summer.

Riley stepped closer, pulling the bottle out of the kit. "Where is it?"

"Riley," Ben said sternly.

"Benjamin," Riley mocked.

Trip pointed to the wound, and she pulled out a tiny brush and started painting it over the cut, which was easily six inches long. "Just dump the bottle on it. It will take forever with that brush."

She dumped the bottle of liquid out, trying to spread it across the wound with the tiny applicator, murmuring words of reassurance to Stumpy the entire time.

"Are you done yet?" Ben was close to reaching his breaking point.

Riley gave the gator one last pat and scurried back up the riverbank. "I touched an alligator!" She and Ada jumped up and down. "Four months ago, I was convinced one was going to eat me within the year."

They were discussing possible hashtags as the guys tried to figure out an exit plan.

"Sharkey, I hope you're fast, because I'm pretty sure you need to be the last one to let go." Trip was so glad he chose the cutting part.

He grunted and gestured that they should get on with it.

Trip handed him the knife, just in case, and then climbed up the bank and grabbed Ada, breathing in her sweet scent and feeling almost as alive as last night when he had that life-altering first orgasm with her.

Ben climbed off the now-thrashing gator and made a dash for the safety of Riley's arms.

Then they all watched with bated breath as Sharkey leaned down and whispered something to the gator, then released the belt and calmly walked away.

Stumpy froze and didn't move until the brewer was a safe distance away, then he walked a couple steps and slid into the river, waving his tail in gratitude.

Chapter Thirty-Three

"Hey, Riley." Ada peeked around the open French door into her hostess's study. "Ben said you wanted to see me."

"Yes! Two things." Riley popped up from her desk chair and waved Ada inside the room. "Okay, I lied. Three things." She leaned against the desk, bouncing on her heels.

Ada sat in one of the chairs situated in front of the desk. She guessed they were old, likely Archie's, and were a combination of wood and leather with brass tacks lining the seams. She ran her fingers over the tacks, feeling apprehension at Riley's excitement.

"First, how was the dance lesson downtown?"

She exhaled. This she could handle. "It was great. We had to turn people away. But it was a lot of fun, and most people were kind enough to leave a donation. Actually, I'd like to pass those funds along to you."

Riley shook her head. "Me? I didn't do anything. You taught people for several hours. And I heard it wasn't the easiest bunch of students. Keep it!"

"Aren't you setting up a foundation or something?" She couldn't recall the particulars, but she was certain she'd read something about it when she first found out about the gala.

"Yes, all the proceeds from the auction are going into the Archibald Kirkman Foundation, which will grant scholarships for future artisans to come stay at Heron House."

"Perfect! I'd like to donate the money to that."

Riley blushed and clapped her hands. "My first donation! I guess things are officially official. Thank you." She clutched a folder to her chest. "Did Mr. Calcut find you last night?"

Ada quirked her lips to the side. "Mr. Calcut?"

"Yeah, he checked in late in the afternoon and when he saw some of the paintings we're auctioning off, he mentioned he was here at the same time as your mother, so I sent him to town to find you."

"Oh, do you mean Barry?" In her defense, a lot had happened since she met the artist last night—several mind-erasing orgasms, her first time on a boat, and alligator wrestling.

Riley nodded. "Yes, Barry."

Ada smiled. "He never told me his last name, but yes, we had pie together."

"Thanks for the leftover pie, by the way. I'd move in with that coconut cream pie and live in sin." She closed her eyes and groaned.

Laughing, Ada relaxed. She didn't need to be anxious around Riley. Although, she did say three things and Ada couldn't really follow how many things this part of the conversation counted as. "Yeah, for a minute I considered licking the plate, but I didn't want Trip and Barry to see me."

"And you slept okay? On the boat?" Her eyes were twinkling, and Ada had the feeling she wasn't asking about the quality of her sleep.

Ada leaned forward like she was sharing a secret. "I slept amazingly well. Like really, really well."

Riley dissolved into giggles. "Oh, I'm so glad. I was nervous, because the first time I slept on the boat, I was up all night long." She gave an exaggerated wink.

Ada really liked Riley. She was a simple gal who enjoyed life to the fullest and didn't put on artifice for anyone. She was truly herself all the time. "Sorry again about making Trip late this morning."

"No biggie. But his list is a mile long today, so don't expect an early bedtime tonight." She opened the folder. "Next, I was wondering what you've decided about *The Ballerina*. I sent Paul a picture of the inscription and he said he could draw up provenance paperwork based on it. Unless you've decided to keep it, of course."

Ugh, the painting. She'd been so wrapped up in everything happening with the dance lessons and Trip that she'd shoved that uncomfortable subject to the back of her mind. "Can I tell you after lunch?" She wanted to have one more conversation with Paul before she made her final decision. Her gut said to move on, and that painting was firmly rooted in the past. But a little voice somewhere near her heart said she should keep the one thing still tethering her to the mother that barely existed now.

"Of course." Riley pulled a sheet of paper from the folder and held it out. "This is the bio I have written up about Charlotte. Can you please read over it and make sure everything is accurate? Or if I've left anything major out?"

Ada took the paper. "Sure. Is this going to be in the auction guide?"

"Yes, and I've got to have the final draft to the printer by two."

"I'll get right on it. And if you need any help after lunch, I'm free."

Riley dropped the folder on the desk. "I'm not going to say no to that. My to-do list is even longer than Trip's."

Ada would have loved to get another shot at Archie's papers, but it didn't look like that was happening today. She got up and started to leave the room, then turned back. "I know I left my reservation pretty open-ended, but I'll definitely be staying at least another week, if that's okay."

"I'd love that." Riley threw her arms around Ada, who returned the hug. "You can stay here as long as you'd like. I'm sure Trip won't mind one bit."

Hopefully after Mrs. Westinghouse and her annoying Italian gnat left, she could get her suite back. Although she'd likely invite Trip for a sleepover.

***

> *Charlotte Maddox is one of the most widely recognized artists of modern times. Her painting style is a mixture of realism with bursts of surrealism and sometimes social commentary. She began her career in her late twenties when she was discovered by Paul Mallory, a NYC gallery owner, who has remained her manager for her entire career. She sold out her first solo show at the age of 28. Soon after, she was in residence at Heron House for a summer, where Archibald Kirkman further encouraged her to adopt her own unique style. She traveled widely and much of her art is influenced by other cultures and locales. She never married, but was blessed with a daughter, Ada, who is a very talented dancer and teacher. Charlotte has retired due to medical issues, so it is expected that her work will only increase in value.*

As usual, the piece made Charlotte sound like the most interesting person in any room. Ada supposed it was accurate, but wasn't there more to life than being the center of attention? She shot off a quick text to Riley that the bio looked good, then she dialed Paul's number.

"Hey, kiddo. How are things going?" There was a lot of background noise, like maybe he was on the street.

"You on your way to the gallery?"

"Yeah, the artist who's showing this weekend wants to talk about changes. You know, only a few hours before the opening. Typical."

Ada smiled despite the churning in her gut. Paul always complained about the artists, but he thrived on the rush of opening new shows monthly, not only in his New York City gallery, but also in the San Francisco one he'd opened a few years ago. "You always say you'd rather an artist have passion than be a pushover."

"Once again, my words come back to bite me in the ass. Maybe I'm just too old for the bullshit. But enough about my drama. Tell me about Eastport Beach."

"It's adorable. Almost like one of the boroughs, but without the convenience of a city nearby. Word got out that I'm a dancer, so I ended up giving impromptu lessons last night in this amazing space that used to be an art gallery."

"Aw, I hate to hear about a gallery going out of business, but it's great that you got to show off your talents."

Ada walked to the window, which looked out over a parking area and storage shed. Right then, Ben and Trip rounded the corner, lugging something heavy. It was wrapped in a tarp and the weight of it swung between the two men. Her first thought was that it was a dead body. But that was ridiculous. "It would make a perfect studio."

"Ada, are you thinking about staying down there?" Horns honked in the background.

As the guys got close to the shed, they set the tarp down to open the door. The sides flopped open, revealing several tree stumps. Definitely not a body. "It's not like I have a better idea. The studio in Virginia is closed and all I'm qualified to do is teach dance. Or go back on the road, which I'm not even sure I could do at this point."

"Well, you are certainly talented enough if that's what you want to do."

She shook her head, even though he obviously couldn't see her. "I'm not in the kind of shape I would need to be to compete against teenagers. I have zero interest in auditioning for a company."

"Is there some other reason you're considering staying?"

Trip bent down and hoisted one of the stumps, his t-shirt straining against his back and his biceps popping. "Well, I have kind of met someone."

"I see. I won't bother lecturing you, because you're the most responsible, conscientious young person I know—although most of the young people I know are spoiled, selfish artists. Just be careful."

"I will." She started to say goodbye, then remembered the reason she'd called him. "Riley has offered to give me The Ballerina, but I feel like it belongs to Archie's estate. It was clearly intended as a gift."

Paul chuckled. "Like I said, conscientious. But I agree with Riley. You should keep it."

"If I decide to, is there some way we can make a donation to the foundation Riley's set up? If she auctioned it off, she'd probably get good money for it. It's a large piece."

"It's a stunning piece and it shouldn't sell for under twenty grand."

Ada leaned her head against the glass of the window, watching Ben and Trip carry the stumps into the shed, breathing to calm herself. She didn't have twenty thousand dollars to donate to Archie's foundation. After she broke her lease in Virginia, she wouldn't have two dimes to rub together. "I should probably let her sell it. That would be huge for the foundation."

"If it's a matter of the money, we can take care of that. Keep it, Ada."

She'd almost talked herself into keeping it, but now she was more conflicted than ever. She didn't like to argue with Paul, so she changed the subject. "I met a guy last night who was here at the same time as Charlotte. He said it's possible she had something going on with Archie. I mean, the timing is right."

Paul sighed. "Ada, I seriously doubt that Charlotte had a relationship with Archie."

"What if I never know?"

"Know what?"

"Who my father is," she whispered, her voice cracking.

"Aw, sweetheart. I'm sure there are reasons Charlotte didn't tell you."

A tear escaped and rolled down her cheek. "I'm practically an orphan."

The line was quiet for almost a full minute. He must have gone into the gallery, because the street noise was gone. "Ada, you will always be part of our family. Elaine and I are always here if you need us."

"I know that." But it wasn't the same. Now that she was an adult, she couldn't just hang out baking cookies and watching old movies with Elaine or go on a hot chocolate date with Paul. They'd always been there for her when she was growing up, but now she was on her own.

"Sweetheart, my artist is walking in the door, so I have to go. We'll talk about this more later, I promise. And keep the painting. Love you, kiddo."

"Love you too." The phone went quiet, Trip and Ben walked around the front of the house, and Ada was all alone. She didn't know her father and her mother was practically gone. Maybe her best bet was to make her own family. Maybe she could do that with Trip.

Chapter Thirty-Four

He stuck his head in the study. "Riley, have you seen Ada?"

"She was down here earlier, but I haven't seen her since." She moved a stack of books off the desk and piled them in a bookcase. "She did text me though. She said we should sell The Ballerina."

Trip had wanted the painting before he knew Ada, but now, the thought of someone else taking it home caused him to clench his hands into fists. "Do we even have provenance for it?"

"Yeah, Paul is sending a formal letter over, but he said the inscription is enough. I don't know, I just feel weird about it."

"Maybe we could leave it in the collection?"

"I thought about that. But Paul also said it should bring five figures. That would be a huge boon for the foundation."

Maybe he could convince his mother to buy it. The foundation would get its money and at least he'd know where it was. And if Ada ever changed her mind… "I understand. That's hard to pass up."

"Did you guys get all the chairs and tables set up?"

"Mostly. I came up to make some wraps for lunch. You want one?"

She waved him off. "I'm too nervous to eat."

"Riley, everything is under control, and you need your strength, or you won't have the energy to order us around."

She pursed her lips at him. "Turkey please."

"I've got you covered." He took out his phone as he headed into the kitchen, shooting off another text to Ada. When she didn't answer the first one, he figured she was busy or maybe catching a nap—after all, they hadn't slept much the night before. But now he wondered about her state of mind. Was she upset about the painting? She had a complicated relationship with her mother.

She still hadn't answered when he finished making lunch. He tossed the wraps, a bag of chips and three Gatorade's into a reusable bag. He kept Riley's turkey wrap—with Swiss cheese, spicy mustard and pickles—out and grabbed her a bottled water. When he poked his head back in the door of the study, she was gone. He left her meal on the desk and sent her a quick text to let her know.

He was on his way out the front door when he decided he couldn't wait until after lunch. He needed to know that Ada was okay. He set the bag on the bottom step and took the stairs two at a time. His timing was shit, because his mother opened her door just as he reached the top of the staircase.

"Oh, good, Carlton, I'm glad I caught you. We're going into Wilmington for the day."

Yes, his mother's day did usually start around noon. As a child, the housekeeper made his lunch for school and his nanny made sure he got out the door in time. "Have fun, Mother."

"Would you like to join us?"

Has hell frozen over? "As fun as that sounds, Riley's got me tasked until sometime into next week."

She tittered. "Well, she's going to have to learn to do without you, since you're coming home on Monday, right?"

Trip didn't have time to have this particular "discussion." "Sorry, Mom, I've got to grab something out of my room and get back outside. Have fun in Wilmington."

"You didn't answer my question, Carlton."

He was halfway down the hall and didn't risk turning around. She may not be maternal, but she knew when he was lying. "Bye, Mom." He sailed up the steps to the third floor and prayed that she'd be gone before he came back down.

His room was at the top of the stairs and empty. Ada's luggage sat in the corner and the clothes she'd worn yesterday were folded neatly on the straight back chair. He continued down the hall, peeking into the other rooms, which had been set up as studio spaces. Gina's door was closed, and he was pretty sure she was working the lunch shift at the diner.

The last room, which sat at the front of the house, had been Ben's wife's studio before she died. The red door was propped open, her art covering every inch of the walls and several pieces displayed on easels. Trip had never met Sarah, but her art was vibrant and happy. Ben had selected a few pieces to be included in the auction, but Riley had insisted that her studio remain mostly intact. They spoke about Sarah freely and Trip knew her sister was coming to the gala.

His phone chimed with a text. Instead of Ada, it was from Robert, once again insisting on the meeting with his grandfather on Monday. Trip ignored the message and stuffed the phone back in his pocket. He needed to get lunch to Ben and Chesnee and get back to his monumental to-do list. Hopefully his mother wasn't standing by her door waiting to attack.

He crept down the stairs and leaned around the corner. The hallway was clear. Whew.

As he was passing his mother's room, his phone trilled. Shit. He grabbed the phone out of his pocket and swiped the screen to make it shut up, then rushed down the stairs, grabbed the bag and slipped out the door before saying, "Hello?"

"Hey, it's Ada." Her voice was quiet and laced with a hint of sadness.

The thought of her hurting gutted him. He continued down the porch steps, trying to put distance between himself and the house, just in case his mother was still around. "Thanks for calling me back. I made you some lunch."

"That's sweet, but I took one of the bikes into town. I'm going to grab a bite at The Spicy Mermaid. Gina said she'd be working." The sound of wind whistled in the background. He could picture her flying down River Rd, her hair waving behind her.

"Okay, be careful, and when you get back, I'd love to see you." Trip was walking the tightrope between concerned possible boyfriend and needy almost stalker. But after last night, things had shifted for him. It was so much clearer now. He wanted away from his family, and he wanted Ada in his life.

"I'll come find you, but I told Riley she could put me to work."

"You'll regret that. She's on the warpath."

She laughed, and his heart felt lighter. "She seemed a bit stressed, so hopefully I can take some of the load off."

"Yeah, it was nice of you to offer."

"She's really easy to like."

Trip nodded, even though she couldn't see. "Riley's the best. Ben too. They are solid people."

"Everyone in Eastport Beach is. I like it here."

Maybe there was a chance she'd stay. "I'm glad. It's a special place."

"I'd better focus, there's a lot of traffic on Main Street today. I'll see you soon."

"You better."

Her laughter was cut off as the call ended.

Damn he had it bad for this girl. They'd only been apart for a few hours, and he was itching to get his hands back on her. Even just to hold her hand, although he'd prefer something a little more private.

"Dude, you bringing that food over here sometime today?" Chesnee hollered from across the lawn where the tent was set up.

Yup, he had it real bad. He was standing in the middle of the driveway daydreaming about a girl he'd met less than a week ago. And Chesnee would never let him live it down.

Chapter Thirty-Five

Ada was securing her bike outside The Spicy Mermaid when a two-seater Mercedes pulled up to the curb and parked. It was a handicap space and the man who emerged from the car seemed fit and spry. He slid his sunglasses down his nose and made a show of checking her out.

The attention gave her the creeps, but as she got a good look at him, she realized how much he looked like Trip. She knew his father was attending the gala, so there was a chance this was Win Westinghouse.

"Hey there, sugar. You heading in for lunch?"

She considered unhooking the bike and pedaling back to Heron House as fast as possible, but she was really hungry, and she was hoping to talk to Gina. "Yes."

"Great! You can keep me company." He grabbed her arm and started toward the restaurant.

The overly familiar gesture stunned her, and she jerked away. "No, thank you."

"Come on, a pretty little thing like you can't eat alone."

"I don't want to be rude, but I don't know you, and you're old enough to be my father."

He snickered and held out his hand. "It's Win, nice to meet you. Any chance you have daddy issues?"

Seriously, what kind of luck was this? She'd come to the diner because Riley told her Gina didn't know her father either, so she was hoping to speak to someone who would understand. And pie. She definitely never expected her boyfriend's father to hit on her. Was it weird to think of Trip as her boyfriend? It was probably too fast, but she felt deeply connected to him after last night. She sorted through several responses in her head, each one snarkier than the last. Finally, she settled on cordial. If this thing with Trip did last more than a weekend, she may have to see this man again. "It's nice to meet you, Win. My name is Ada and I'm dating your son."

After the shock wore off his face, he threw his head back and roared with laughter. "Chip off the old block, I guess. Now you absolutely must let me buy you lunch."

From what she'd heard, Trip was nothing like his father. "That sounds nice." She'd rather have someone yank out her fingernails one at a time, but she'd probably survive a meal—as long as there was a table between them.

He opened the door for her, and she immediately caught Gina's attention.

"Hey girl. Table for two?" Her expressive eyes were asking who the heck was the silver fox?

"Can we have a booth?"

"Sure." Gina grabbed a couple menus and led them to the same booth Ada had shared with Barry last night. A not-creepy dinner companion. Pie counts as dinner, right?

"Gina, this is Trip's father, Win Westinghouse."

Realization dawned on her face. She snapped her fingers. "I see the resemblance."

"This town is full of young, attractive women. I can see why Trip likes it here." He leered at Gina, not even attempting to hide it.

"Okay...Hey, Ada, I need to ask you about something." She turned to Trip's dad and put on a 1000-watt smile. "Can I steal her for a minute? Girly stuff, you know." She winked at Win, then grabbed Ada's arm, not waiting for an answer for either of them. She dragged her back to the hallway that led to the restrooms. "No judgment, but WTF, Ada?"

She wasn't going to point out that WTF was basically judgment, because she was on the same page as Gina and she didn't even want to be reading this book. "He accosted me outside. I thought he looked a little familiar, but when he said his name was Win, it all clicked. How do I tell Trip that his dad hit on me?"

"Um, you don't tell Trip, but you should also have told Senior no."

"Technically, he's Junior and Trip's the third." Then she realized that she was having lunch with the man who would likely take over when Senator Westinghouse retired. "I can't be rude. If this thing with Trip goes anywhere, I'll probably have to deal with his family."

Gina rolled her eyes. "I've met the mother. Trip would be better off as an orphan."

"Yeah, he's not a big fan of either of his parents. There are a lot of expectations."

Someone behind the counter gestured at Gina. "I've got to get back to work. I'll play interference as much as I can, but we should probably have a safe word in case you need a quick exit."

Ada laughed. "Okay, 007."

"I'm more of a Bourne fan. That's it. Jason is your code word."

"Sure, I can slip that into a conversation." Ada was still chuckling to herself as she walked back to the table.

"Did you girls talk about me?" Trip's father was spread out in the booth, his arms stretched out along the back of the seat, looking comfortable as could be as if he was holding court with the entire diner.

"No, she just needed some advice about a female issue."

He became suddenly engrossed in the menu.

Female issues—a surefire way to keep a man out of your business. "What brings you into Eastport Beach? Trip said you're staying up in Wilmington."

"I came down here to try to talk some sense into him, but he was too busy to get away." Win huffed like a petulant child.

"There is a lot to do to prepare for the gala. I'm planning to pitch in when I get back."

"That's what the help is for."

Ada narrowed her eyes at the older man. *Is he for real?* "You do realize that Trip works for Riley and Ben?" *He's "the help."*

"Well, that will be over soon enough. He has responsibilities at home."

She didn't bother to remind him that Trip was staying in Eastport Beach. "He'll have more time to talk after the gala."

Gina appeared, interrupting the awkwardness. She set two glasses of water in front of them. "Have you had a chance to look at the menu?"

"I'll have a scotch neat. None of that watered down shit."

Gina gave Ada an is-this-guy-for-real look. "I'm sorry, sir, but we don't have a bar."

"Oh, God. Please tell me I'm not trapped in some little dry county."

"No, sir. Eastport Beach loves a good alcoholic beverage or two, just not here at The Spicy Mermaid."

He gave her a bored look. "Do you at least have sparkling water?"

"We have bottled water. I could blow some bubbles in it if you like."

Ada snickered, not even attempting to hide it. The man was ridiculous. "The Landing is just down the street, and they have a full bar." She didn't bother to tell him it was where Trip and she had their first date. He didn't seem like the sentimental type.

Win sipped the water in front of him and made a face.

He was basically a toddler in Ralph Lauren.

"I think I'll grab something to go so I can get back to Heron House and help out. I can show you where The Landing is." Ada briefly glanced at the menu.

"After the morning I've had, I need a drink. You're sure you won't join me?" He was already sliding out of the booth.

Ada shook her head. "No, thank you. I should get back. Gina, can you order me a tuna melt to go?"

"You got it." She headed for the kitchen, then turned back. "It was great to meet you Mr. W. I'll see you at the gala."

"The waitress is coming to the gala?"

Ada couldn't believe the things that came out of this man's mouth. "Yes, everyone in town is welcome." She slid out of the booth and led the oaf out the door. They reached the street, and she pointed down toward the water. "The Landing is right down there.""Will they have valet at least?" He opened his car door.

"I really wouldn't know, I'm only visiting." She crossed her fingers behind her back and prayed that Captain Percy would happen by. He'd probably appreciate seeing someone more outrageous than him for once. "See you tomorrow." She slipped back inside before he could say anything else. It was a wonder Trip had turned out so well with parents like that.

Chapter Thirty-Six

S unlight slanted through the window, warming Trip's face. He stretched, realizing he was alone in the bed. His eyes popped open, scanning the small room. Ada was gone. Just how late was it?

He sat up and checked his phone. It wasn't seven yet, and Riley wouldn't be crawling out of her cave for another half an hour at the earliest—unless she hadn't gone to bed. She was pretty manic last night, which was why Trip got to his room after two a.m. and Ada was already asleep. He'd happily curled around her body in the tiny bed and fallen quickly into a deep slumber.

Hard work and a warm body were the perfect sleep supplement.

Pulling on a pair of board shorts and a tank top, he crept down the stairs, careful not to wake any guests. He used the facilities, then slipped down the main stairs, where the smell of coffee and something yeasty drew his attention toward the kitchen. Crap, did Riley make another batch of cinnamon rolls?

"Morning." Ada greeted him with a cup of coffee prepared exactly right. When had she noticed how he took his coffee? She didn't even drink the stuff. She pushed up on her toes and kissed his cheek, running her hand through his hair, likely trying to tame his permanent cowlick.

"Hey sweetie pie." Ben sat at the table, artfully arranging fruit on a platter.

"Good morning, sugar dumpling," Trip quipped back and Ada laughed. "Where's Riley? And what's that delicious smell?"

Ben jerked his head toward the butler's pantry which held a not-so-secret passage to the master suite. "We're letting her sleep in. She was up past four. And Ada made a casserole."

She was leaning against the counter, sipping orange juice, wearing a simple black tank and shorts. She had flour on her shorts and a spot of something wet on her top. Her eyes were dancing with merriment like someone had just told a dirty joke in mixed company.

"You cooked?"

"I'm not completely useless in the kitchen. I had to fend for myself growing up. If I didn't cook, I didn't eat." She grinned. "Until I learned how to order in."

Trip opened the oven door, and a heavenly scent escaped. "What is it?"

"French toast casserole. It's really easy—just a bunch of torn up bread and some eggs, milk and cinnamon."

Ben waved a banana at her. "Don't let her downplay it. When I came in, she was whipping fresh cream."

Trip arched his eyebrows. "Well, aren't you full of surprises? Riley's gonna kick me out and beg you to move in. I've never whipped fresh cream." He leaned next to her, and she smelled like strawberries and cinnamon. It was intoxicating, but he was all too aware of Ben's presence, so he kept his hands to himself. "You should have woken me up. I could have helped."

"You were zonked. And I know Riley will have you back at it as soon as she gets up, so I figured someone should make breakfast for you for once."

"Breakfast is for everyone, hence the half ton of fruit and tray of bagels already in the dining room." Ben gestured to the hallway with a bunch of grapes.

Trip's stomach rumbled. "Did you get bagels from Coastal? And those crazy cream cheeses?"

"No licking the lids this time. We have a house full of guests."

"That was one time, and I don't even regret it." Trip turned to Ada. "You've got to try the honey walnut dip. It's insane."

Ada's phone beeped and she sprang into action, putting potholders shaped like trout on her hands. She opened the oven door and slid the casserole onto a trivet on the counter. "I hope this comes out okay. I usually make a much smaller portion."

Trip slid his arm around her waist and leaned over her shoulder. "I'm sure it will be great. It's golden brown and it smells like a freaking bakery in here."

The door slid open in the pantry and Riley shuffled into the room. "I was going to make cinnamon rolls, but I overslept."

Ben jumped up and made her a cup of coffee, then handed it to her with a kiss on the forehead and whispered words. She smiled and sipped the coffee.

"I don't think three hours of sleep can be considered oversleeping." Ada used a spatula to loosen the casserole around the edges and then cut it into portions.

"We've got breakfast under control, Ri." Ben guided her into the chair he'd been sitting in and picked the fruit platter up. "Everything will be set up in the dining room for when our guests wake up." He headed down the hall, platter in one hand and fresh-squeezed orange juice in the other.

Ada had been very busy if she juiced that much fruit this morning too. Trip leaned close to her and whispered, "Just how long have you been up?"

She shrugged, then lifted a serving of the casserole onto a plate and set it in front of Riley, along with a pitcher of syrup.

"Did you milk a maple tree, too?" Even at Trip's house, they'd used syrup straight from Mrs. Butterworth's head.

She laughed and bumped against his hip. "No, silly. There's all this fancy serving ware in the pantry, so I figured why not use it." She gasped and spun toward Riley. "I asked Ben's permission, of course."

Riley had already smothered her French toast in syrup and was cutting into her second bite. She waved her fork at Ada. "Girl, if you're going to cook like this, you can use anything in this house. Hell, we'll set up a bedroom for you upstairs." She grinned. "Or maybe just get Trip a bigger bed." She laughed as she slid another bite into her mouth.

"That'd be okay with me." Trip grabbed Ada's waist and pulled her close. All those months of watching Ben and Riley together and now he had someone he wanted to have his hands all over. Maybe things were looking up.

"Please tell me there's a French press." The sound of his mother's voice was like a wrecking ball smashing into his little bubble of happiness.

He rolled his eyes. "Good morning, Mother."

***

Breakfast had been a hit for all the normal, grateful guests staying at Heron House. Karina had called her driver to "find her some decent coffee and half a grapefruit."

Honestly, he might murder one or both of his parents before this weekend was over.

But he couldn't deal with them now, because Riley had a day-of list that rivaled a CVS receipt. Chesnee had shown up as if he smelled the food all the way from his apartment and now the two of them were rearranging tables and chairs because they hadn't left enough room for the dance floor.

"Where's Gina? She's still helping tonight, right?" Chesnee dragged a table across the wooden floor that had been set up under the tent.

Trip shook his head. "Why don't you just tell her how you feel and get it over with?"

His deluded friend held his hands up. "Whoa. I just asked why she wasn't helping."

"Just keep telling yourself that, buddy." Trip grabbed two chairs and slid them around the six top table he'd just moved. "She had a shift at the diner this morning. She's going to help us with the auction, as planned."

"Speaking of the diner, someone said they saw Ada eating lunch with some old dude yesterday."

Tension crept across Trip's shoulders. He was still seething from what Gina had told him last night. "That was my father. Apparently, he hit on her." His hands curled into fists.

"No shit. She told you that?"

"No, she told me she ran into him. Gina told me he hit on her—well, both of them somewhat."

"Hey now. Your pops better back off."

But you don't have a thing for Gina. Okay. "It turns out neither of my parents know how to behave in public. I never should have even told them about this gala. I just know they're going to cause trouble tonight."

"I'll help you keep an eye on them."

"Help me keep them separated or there'll be bloodshed." Luckily, only one of them was bringing a date.

"Did they get divorced, and you didn't tell me?"

Trip sighed. "I wish. No, they still pretend to be married when it's politically expedient. They live in separate wings and basically communicate through a third party. Me, if I'm unlucky."

"No wonder your sister fled the country."

"Yeah, she had the right idea."

"Is she coming back to help with the campaign?" Chesnee picked up two chairs and then backed into one of the tent supports.

Both men froze as the entire tent shook like they were in LA and the big one had hit.

When the entire thing didn't collapse on top of them, Trip answered the question. "No, somehow having two 'X' chromosomes precludes her from the responsibility of entering the family business."

"Yeah, I've met your grandfather. No way he'd allow a woman to run anything."

Trip gritted his teeth. "His beliefs are archaic. That's one of the main reasons I don't want to be involved in Dad's campaign. I'm diametrically opposed to most of what he stands for."

"Who? Your dad or your grandfather?"

"Is there a difference at this point?" Trip stepped back and surveyed their work. Hopefully it would pass the Riley test, because it was hotter than sin out here, even under the tent. Thank goodness the gala was late in the day, otherwise, he wouldn't be able to bear wearing his tux.

"I'm lucky my parents are so wrapped up in their practice they don't have time to worry about what I'm doing. It helps that my sister is a kiss-ass and became a chiropractor too." Chesnee was staring at someone or something over Trip's shoulder.

He turned, and sure enough, Gina's VW bug was pulling down the driveway.

"Thanks for helping with the chairs. I'm going to hit the shower. Maybe Riley won't be able to find me to give me another task."

Chesnee was already walking toward the driveway. He waved his hand over his head, completely focused on the woman he claimed he wasn't obsessed with.

Chapter Thirty-Seven

Ada skipped down the steps leading to the second floor. Every time she crossed the hall to the main staircase, she worried she'd run into Maurico. Luckily, he and Mrs. Westinghouse were gone a lot. Doing God knows what. She really didn't want to know.

She peeked through the doorway. The door to the Maddox suite was closed and as she leaned farther into the hall, she saw Trip coming up the main stairs. All thoughts of her ex fled, and her entire disposition transformed.

When he spotted her, a smile lit his face, and he gestured for her to keep quiet—likely worried that his mother would hear them. He wiggled his fingers, waving her to him. They met in front of the door to one of the shared bathrooms. He grabbed her and kissed her—right there in the hall for anyone to see. While they were still kissing, he opened the bathroom door and pulled her inside with him.

Pinned against the door, Ada could feel his heat and hardness. It made her feel alive.

Trip reached behind her and turned the lock, then reached back and yanked his t-shirt over his head.

She covered her mouth as she giggled. "What are you doing?"

"I need a shower. You need a shower. Water conservation." He grabbed her tank and pulled it over her head.

"Someone will hear us."

He grinned. "Guess you better control your screaming then." He lost his shorts and briefs with the same motion.

She blushed. Ada had never showered with a man before. It seemed to merit a certain level of intimacy she'd never shared with anyone. She'd known Trip for less than a week and here she was stripping in a bathroom, feeling like she'd won a dream experience. "I'm supposed to help Riley organize the auction materials." She climbed into the tub/shower combination with Trip.

"Riley needs to chill. She made us rearrange the entire tent, call the caterers to change the order of the hors d'oeuvres, and now she wants to reorganize the auction materials?" He leaned out of the shower and typed something on his phone. "I'm activating operation save-Riley-from-herself. Ben and I have a plan. She was bound to lose it eventually. It's actually later than I guessed, so I'm out twenty bucks." He tossed his phone onto his pile of clothes and refocused his attention on Ada.

"What does this plan involve?" He was standing so close she could feel every inch of him. All the inches.

"Her entire family is here minus her niece and nephew. They can help manage her. So, you're officially off the clock. Nowhere to be for hours." He dove into the space between her neck and shoulder, exploring with his mouth, his tongue, nips of his teeth.

Goosebumps formed in the wake of his kisses and despite the warm stream of water, chills raced up and down her skin. She was trying to work out the mechanics of shower sex when Trip knelt in front of her and placed a kiss in a very different location.

How the hell am I supposed to keep quiet with him between my legs?

His hands slid up the backs of her legs and squeezed her ass. "Damn, you're freaking perfect." He nipped at the tender skin of her inner thigh, then licked his way to the glory land.

Ada gripped his shoulders, holding on for dear life as he took her on a spiritual journey of pleasure. It didn't take long before her core was clenching, and she tipped over the edge. The orgasm came in waves, so intense at first that she forgot to breathe. Before it was over, Trip had her pinned against the wall, his mouth covering hers, the tart flavor of lust on his tongue.

He grabbed his penis and rubbed it through her soaking wet folds, teasing her, making her want to feel full like she had that night on the boat. Suddenly, he cursed and stepped back. "Fuck, I don't have a condom with me."

"That's okay. I have a better idea." She knelt in front of him, his glorious physique rising above her, water streaming down his back.

"Ada, you don't have to..."

He trailed off as she grasped his cock and smiled up at him. "I don't have to, but I want to." She licked her lips, and he groaned. By no means was she an expert at giving head, but being with Trip made her feel sexy, and safe. Confident. She ran her tongue around the tip, keeping eye contact with him until he closed his eyes with a moan.

"Darlin', you're gonna kill me with that tongue."

Ada let out a breath, and Trip's member jerked in response, so she played with that a bit, licking, then blowing softly over the same area. By the third time, he had clutched her hair and was whispering her name repeatedly. She'd never really understood how women could enjoy giving head—she just assumed it was something they suffered through to bring their man pleasure.

But this was different. She felt immense power—and pleasure—with every moan. As she lowered her mouth over his penis, she slid her hands around the back and grabbed two handfuls of his ass.

Trip pushed his cock farther into her mouth.

Soon, she had a rhythm going, and played around to see what he liked, and what really got him going. She wasn't sure how long she was down there, but when she cradled his balls in one hand and gripped his base in the other, he pushed deep in her mouth and came.

When he was spent, he knelt down to her level and wrapped his arms around her. "Darlin', that was so damn good. I may never walk again."

She understood the sentiment, because that first night when he ate her out, her legs had been like gelatin for hours afterwards. Her cheeks heated from the praise, and she nestled into his arms, content to stay there, under the stream of water, until it ran cold.

Trip pulled back enough to kiss her, holding her face between his hands and whispering her name when he took a breath. When his phone rang, he muttered but didn't stop the kiss.

They were getting worked up again when the pounding started on the bathroom door.

"Trip, we need you outside ASAP."

He cursed under his breath, then held a finger to his lips as he turned the water off.

Ben knocked again. "Riley's looking for Ada, if you happen to know where she is. But Sharkey's beer trailer is stuck and it's all hands on deck."

Footsteps traveled away from the door, and they could hear shouting downstairs.

"Do you think he knew I was in here?" Ada was mortified to be caught having sex in a shared bathroom.

"He definitely knew you were in here. Did you hear how loud I said your name when I came?"

She buried her face in his chest, groaning—and not for sexy reasons.

"Hey, it's fine. We're all adults." He squeezed her tight, then pulled the shower curtain open. "Guess I'm putting these stinky clothes back on. Not like we got around to the washing part of the shower anyway." He shot her a grin over his shoulder as he stepped out of the tub and grabbed a towel.

She wasn't as urgently needed, so she was going to put on clean clothes. He handed her a towel, and she wrapped it around her body, checking her reflection in the mirror over the sink. If the whole house hadn't heard, her "sex hair" would definitely give it away. She tried to smooth out the tangled knots but quickly gave up. "I'm going to run upstairs and grab some clothes." She bent and gathered her black tank and shorts, clutching them to her chest.

Dressed, Trip opened the door and stepped out into the hall. Ada followed, running into his back when he stopped suddenly.

"What's wr…" Ada started to ask but became mute when she saw Karina Westinghouse and Maurico staring back at them.

Chapter Thirty-Eight

As Trip jogged across the lawn, he chuckled to himself. The look on his mother's face when he and Ada came out of that bathroom half dressed would be a memory he'd recall anytime he needed a pick me up. She was so outraged that she turned around and went down the stairs without a word.

Ada had molded herself to his back, asking the Earth to open up and swallow her.

Trip had beamed with pride while that little Italian prick tried to get a good look at Ada in only a towel. *Keep on walking, buddy.*

He'd spent the next few minutes calming Ada down and assuring her that his mother probably didn't hear him scream Ada's name. So now he was booking it across the grass to where all the men (which is why Maurice wasn't in attendance) on the property were gathered on the far side of the giant tent.

"Nice shower? Did you forget to use soap? 'Cuz you still stink." Chesnee wiggled his eyebrows at Trip and gave him a knowing wink.

No wonder Gina wouldn't give him the time of day. He was an overgrown man-child. Trip shook his head, then addressed Ben and Sharkey, who had their heads together over by the truck. "What's the plan?"

From what he could tell, Sharkey had driven the truck, with the beer trailer hitched behind it, along the riverbank from his property behind Heron House. A driveway approach wouldn't have worked because of the tent. But the soil near the river was loamy and sand didn't mix with heavy vehicles.

Sharkey crossed his arms over his broad chest and nodded to Ben, who stepped forward. "We're going to unhitch the trailer and see if he can get the truck out without the extra weight. But that means we're going to have to manually move the trailer closer to the tent."

Normally, that wouldn't be a huge deal. There were six of them and most were in decent shape. But the trailer had seven full kegs on tap and likely backups as well.

"And ideally we get it done before Riley knows there's an issue." Ben winced.

All the men in the group nodded in agreement. No one wanted a Riley meltdown just three hours before the gala.

Trip clapped his hands together. "I asked Ada to keep Riley at the house until we give her the all clear, so let's get this done."

Riley's dad, a career Navy guy, and probably the most fit member of the group, looked doubtful. "Is there anyone else who can help?"

Chesnee's face brightened. "What about that foreign guy? With the scarf?"

"We don't want to raise suspicions by asking guests to help. We need to keep the circle tight."

Trip didn't care what Ben's reasons were, he was just glad they weren't involving the European creep. He couldn't be certain which he hated more—the fact that his mother was twittering over a man half her age or that Ada obviously had a history with him that she wasn't willing to discuss. All he knew was that he ranked crazy high on the skeeve meter.

Sharkey unhitched the trailer and started the truck. He was easily able to drive it away from the trailer and park it near the edge of his property.

He returned to the group and stood with his hands on his hips assessing the situation. Finally, he pointed at Riley's brother-in-law, Roger, and then pointed at the trailer tongue.

Roger didn't move immediately.

Trip leaned closer to him. "He wants you to grab the tongue."

Roger still looked confused, but he walked over and grabbed the metal piece that stuck out the front of the trailer.

Ben pointed to where the trailer needed to end up and then everyone else moved to the back to push.

"Maybe we could lighten the load by having a beer before we start." Chesnee started to laugh at his own joke, but the look on Sharkey's face stopped him. "Or we could just push."

"On three." Ben counted down and the five men let out a chorus of grunts as they heaved their bodies against the mini brewery on wheels. The trailer rocked forward, then settled back into the groove it had created in the lawn.

They repeated the process three more times with the same result.

Without a word, Sharkey went around the trailer and grabbed the tongue away from Roger and pointed as if to say, "To the back of the line, minion."

With Sharkey at the helm, the trailer rolled about two feet before the humans at the back of it had to stop and breathe.

"Wouldn't it be easier to move that with a truck?"

All their heads swiveled to find Riley standing under the tent, about thirty feet away, her hands on her hips. Ada was behind her mouthing an apology and throwing her hands up in the air.

Yeah, they couldn't fault her. Riley was a force. She'd started the summer in a new city, with a rundown house and a touch of meekness, but she'd grown in so many ways. She was physically stronger, way more headstrong, and ready to tackle anything the universe threw her direction.

"Come on, Ada. Let's show them how it's done." Riley grabbed Ada by the arm, and they joined the five men at the back of the trailer. "On three." She took over, yelling the countdown, and damn if that trailer didn't roll right over the grass like it was full of marshmallows instead of beer.

Once they had it settled in the right spot, she brushed her hands together and headed back to the house. Ada waved and followed her.

The men stood dumbfounded—whether from shock that the girls were so strong or the fact that Riley didn't freak out—remained to be seen.

After a few minutes of shocked silence, Chesnee piped up. "I think we deserve a beer."

Sharkey didn't even argue with him.

***

Their beer break was short-lived because the band arrived. Sharkey locked the trailer up, shooting a suspicious glance at Chesnee. Riley's father and brother-in-law went back to the house and Ben, Chesnee and Trip stayed to help the band get set up.

Most of the guys were from Myrtle Beach, but the drummer had grown up in Eastport Beach. He had played his first gig at Heron House as a teen. Between the incredible shower orgasm, the beer, and the nostalgia, Trip was feeling like nothing could go wrong.

So, when his father arrived early, he didn't immediately go on high alert. The band was performing a sound check, Chesnee was dancing—horribly—and Trip and Ben were relaxing before Riley figured out where they were.

All of a sudden, Win had joined them at a table, dressed far too casually for the high-end event. "The real music is a good choice. Usually it's a four-string quartet at these things."

"Seeing as how you're an expert, one would assume you'd at least wear dress shoes." Trip pointed at his father's golf shoes.

Win waved him off, the picture of nonchalance. "I've got my tux in the car, don't worry. I communicated with your mother, and we'll be on our best behavior tonight."

Trip choked on his last swallow of beer. "You talked to Mom?"

"Son, we conceived two children together and live in the same house. We do speak occasionally."

Had she told him about the little Italian tag-along? "Well, I appreciate the effort. This event is really important to my friends."

"Yes, yes. That's why I came early. That way we can get business out of the way before it begins."

Trip knew Win was beholden to Carlton Sr, if he wanted the money to keep rolling in—but Trip couldn't care less about the trappings that came along with that level of wealth. "Listen, I know the plan was for me to help with the campaign. But I've learned something about myself this summer. I prefer life to be quiet and simple. I'm not interested in politics or the law at all."

"Son, your life has been simple, trust me. You've had it made because of who your family is. Now it's your turn to step up and take on some of that workload."

Work? His father hadn't worked a day in his life. He floated on the family dime, playing golf and fucking his secretary. "I've worked my ass off this summer. Real work." He held out his hands. "These calluses aren't from swinging a golf club. I've been doing work that matters to people."

Chesnee was watching the argument like it was a tennis match and Ben shifted in his seat, obviously uncomfortable.

"I'm talking about real life, son. Money makes the world go 'round, and this family's influence determines which way it will spin."

Ben and Chesnee rose, like scared gazelles looking for an escape from two warring lions.

Trip leapt up, his chair falling backward. "You don't have to leave, because I am." His father would never get it. It was a waste of energy to argue. Maybe he'd just get in his car and drive back to Virginia. It'd be one less thing Trip had to worry about tonight.

As he left the tent, heading for the house, he heard his father ask when the bar would be open.

All the bliss from his shower with Ada evaporated after one argument with his dad. He didn't want to completely cut ties with his family, but they made it so hard to get along. His sister was able to jet off and do her own thing on their dime, but they wouldn't even let him pay his own way. It always had to be *their* way. Well, he was done with that. They could decide if they wanted to maintain a relationship with him, but he was done following their commands. He was staying in Eastport Beach and hopefully staying with Ada.

It felt like his insides were boiling and the only thing he wanted right now was to see her. Maybe she would be his family.

Chapter Thirty-Nine

"Lot 58. It's a photograph of the Grand Canyon at sunset." Riley read from her clipboard while she bounced from foot to foot. Time was ticking down, and this was the third time they'd checked the lots.

Ada held up the framed picture. "Got it." Everyone dealt with stress in their own way, so she wasn't going to complain.

Riley practiced pronouncing the artist's name again. "This is tricky. I should make a note for the auctioneer."

"You told me he's had the list for over a week. I'm sure he'll do great."

Trip appeared in the doorway, his forehead wrinkled—either from consternation or confusion. Ada guessed it was the former. His mother was on the property after all.

"Riley, can I steal Ada?" He grabbed her hand and pulled her toward the hallway, not waiting for an answer.

"Sure, don't worry about me. I don't have twenty more lots to check before the gala or anything," Riley shouted, a screechy edge to her voice.

Trip leaned close to Ada and whispered. "How many times have you been over them?"

"Two and a half. And that's just today."

"Riley, take a break and have some lemonade. You're dehydrated. I'll have Ada back in a jiffy."

Ada assumed he'd take her upstairs to finish what they'd started in the shower, which was A-okay with her, but instead, he opened a door underneath the stairs and shoved her inside.

"Trip, what the hell?" She waved her arms, swatting something soft in the darkness.

There was a click, and the small room lit up, revealing a coat closet.

"What are we doing in a closet? Is this my latest room change?" She put her hands on her hips, feeling a little put out and a whole lot sassy.

"I just needed to see you. And not see anyone in my family." In his defense, he had a tortured look on his face, and he kept squeezing her hand.

"What did your mother do now?" Ada was still mortified about Trip's mother basically catching them in the act in the bathroom. And a little proud, because Maurico was there too—and haha, *look at me now*!

He pulled her into his arms, his breathing ragged—and they weren't even making out yet. "Nothing since the bathroom thing. This time it's my father. He can't get it through his thick skull that I'm not going back to Virginia and I'm not going to work for my grandfather." He buried his head in the crook of her neck and sighed loudly. "I wish I could disown them."

"Trip, don't say things like that. They're still your family."

"Well, maybe I don't want them to be."

She pushed out of this embrace, backing farther into the closet. "At least you have parents, and they care enough to be here." She bumped against the wall, and it felt like it was moving.

"They're here for their own selfish motives, not to support me." He crossed his arms over his chest. "I thought you would understand growing up with a narcissistic mother."

"I do. But I'd give anything to have her know me again. Even if it was like before." She leaned back against the wall and suddenly she was falling. "What the?" She landed with a thud on a plywood floor.

"Ada, are you okay?" Trip stepped forward and reached out. "Grab my hand."

Her eyes were adjusting to the darkness, and she could see slatted walls and lots of dust. She sneezed. "I'm okay. What is this?"

"It's a passageway to the cellar. Archie had all kinds of secret entrances and exits and passageways. I haven't been down that one because I don't do spiders."

She felt for his hands, grabbing them and let him pull her to standing. "Archie sure sounds like an interesting guy." Not for the first time, she wondered if she could find a sample of his DNA somewhere in the house.

"I never met him, but yeah. You should have seen his wardrobe. I took most of it to the church rummage sale, but he had quite the style." He pulled her back into the spider-free and well-lit closet. "Sorry, I forgot about the door. And I'm really sorry about what I said about my family. It was insensitive."

"You're frustrated. I get it." She brushed off the back of her shorts and slid the door closed again. "Maybe you should go back to Virginia and try to reason with them."

Trip shook his head emphatically. "I'm twenty-seven years old. I don't have to do what they say anymore. They're just bored socialites with too much time and money and usually they can buy their way out of anything. Well, they can't pay me off. I'm staying."

"Listen, let's get through the gala. Maybe try to avoid them. Talk to them tomorrow. I'll back you up, no matter what you decide." *But if I knew my father, there is no way in hell I'd ever jeopardize that relationship.*

He pulled her in for another hug. "Thank you. That means a lot to me."

Their embrace was interrupted by pounding on the door. "Hey, lovebirds. We could use some help out here," Chesnee shouted. "Did you get over your fear of spiders, Trip?"

Ada groaned. "It is impossible to have any privacy in this house, huh?"

"What's sad is we aren't even making out." A half grin slid across his mouth.

"Gotta give the people what they want." She pushed him against the opposite wall and when it didn't open to a new dimension, she pressed up against him and kissed him like there was no tomorrow.

***

Trip whistled as Ada descended the stairs. He was dapper in his tux, all long, lean lines. The suit fit him like a glove, and she immediately knew it wasn't a rental.

She'd bought her dress years ago, for a red-carpet event at the beginning of one of the dance companies' runs. It was flowy, had an asymmetrical hem, and the rose gold hue had a subtle sheen to it. The dress felt like a more sophisticated version of a dance costume. Her heels were a little higher than she normally wore, so she was hoping to stay on the wooden floor that had been erected on the lawn. Riley had the foresight to have a boardwalk extend from the driveway all the way to the party tent.

Ada descended the stairs, holding onto the railing so she didn't take a spill. She'd already flashed Trip that night she fell out of the hammock, and while he'd since seen what she had to offer, she'd still rather stay upright. When she reached the bottom step, Trip stepped forward and reached for her hand, helping her down and smoothly kissing it in the same motion.

"You are stunning." His gaze roamed her body, hunger blazing in his eyes. "Maybe we could be fashionably late?"

She grinned. "I appreciate the sentiment, but I'm pretty sure Riley expects you to be early. I'm just along for a good time."

"You are definitely a good time." He slid his arm around her waist, trailing his hand over her ass on the way to its destination.

"Sei bellissima!" Maurico appeared in the doorway to the parlor, pinching his fingers together like he'd just complimented the chef on a nice ravioli.

Trip glared at the older man, his grip on Ada's waist growing tighter.

"Thank you, Maurico. I'm sorry, but we've got to go help set up." She took a step toward the door, but her ex ignored her efforts to get away from him.

"I wait for Karina. She is—how you say?—lenta?"

Trip vibrated next to her. She needed to get these two separated quickly. "I believe you mean slow. And yes, some women take a while to get ready." *And some men are selfish, entitled perverts.* She covered her mouth, afraid the words might pop out. "Let's go, Trip."

He growled and led her out the front door. Once they were on the porch, he mumbled, "I hate that guy."

Me too.

They were on the porch steps when Chesnee appeared from the side of the house. "Damn, Ada. What are you doing with this riffraff?"

Trip straightened. "At least I wore a tux."

"Mine's at the cleaners." He popped the collar on his dress shirt. "Besides, tuxedos are so 1990s."

Ada had to admit Chesnee looked good in dark slacks and a button-down shirt with a bold print. *Were those flamingos?* "I like your shirt, Chesnee."

He puffed out his chest. "Thanks, Gina picked it out for me."

"Where is she, by the way?" Trip glanced at his watch. The four of them were supposed to help with some last-minute details.

"She was getting dressed when I was upstairs. I'm sure she'll be down any minute." Ada hoped Maurico didn't ambush her too.

"Maybe I should go check on her." Chesnee had one foot on the stairs when Trip grabbed his shirt and pulled him back. "Hey! Hands off the duds."

Trip tapped his watch. "She can catch up. Riley's expecting us."

"Yeah, yeah, yeah."

The three of them followed the wooden walkway down to the tent.

The setting was magical. All the trees around the tent were draped with white lights and little fairy lanterns. Underneath the tent, more bulbs were strung, and the centerpieces on the tables even twinkled. When the sun went down, Ada imagined it would be even more enchanting. "You guys did a great job with the lights. It's so beautiful."

Trip leaned close to her. "Not as beautiful as you."

Ada felt her whole body warm up from the inside.

"Keep saying sweet stuff like that, and I'll take you to bed myself." Chesnee stuck his head between them.

She laughed as Trip swatted at the invader's head. "Grow up, man."

Chesnee scoffed. "I ironed my own shirt, dude. I had to buy an iron, but I did it myself."

Trip put his head in his hand, laughing. "I can't even argue with that."

"I can't believe you actually wore that shirt." Gina was making her way toward the tent wearing a long black dress with a sheer panel across her midriff. Her hair was set with exaggerated curls, and her makeup followed the same 30s vibe. She had such a unique sense of style.

Chesnee looked crestfallen as he stared down at his shirt. "You picked it out."

"As a joke, dude." She joined the group on the dance floor. "I love your dress, Ada. It shimmers when you move."

"I'll give you fifty bucks for your shirt, Trip," Chesnee pleaded.

"No way, bro."

Ada laughed. "Chesnee, I don't know what you're worried about. You look great. Very fashionable." She was trying to be sincere, but everyone was laughing by this point. Except Chesnee.

"I bet Ben's got a boring white shirt I can wear." He turned toward the house, but Riley and Ben were headed their way. "Riley's gonna freak."

Ada had witnessed Riley's stress over the event, but right now, as the couple walked toward them, she was radiant. Glowing. Ada had a sneaky suspicion of what Ben had done to help her relax before the gala.

"Chesnee, I'm glad to see you dressed up for the occasion," Riley said without a trace of sarcasm. "And you even ironed."

"I did!" He pushed lightly on Gina's shoulder. "Thank you for noticing."

Gina snickered behind her hand.

"You look great, Riley. I'm glad you picked that dress." Ada had helped her choose her dress for the gala earlier in the week, but Riley had only narrowed it down to two as of yesterday. The dress was the color of sea glass, and the skirt would flow nicely while she danced.

Everyone expressed a similar sentiment, until Riley waved the compliments off. "I may be in a good mood"—she shot a quick smile Ben's way—"but there's still a few things that need to be done before the guests arrive."

"And knowing Eastporters, they'll be early." Ben wore a linen suit and white shirt that complimented Riley's outfit beautifully.

"Especially because there's a beer truck," Chesnee added.

"True, so we need to snap to it." Riley consulted her clipboard and assigned tasks to everyone, including her parents, sister and brother-in-law who showed up just in time to help.

Soon, they had all fanned out—checking centerpieces, fixing lights and making sure the servers had extra napkins and silverware.

The band was warming up and when they played the first few strands of *Why Don't We Just Dance*, Trip grabbed Ada and started spinning her around the open dance floor. They'd danced informally a few times this week, but mostly as a demonstration, so she hadn't experienced the full extent of his dance knowledge.

His form was impeccable, he led her flawlessly through several different steps as the tempo of the song changed, and when he pulled her in close at the end, her heart fluttered in her chest. This might just be the perfect man for her.

Chapter Forty

The gala was in full swing. Beer was flowing from Sharkey's trailer, the band was playing, waiters were passing out mini crab puffs and stuffed mushrooms and the locals were trying out their new dance moves.

Trip was a little annoyed, because after their first spin around the dance floor, he hadn't had a chance to dance with Ada again. Every guy within fifty miles was lined up to get a dance with his girl.

All he wanted was a little alone time with her.

Luckily, the auction would start soon. Ada, Gina, Chesnee and himself had agreed to be Riley's very own Vanna White by displaying the lots as they were auctioned off. And once their duties had been performed, he had plans to whisk Ada away.

Ada seemed to be having a great time. She was currently dancing with Manny, who's hands were a little too low for Trip's liking. The only dance she'd turned down was with Maurice. Trip got immense pleasure from the look of disappointment on the tiny Italian's face.

Really, who wears a pink scarf with a suit? Only some pretentious European. That's who.

"Ada's the life of the party." Ben joined Trip, handing him a fresh beer.

"Yeah, she's Miss Popular, all right," Trip mumbled.

"Riley told me she extended her stay."

Trip's mood lightened considerably with that news. "We're both staying."

"Glad to hear it. She's great."

"I think it could go somewhere." It was weird to say the words out loud, but he was no longer afraid of pursuing something long term. Once he made the decision to go against his family's wishes, it freed him up to have a real relationship and not constantly worry about how his family would mess it up.

Ben clapped him on the back. "You better go rescue your girlfriend from Manny. His hands are heading south fast."

Trip stepped onto the dance floor to cut in, but a commotion just outside the tent drew his attention. He couldn't see who was involved, but he spied a flash of hot pink. Anxiety simmered in his gut as he crossed the floor. It came to a full boil when he saw his mother, father, Maurice and Amber having a lively "discussion." What the hell was Amber doing here? So much for best behavior.

"At least Trip has the balls to follow his own path," Win's words shocked Trip, since his dad had been beating the "responsibility" horse until it was dead.

"Trip is just sowing his oats. Soon enough he'll realize what he's missing out on," Karina shot back. "You don't think I'd like to have a little action on the side? But one of us has to have a little decorum."

It felt like Trip was a hundred yards away and his feet were stuck in cement. He couldn't get over there fast enough to stop this train from plowing into Riley's event.

"Decorum? You think banging this little European loser shows decorum?"

Karina Westinghouse smoothed her dress and held her head high. "I do not bang, Wingate."

"Which is precisely why he came to me to meet his needs," Amber joined the conversation, setting Trip's "oh shit" meter on its highest level.

Trip finally reached the group and attempted to coral them away from the tent and toward the house. "Keep your voices down."

"You've destroyed our family! Don't you talk to me about what he needs."

"Karina, settle down. Nothing's destroyed. We'll figure it out."

The fury in his mother's eyes burned through the twilight. "I will not settle down. I've spent thirty years of my life making sure this family maintained its position. Now, your father is finally ready to retire, and you pull this!"

"It's fine. No one has to know about Amber." Win's words were slightly slurred, and Trip wondered how many of Sharkey's brews he'd had.

"What the fuck, Winny? You told me you were leaving this old hag and we'd be a family." Amber stuck her bottom lip out and rubbed her flat stomach.

No, no, no. Alarm bells rang in Trip's head as he continued to push the pack of screaming hyenas toward the house.

"I am not giving up everything I've worked toward because you knocked up some white trash skank."

Ah shit. Amber was pregnant. His father's campaign was supposed to kick off in a week. No wonder his grandfather had been trying to get Trip back to Virginia. This was a political powder keg. "Everyone in the house." He shooed them up the steps and through the door, mortified that his worst fear had come true and his freaking family ruined Riley's big night. Plus, he couldn't blame Ada if she wanted to stay as far away from the drama as possible.

So, he was stunned when he felt her hand on his shoulder. "I'm here. Hardly anyone noticed and the band's going to play a few more songs."

With Ada backing him up, he felt hopeful and strong. "What the hell is wrong with you people?" he roared.

The group stopped arguing and looked at him in shock.

Karina was the first to speak. "We don't speak like that, Carlton."

"Are you fucking kidding me?" Ada yelled back at Karina. "You people are acting like children and embarrassing your son, and you're going to say something to him about his language. You are crazy, lady."

Karina leveled one of her death stares at the woman Trip might just love after that speech. Maurice had the nerve to try to touch Ada, his eyes sparking with hunger.

Fuck no. Trip clapped his hand down on the Italian's arm. "Back away, Mario."

The little prick had the sense to leave the room.

Somehow, in the mist of the melee, Win had found the bar in the corner of the room and poured himself a scotch.

Sure, let's throw a little more alcohol on this fire. "Dad, you've had enough." He yanked the drink out of his father's hand and set it on a side table. "Sit."

Win's eyes widened, but he flopped onto one of the couches. Amber sidled up beside him, but when Karina turned the death stare on her, she moved to a chair.

"What were you thinking, Dad? She's younger than me." Did this mean he'd be a brother again?

"Obviously, I wasn't thinking about a baby. I was just letting off some steam."

Because your life is so stressful?

"Winny," Amber whined. "You told me you loved me."

His father shrugged and stared longingly at his drink.

Amber rose from the chair, hands on hips. "I'm going to drain your fancy-ass family of every penny, Wingate Westinghouse. You messed with the wrong skank." She flipped her hair and stormed out of the house.

"Great job, Win. It should make the 11 o'clock news now. There goes your campaign." Karina crossed her arms over her chest.

"Maybe Trip can run instead," Win offered from the sofa.

A manic laugh escaped. "Now I know you've lost your minds. I don't even want to help with the campaign, let alone run for office." He didn't want to think about what would happen when his grandfather found out. If he didn't already know. The man had ears everywhere.

"Karina, what should I do?" Win leaned forward, resting his elbows on his knees, looking like he'd aged ten years in the last five minutes.

"If you have to ask, then you don't deserve to be in Congress."

He heaved his body off the couch and dragged himself after Amber.

The silence in the parlor lingered for long minutes. Ada looked stunned and Trip just prayed she wouldn't hold this against him.

"I'll call my driver, Carlton. I apologize for your father's behavior." Karina rose, dusted off her skirt and climbed the stairs.

"Self-awareness must not be an inherited trait." Ada stepped closer to Trip, sliding her arms around his waist. "I'm so sorry, Trip. Your parents officially suck the worst."

Chapter Forty-One

Trip's parents left in separate vehicles—Win in a hired car and Karina in her personal town car with her trusty driver at the wheel. Ada wondered what the driver did in between wheeling Ms. Daisy around town. Did he read? Sleep? Watch porn in the back behind the tinted windows?

Unfortunately, Mrs. Westinghouse left her guest behind, and Maurico was currently chatting up a woman who was older than Karina and from her jewelry and designer gown, likely richer.

Ada wasn't sure what the etiquette was here, but she hoped Riley would kick him out now that his meal ticket had departed.

The auction was in full swing. The auctioneer, doubling as emcee, was a pro, and Ada was struggling to keep up with his motor mouth. They'd sailed through the first thirty or so lots and money was flowing right alongside Sharkey's beer. The first of Charlotte's pieces had gone for almost five grand and it was just a small landscape. Gina was currently on stage, holding one of Charlotte's earlier pieces.

The brush strokes weren't as confident as in her later works, but even Ada's untrained eye could see the potential in it. It was a cherry blossom in full bloom, the Washington monument in the background. It was what Charlotte referred to as a couch piece. Large enough to display over a sofa, but not a statement piece. Those tended to be quite large with the intention of being the centerpiece of a room. The Ballerina was statement sized, and coming up next.

Ada was just off the stage, balancing the painting on the tops of her feet. With the gold frame, the piece was quite heavy, but there was an easel set up, so she just had to carry it out and then lift it up.

Bidding for the cherry blossom piece was lively, and she could see Riley on the other side of the stage, bouncing on her toes and watching the crowd with excitement. Ada was glad her mother's pieces would help Archie's foundation, especially since it appeared he'd had a significant impact on her career and possibly her life.

She was still working up the nerve to ask Riley about any personal effects she might have of her uncle's that could be tested for DNA.

The auctioneer banged his gavel and yelled "Sold!" No one expected the piece to bring almost eight thousand dollars. She looked down at the painting she held and felt an overwhelming mix of emotions.

The crowd was cheering, and Ada knew she should be moving onto the stage, but her feet were nailed to the ground. The auctioneer looked at her expectantly, but she was frozen to the spot.

Had she made the wrong decision? Should she have kept it? It would surely sell for a considerable amount, and she knew the money would be put to good use. It was about Archie's legacy—but Charlotte's too. If she was aware, she'd be happy to know she could help an aspiring artist grow their craft.

"Darlin', pretty sure it's your turn." Trip appeared beside her, whispering close to her ear. "Is everything okay?"

She nodded, but it was a lie. It was definitely not okay. But there was no way she could back out now. She couldn't do that to Riley.

"Is it too heavy? Do you want me to carry it out?" He rubbed soothing circles on her back, which made her feel marginally better.

I can do this. It's just a painting. It's not even an accurate representation of my relationship with Charlotte. Or maybe it is, because she never intended for me to see it. Fuck this. Fuck her.

Ada lifted the painting and propelled herself forward. Trip shadowed her up the steps, likely thinking she was nuts. But she made it up on stage and lifted the piece onto the easel.

The crowd was hushed as the auctioneer spoke about the origin of the piece—the little they knew anyway—and then the murmurs began as people realized they were staring at the subject of the painting right beside it.

She tried to track the bidding, but it went quickly, like a three-way ping pong match if such a thing existed. Then as it reached the twenty-thousand-dollar mark, a new bidder jumped in, and she immediately zeroed in on the new guy. She'd know that voice anywhere.

Paul was here and he was bidding on her piece. It made no sense. He had plenty of Charlotte's pieces in his personal collection. And why hadn't he told her he was coming?

The crowd was enraptured by the bidding war between a grim man in an ascot and Charlotte's manager. Paul didn't appear to be backing down.

Ada glanced over her shoulder, where Riley was holding on to Ben for dear life. She looked ready to faint—or break into a happy dance.

On the other side of the stage, Trip stood staring at Ada, a concerned look on his face. He had also told her to keep the painting. But how could she deny the foundation this much money?

Then a strange thought hit her. Was Paul bidding on the painting for himself or for her? He had pleaded with her to keep it. Told her Charlotte would want her to have it. But if that was the case, why send it to a man Ada had no knowledge of? Her mother couldn't have known Ada would end up at Heron House.

It was surreal. The bidding was now at forty thousand and neither of the men seemed to be backing down. It was just a picture of a teenage ballerina. The only thing that made it special was her mother's signature at the bottom.

When the gavel finally descended, Ada jumped. She was lost in an alternate reality—one where life made sense.

"Sold! $67,500 to bidder number 78."

The crowd cheered and Riley rushed onto the stage and threw her arms around Ada. "Oh my gosh, Ada! Can you believe it? They love your painting."

Ada didn't bother to correct her. It was Charlotte's painting, not hers, and now she had to live with the guilt that Paul had spent a ridiculous amount of money on a picture of his famous artist's daughter. Once again, it was all about THE Charlotte Maddox.

She walked off the stage in a daze, winding her way around the crowd, focused on finding Paul. He was easy to spot with his full head of white hair. Elaine liked to call him a silver fox, and Ada had to admit he looked good for an older guy.

The auction continued, and the crowd cheered for one of Archie's pieces. Bids rang out like fireworks. Everyone wanted a piece of the local legend.

Paul was focused on the bidding, so he didn't see her until she was right beside him. And she didn't see Elaine until that moment either. Paul's wife was petite and frail. She'd suffered from MS for as long as Ada had known them. It was surprising she'd made the trip down with Paul.

"What are you guys doing here?"

The couple turned in unison, their faces lighting up when they saw her.

Paul hugged her first. "After you called yesterday, I knew I had to come down here."

"And I insisted he bring me along, even though I'm a nuisance to travel with." Elaine hugged Ada with one arm, the other grasping a cane.

"I wish you had told me. I could have met you at the airport."

"It was very last minute, and we weren't even sure we'd make it in time. The auction had already begun when we arrived, so we didn't even have time to find you." Paul grasped Elaine's elbow and helped her to a table away from the raucous crowd.

"I'm so happy you're here, but I don't understand why you spent so much money on that painting." She grasped a cloth napkin and fidgeted with it in her lap. She'd never been nervous around Paul and Elaine before, but right now she felt like she was responsible for the extravagant purchase.

The couple exchanged a meaningful glance which ended with a small nod from Elaine. Paul cleared his throat and wrung his hands together.

Is he nervous too? "Maybe we could ask the other bidder if they want to buy it for their last bid. It'd still be a lot of money for the foundation."

"Ada, this isn't about the money. That painting needs to stay in the family. It's you."

"It's too much."

Elaine leaned forward. "Honey, the money isn't an issue."

"I don't even have a place for it. Who knows where I'll be next week, let alone in a year or two?" Her life was in limbo right now. She felt completely untethered.

Paul shook his head. "I didn't buy it for you—unless you want it, that is." He grabbed her hand. "I didn't even know it existed until Riley emailed me a few weeks ago. Charlotte ran all her pieces through me, so I was shocked to see such a significant piece, and even more shocked to discover she had gifted it to Archie."

"Because he's my father." *Why else would Charlotte be so secretive about it?*

"I didn't just come here for the painting. Twenty-four years ago, I made a promise to your mother, and it's time for me to break that promise." He glanced at Elaine again and she squeezed his arm. When he looked back at Ada, he had trouble meeting her gaze. "Ada, I'm your father."

The twinkle lights in the center of the table swam in front of her eyes and the entire world turned on its axis. She pitched to the side and nearly face planted on the wooden floor. But Paul's strong arms caught her, swept her up.

"Ada, I'm so sorry." He held her tight, and even though part of her wanted to kick and scream, a bigger part wanted to be held. By her father. "It's such a complicated story, but when you're ready, I'll tell you anything you want to know."

"I can't breathe."

Paul loosened his hold on her, easing her back into her chair. "Can I get you something? Water?"

She nodded, unable to form words or coherent thoughts.

He jumped up from the table and ran somewhere, returning with a goblet of ice water. She sipped it, afraid her throat wouldn't work. Suddenly, breathing seemed complicated, so she focused on drawing breath in and blowing it out again.

When she felt like her lungs were working properly, she looked up at Elaine, trying to read her. She thought back to all the time they spent together when she was growing up. She'd never felt anything but love from her. *How? How could she love the evidence of such a betrayal? How could Paul cheat on this amazing, beautiful, supportive woman? Especially with a narcissist like her mother? She'd always held him in the highest regard. He was one of the best people she'd ever known. How could he have done something so awful?*

She couldn't stay here. She couldn't look at either of them.

Ada scanned the tent, searching for Trip. The auction appeared to have ended, and the band was warming back up. People were milling about, getting refills from Sharkey. *Where is he?* Usually, he was a full head taller than most people. She pushed up from the table, gripping the edge to keep from crumpling into a pile on the floor.

"Ada, wait. You've had a shock, let me help you." Paul stood with her and tried to offer her support, but she waved him off with a glare straight out of her mother's toolbox.

Luckily, Trip found her at that moment, and he appeared by her side, concern painted across his face. "What is it, darlin'?"

She grabbed him and used him to keep from falling. "I need to go."

He looked to Paul and Elaine, obviously confused about who they were and why they had upset his girlfriend, but he didn't ask questions. He just led her away from the couple and toward the house.

All she could think of was how he'd basically lost his family tonight and she'd found hers—yet it was nothing like she'd imagined. It was a betrayal. One more giant fuck you from Charlotte.

Chapter Forty-Two

Trip had no clue what had happened to Ada, but she was in a state of shock. The painting had fetched a huge price and he'd been looking for her to make sure she didn't regret selling it. When he found her with the winning bidder, she appeared to know them.

He couldn't get anything out of her on the way to the house, but as they walked by the staging area, she snagged a bottle of champagne.

His plan all along had been to take her somewhere private—maybe even with a bottle of champagne—and tell her that he wanted to pursue a long-term relationship with her.

This was not what he imagined.

They climbed the porch steps, and she stopped, clenching the bottle between her legs and working the cork out of it. He watched as the cork shot up, pinging against the bead board, leaving a mark in the white paint.

He opened his mouth to offer to get a couple glasses, but she'd already tilted her head back and was chugging from the bottle.

She swiped her hand across her mouth and then tilted the bottle toward him in question.

It was only eight o'clock and there was a lot of gala left. He grabbed the bottle and took a swig.

Strains of music from the tent floated over the lawn toward them. He couldn't make out exactly what the song was, but hopefully the guests were dancing, and no one was wondering about the drama thus far.

"Dance with me." Ada whispered the words, her body swaying to the music.

Don't have to ask me twice. He set the bottle on the bench and pulled her into his embrace. It was just the two of them, dancing on the porch, so he didn't worry about a proper hold or counting steps. He just held her close and moved to the music.

After a few minutes, she slumped against him, tears flowing steadily. He tightened his embrace and rubbed her back, murmuring encouragement. He didn't know what say, so he just told her how much he liked her and that they could figure it out together.

Eventually, her sobs lessened, and she pulled away from him. Her face was streaked with tears, her makeup mostly gone, strands of her hair stuck in the moisture. It didn't matter. She was still the most beautiful woman at this party.

He swiped her hair back off her face, stroking his thumb under her eye, wiping away the tears. "Who are those people, Ada?"

She sniffled, then grabbed the champagne and took another drink. "Apparently, he's my father."

Trip staggered back. From what Riley had told him, they were convinced Archie was her dad. He regained his footing and grabbed her, leading her to the swing. She clutched the bottle of champagne tightly between her legs. "But you know him?"

She nodded. "That's Paul, my mother's manager." She sucked in a huge breath and forced it back out. "And that was his wife, Elaine," she gritted out between clenched teeth.

Ada had spoken highly of the couple, saying they'd been there for her throughout her childhood when her mom wasn't. Even now, Paul was handling the sale of the condo and had set up Charlotte's care.

It didn't make sense. And he was willing to bet Ada was as clueless as he was from the tortured look on her face.

"I left before he could explain. I just couldn't..." She trailed off, staring down at the party tent near the water.

It was mostly dark now and the whole area twinkled with the lights they'd strung through the trees. Riley had planned it well—it was beautiful. Trip wished they were down there, under that tent, dancing the night away without a care in the world.

Instead, it seemed both their worlds had come crashing down tonight. Right now, they had each other, but would they be able to withstand the fallout?

He held her hand and she leaned her head on his shoulder. They swayed on the swing, listening to the sound of the party below. Ada had stood up for him with his family earlier and he was prepared to do the same for her. Whenever she was ready—he'd be here.

***

They'd been sitting that way for a while when he noticed two people walking up the wooden path toward the house. Paul's white hair stood out even in the darkness.

"Darlin'," he whispered, jostling her from a light snooze. "Paul and Elaine are coming this way. Do you want me to get rid of them?"

She cut her eyes up at him and the sadness there gutted him. She shook her head and slowly sat up. "Can you stay with me?"

"Of course. Whatever you need." He grabbed her hand and squeezed it.

The tiny smile she offered him broke his heart into pieces. He couldn't imagine what she was feeling right now.

The older couple scaled the porch steps, holding hands as well. Paul spoke first. "Ada, can we speak to you, please?"

Trip could feel the tension in her body just from his contact with her hand. He was ready to jump up and take this old man out if need be.

She nodded, keeping her eyes fixed on the porch floor.

"Maybe somewhere more private?" Paul gestured toward the tent full of revelers.

She didn't answer, so Trip took the lead. "We can talk inside."

"Is this the young man you spoke of?"

"This is Trip. Trip, Paul and Elaine Mallory." She still failed to meet their eyes.

He rose from the swing, careful to slow it down and keep from pitching Ada out of it. He extended a hand to Paul first. "It's good to meet you. I know you've been a big help to Ada with her mother's illness." He guessed her whole life, but he didn't want Paul to think he was forgiven for this betrayal. Next, he grasped Elaine's hand. "And Ada has told me so many lovely things about you."

Elaine Mallory was frail but her eyes sparkled, and she was quick to smile despite this awkward situation. "It's great to meet you, Trip. Ada is a very special young lady."

"I know." He squeezed Ada's hand and pulled her gently off the swing. "We can talk in the parlor." He led Ada inside, holding the screen door open for the Mallorys.

"Trip, no offense, but we have a sensitive matter to discuss, if you don't mind." Paul was taller than Trip, but he didn't try to act intimidating. He was polite and cordial.

"He stays." Ada sat on one of the sofas and pulled Trip down beside her, gripping his hand like it was a lifeline.

The Mallorys sat on the opposite couch and for a few minutes, the silence was as awkward as a fifth-grade dance.

Trip broke the standoff. "Can I get everyone something to drink? Water? Wine?" He could use something a little stronger right now, but he decided to remain levelheaded.

"Water would be great," Elaine answered.

"Ada, do you want anything?" He stroked his thumb across the back of her hand, and she met his eyes.

She nodded. "Water."

He rose, hesitant to leave her alone. He kissed the back of her hand and then hurried to the kitchen. Grabbing four bottles of water from the fridge, Trip noticed a tray of cheese and grapes on the bottom shelf. He grabbed it as well.

When he returned to the parlor, it was still as quiet as Sunday mass. He passed out the waters and set the tray of food on the coffee table. He retook his seat beside Ada and pulled her close to his side. He'd never felt so protective of anyone—and she'd already stood up for him tonight.

Paul took a long drink of water, then capped the bottle and set it on the floor. "Ada, I want to explain." He took a deep breath, and when she didn't respond, continued. "First of all, Elaine and I love you more than anything. You are just as important to us as our boys. You always have been."

Elaine nodded along with her husband.

Ada cringed when he mentioned his other children. Trip placed a quick kiss against her temple.

"Elaine was diagnosed with MS the year John started high school." Paul glanced at Trip. "He's our oldest. James is a year younger."

Trip nodded.

"Anyway, it was hard, raising two boys, running the gallery, and taking care of Elaine. Our marriage went through a rough patch. And it was during that time

I met your mother. She marched into my gallery one day and announced that I was going to give her a show." He smiled, shaking his head slightly. "She had such confidence and gumption. If she believed something would happen, it usually did."

The man cheated on his sick wife? While she took care of two boys? No wonder Ada wasn't welcoming him with open arms despite their previous relationship.

Paul started to speak again, but Ada sprung off the couch and cut him off. "I can't listen to any more of this." She ran from the room and dashed up the stairs.

"Give her time to get used to the idea, Paul." Elaine patted her husband's knee.

Trip was dumbfounded by the situation. His face must have clearly expressed his disbelief, because Elaine addressed him next.

"The affair was a long time ago, during a time we had separated. But look what we got out of it. I love Ada as if she were my own child. The daughter I never had. After my diagnosis, the doctors said pregnancy wouldn't be safe, so we were unable to try for a little girl. I love my sons, but Ada has filled a hole in my heart over the last twenty-some years."

Paul swiped his eyes. "I'm not proud of what I did, but I am proud of Ada. Please tell her we love her—just as we always have. We're staying in Bluffville. We'll be here until she's ready to talk." He rose, then helped his wife up from the sofa. "Please go comfort our daughter."

Chapter Forty-Three

It felt like she was in a dream—or an alternate universe. Just an hour ago, everything she thought she knew had been turned on its head and she couldn't grasp the new reality. She lay on Trip's small bed, staring up at the sloped ceiling. Her tears had dried up and now she was just numb.

There was a knock on the door and Trip asked if he could come in.

Earlier tonight, he'd found out his father was having a love child, his mother was even crazier than he'd originally thought, and they expected him to run for political office. He'd basically had to sever his relationship with them. On the very night he lost his parents, Ada had found not only her father, but another mother too. One that she already loved.

So why was this so hard? Why did it feel like her heart had been yanked out of her chest and had the Mexican hat dance performed on it?

She wasn't sure how long had passed since Trip knocked, but she was finally able to croak out, "Come in."

He'd lost his jacket and bowtie, and the sleeves of his white dress shirt were rolled up to his elbows, revealing his sexy forearms. She stared at the sinew bulging under his tanned skin, focusing on his arms because they were more interesting than the ceiling.

"Darlin', I can't even imagine what you're going through." He climbed into the bed with her and pulled her close. "They're gone, but they wanted me to tell you they love you—they always have—and they're staying nearby whenever you're ready."

"They aren't going back to New York?"

"It didn't sound like it."

She sighed and burrowed closer to him, finding safety in his arms. "I do love them. I just don't know how to process this. My whole life I've asked about my father, and he was right there all along? That's messed up."

"It's epically messed up." He rubbed her back in soothing circles.

"I'm sorry we're missing the gala."

"It's okay. I'm sure by now it's become a drunken spectacle."

She laughed. "Well, now I'm really sorry."

He chuckled and kissed her forehead. "Don't worry, Eastporters love to imbibe and cut loose. I'm sure there'll be another opportunity real soon."

"I hope Riley isn't missing us."

"The auction's over, so I'm guessing Riley has lifted her self-imposed champagne ban and is acting just as foolish as the rest of the guests."

"I'd kind of like to see that." She sniffled and pulled back so she could see his face. "I don't want to hide up here and pout. I want to be a drunk Eastporter."

He smiled and brushed the hair back from her face. "I know for a fact they will welcome you with open arms." He climbed out of the bed, then helped her to her feet. "One drunken night of debauchery coming right up."

A little debauchery sounded like the perfect remedy for her crappy mood. "Can we please make up a story about where we've been? I don't want to hash all this out tonight."

He grabbed her hands and got a devilish twinkle in his eyes. "Well, if we fool around before we go back down, we can just tell everyone we needed a little private time."

"Well, you better make my sex hair convincing." She raised up on her toes to kiss him, pulling him down onto the bed with her. She'd heard sex was the best cure for grief—and Lord knows they'd had plenty of that tonight.

***

When they returned to the party tent, the respectable guests had left and what remained were the Eastport Beach party set. The champagne and beer were flowing freely, the band had long since taken their leave, and whoever was in charge of the music had lost their mind.

"I'm pretty sure Riley didn't intend to do the Electric Slide at her fancy gala." Ada laughed as a group of partygoers attempted to perform the easiest dance in history.

"Then we should document this, so she'll have evidence." Trip pulled out his phone to film the group—which included Riley, Ben, Chesnee, Gina and half of Eastport Beach.

Chesnee saw them and left his place in the line of "sliders." "Dude! Where have you been? The trailer is almost out of beer. You better catch up." He winked at Ada, then filled another cup from the tap.

"You want one?" Trip asked, his fingers trailing down her bare arm, leaving goosebumps.

Ada shook her head. "I better stick to champagne." She wanted to get hammered. To forget about this whole stupid evening. But she didn't want to feel like shit tomorrow.

The song ended and Riley spotted her. She listed from side to side as she walked the few feet to where Ada stood. Ada reached out to steady her when she got close.

"Ada! We raised so much money tonight!"

"I know, I'm so happy for you."

"It's not for me! It's for the foundation. Can you believe how much your painting sold for? $67,500!" She thrust her hand up in the air in victory. "And that man who bought it? Wow-wee! He's a looker!"

Ada wasn't drunk enough to have this discussion. "Is there any champagne left?"

"Heck, yeah! We should celebrate!" Riley spun around, losing her balance. Luckily, Ben appeared in time to catch her.

"I think you've celebrated enough for one night, Ri." He tried to keep a straight face, but it was hard not to laugh at Riley in her current drunken state.

"Psstshaa!" Spittle sprayed out of her mouth and onto Ben's shirt.

He sighed, then hoisted her over his shoulder. "Say goodnight, Riley."

"Good night, Riley!" Riley yelled in a high-pitched voice.

Half the crowd echoed back, "Good night, Riley!"

Trip returned with a beer as Ben was carting Riley toward the house. "I definitely don't think that's how she planned on leaving the party."

"Not a chance. I'm going to find another bottle of champagne." *Maybe two.* On the way to the bar, she saw Chesnee and Gina slow dancing to Sinead O'Connor's "Nothing Compares to You." *Seriously, who was controlling the music?* Behind the bar, she found the last two bottles of champagne. From what she could see, every other person at this party needed to be cut off. She took them both.

For the next two hours, Trip and Ada danced and drank and danced some more. The crowd started to thin out and the second bottle of champagne was doing the trick. Ada couldn't remember what she was trying to forget and even drunk, Trip was the best dance partner she'd ever had. Certainly the sexiest.

"You'd have thought Riley would assign a DD for the party." Either Trip was slurring his words or Ada was underwater.

"She didn't need a driver, she's already home." Ada wasn't slurring her words, shank you very much.

"No, like a responsible person to oversee shit. You know, make people leave and not destroy the place." He pointed at Chesnee, who was on his ass because he'd managed to break a chair.

Ada shrugged. "Must not have been on the checklists."

The music had gotten marginally better and now they were swaying to "Can't Fight This Feeling."

Trip pushed her hair off her shoulder and leaned closer to her ear. "Wanna do something crazy?"

The night couldn't get too much crazier—unless Stumpy showed up. "Sure."

He stopped dancing, grabbed her hand, and pulled her off the dance floor. She snagged her last bottle of champagne, which was nearly gone.

They stepped off the floor and headed into the trees behind the house, the twinkle lights fading the farther they got from the tent.

"'Member?"

Ada knew the spot well. It was the hammock she'd fallen out of before they'd officially seen each other naked. "You want me to flash you again?"

He nodded and stepped closer, pinning her against a tree. "I really like you, Ada."

"I really like you too, Trip." She grabbed his face and kissed him hard.

His hands slid up into her hair as he deepened the kiss. She was unbuttoning his shirt when he pulled back abruptly with panic written on his face.

"What?"

He spun away from her and vomited violently.

She rubbed his back while he threw up. *Poor guy.* "It's my fault. We shouldn't have drunk so much."

Trip spit and wiped his mouth. "I think it was the not eating anything and then drinking too much."

She wiped his brow, smoothing her hand down his cheek. "Time for bed."

He nodded, his eyes half closed. "It's so far away. I'll just sleep here." He hoisted himself into one of the hammocks. "Twenty minutes and I'll be good to go."

Ada chuckled. He wasn't going anywhere. He looked cozy snuggled up in the hammock, a serene look on his face as he fell asleep. She leaned down to kiss his forehead.

"I want you to be my family."

The words were a mere whisper, but she heard them and immediately remembered everything she'd tried to forget.

Did she know enough about family to be that for him?

Chapter Forty-Four

A horn beeped, startling Trip from a deep sleep. He'd been dreaming about Ada, dancing on a stage somewhere, a crowd of people cheering for them. He tried to roll over, but he was stuck somehow. He reached out to pull her closer, but all he felt was air.

His head pounded like a freighter steaming into port. Fuck Sharkey and that deadly beer. He never drank too much anymore, but between the crap with his family and Ada drinking to forget, he'd figured what the hell. Never make big decisions on the heels of a mind-blowing orgasm.

Squinting, he stared up, only seeing trees and sky. It was a glorious day—Carolina blue skies, fluffy white clouds and blinding sun. He'd napped in the hammock plenty but never spent the whole night here. He tried to sit up and failed, instead flipping head over ass onto the ground. "Ada?"

She didn't answer, so he crawled to the opposite hammock, but it blew in the breeze, empty.

Gingerly, he stood up, using a nearby tree for support. Why would he hear a horn in the woods? He took in his surroundings and in the distance, he saw the shipping container Sharkey had delivered last month, as well as his truck and beer trailer. He must have driven the trailer back and seen Trip in the hammock. There wasn't a road on this side of the house, but you could wind through the trees as long as you stayed clear of the soggy soil closer to the riverbank.

He found his phone in his pocket, surprised to see it was past eight. Maybe Ada had woken up before him. Or she'd rationally spent the night in a bed.

Brushing his pants off, he headed for the house. He'd have to take the tux to the dry cleaners. But there was no hurry. If he stayed in Eastport Beach, he'd have little need for formal wear. The gala last night was the event of the year, and he stayed away from the country club events over in Bluffville.

If his family had their way, he'd be in a tux every night, schmoozing rich donors. No thank you.

Inside, the house was buzzing with activity. The guests who hadn't partied late into the night were munching on pastries from The Coastal. Riley's parents were in the kitchen offering coffee and juice. Trip grabbed a cup of coffee and covered most of the ground floor looking for Ada.

Heading back to the kitchen, he grabbed a juice for her, hoping she was upstairs in his room sleeping all that champagne off.

When he reached the second floor, the door to The Picasso suite was open. He poked his head in, but, sure enough, his mother had cleared out. He needed to change the sheets and put the room back in order.

Just as soon as he found Ada.

At the end of the hall, the door to the Maddox suite was closed. Had the little Italian prick stayed? He'd ridden down from Virginia with Karina. He better not have missed his ride.

Trip scaled the steps to the third floor and as soon as his foot hit the hallway, he spotted Chesnee.

Sneaking out of Gina's room.

Trip raised his eyebrows, too shocked to come up with a pithy remark. To Chesnee's credit, he nodded at his friend, then descended the stairs.

Interesting. He couldn't wait to tell Ada.

He swung the door to his room open, balancing the two drinks in one arm. "Darlin', you will not believe what I just saw."

Ada wasn't in his bed. She wasn't in the room at all.

And neither was her luggage.

His heart plummeted out of his chest. Did she leave? Had he done something in his inebriated state to upset her? Obviously, last night was rough for her, but that didn't have anything to do with him, or their relationship. That was the only solid thing. At least that's how he felt.

He sat on the side of the bed, possibilities racing through his mind—which wasn't easy because of the boulders currently residing there from Sharkey's lethal brew.

She hadn't left him a message, his phone only showed missed calls from his father. Probably calling to ask him to be the baby's godfather or some bullshit.

His finger was hovering over the button to call her when something occurred to him. Maybe Maurice had left with Trip's mother. And Ada had moved back into the Maddox suite.

That had to be it. He stuck his phone back in his pocket and scooped up the drinks again.

When he stepped into the hall, he almost ran straight into Gina. She was in the same dress from last night, carrying her shoes.

"Morning," she grumbled.

"Hey. Have you seen Ada?"

She shook her head and then moaned. "No, I just got here."

Maybe he was still drunk, because he was confused. If she hadn't been here, why was Chesnee in her room? And where had she been? There was no time to ask a bunch of questions he didn't have a right to ask, because he needed to find his girlfriend.

Hopefully, after everything that had happened this week, she wouldn't mind him calling her that.

"Later." As he started down the stairs, he heard Gina's door close. *Seriously puzzling.* Maybe he'd take Chesnee out for a pint later and grill him for the deets.

When he reached the second floor, he juggled the drinks again so he could knock on the door to Ada's suite.

It took a full minute before the door was wrenched open to reveal the pocket Italian in only a towel.

Wow, I can't unsee that. The man was covered in dark hair, except for his chest, which appeared to have been waxed. *Just, why?*

Then an awful thought hit him. What if Ada was in there with the European ape? Maurice was staring at him, arms crossed over his strangely bare chest. Trip dreaded asking the dancer if he'd seen Ada. So, he hedged. "Hey, man. Just checking to see if you need anything. We've got pastries in the kitchen and coffee and juice, of course." He held the two cups aloft awkwardly.

Maurice pulled the door closed and stepped into the hallway.

What's the little prick hiding?

"I've been here several mornings, and no one has stopped by to see if I needed anything." His eyes narrowed. "Are you looking for Ada? Had a lover's quarrel, si?"

No, we didn't quarrel! And no way would she leave my bed to jump into yours. "No, everything is fine. Some of the guests had a long night, so I just thought I'd check in."

From the look on his face, the Italian wasn't as stupid as he presented. "No, we're all good." He winked and slipped back into his room.

Suddenly, the appetizers from the party last night mounted a sneak attack. Trip barely made it into the bathroom, where he proceeded to rid himself of everything he'd eaten or drunk in the last day.

Regret swirled in his empty stomach. Too much beer, too much rich food, too much family drama, and too much hope.

He dumped the coffee and juice out, leaving the cups on a small table in the hallway for dishes, dragged himself back upstairs and collapsed on his bed.

With one last kernel of hope, he shot a text off to Ada, praying she'd told him she'd be back, and he'd forgotten it in his drunken state. But the realist in him buried his head under the pillow and fell back asleep.

Chapter Forty-Five

One Month Later

Charlotte had been sleeping for most of their visit, as Ada flipped through a magazine, not really seeing anything. She'd felt like she was simply going through the motions ever since she left Heron House.

Leaving Trip was hard, but she knew if she stayed, she'd lean on him and never figure her own life out. After Paul's revelation, she was emotionally fragile, and she couldn't trust her mind or her heart to make appropriate decisions.

She also knew if she tried to say goodbye, he'd talk her into staying. Because it's what her heart wanted. But that organ had betrayed her, and she knew she had to make a clean break.

Most every day, she thought about reaching out. But how could he possibly forgive her for how she ended it? She wouldn't.

Besides, it's not like she'd figured anything out. She was still the same emotional mess she'd been that morning, watching him sleep peacefully in the hammock beside her. She didn't deserve him.

The door to Charlotte's room swung open and Ada dropped the magazine. "What are you doing here?"

Elaine's face transformed into a vibrant smile, and while she still had her cane for support, she looked stronger than the last time Ada had seen her.

The night that changed her life.

"Ada, love. It's so good to see you." She tottered across the room and wrapped her arms around Ada, who was frozen with shock. Elaine pulled back with a smile, taking the chair next to her and patting her knee. "It's okay. You don't have to forgive me. I understand."

A vortex of questions swirled in her mind, but it was the last one that popped out. "Why would I need to forgive you? You're the victim in all this!" Ada had also thought about reaching out to Elaine many times in the past month, but it would have made it too hard to avoid Paul, and she didn't feel ready to face him.

"Sweetie. I'm no victim." She sighed and settled into her seat. "I really wish you would have let us explain further. There's much more to this story than you know."

Another pressing question bubbled to the surface. "Why are you visiting my mother?"

"Charlotte and I have a standing coffee date once a month. We have since you were born."

It felt like her eyes had bugged out of her head. She had no idea Charlotte and Elaine socialized. Ada couldn't even remember an occasion when they were in a room together. *Maybe high school graduation?* "I'm so confused."

"Can I tell you everything? Without you jumping to further conclusions? It's a winding story, so I need you to stick with me."

Ada had grown up wishing Elaine was her mother. She was so much more loving and present that Charlotte—even before her mind had betrayed her. Ada had been visiting Charlotte weekly, trying to feel some sort of connection, and she still felt empty inside. Paul and Elaine had always been there for her, but she felt so hurt by their deception. She didn't know if she could trust herself again, let alone anyone else. But this might be a way to move forward or completely close that door. "Yes."

"Good." She patted Ada's knee again, leaving her hand there. "After I got sick, I saw the toll it was taking on Paul. He was working like a dog trying to get the gallery off the ground, helping me with the boys and taking care of my pathetic body when it railed against me. When my MS flares up, it's like my skin is on fire, and I can't stand being touched." She bent down and grabbed a bottle of water out of her bag, taking a long drink. "Paul is the love of my life. He's a kind, generous man. It wasn't fair to him, having to go months without any affection. So, I made him leave."

Ada gripped her chest. The pressure building there was intense, like a volcano getting ready to erupt. "And he did?"

"Not at first. He's such a loyal man. But I was so sick and the guilt I felt was overwhelming. So, eventually he relented. He moved into one of the apartments over his gallery and then he met your mother."

Charlotte stirred in bed, but didn't wake up. Ada took a moment to collect herself by fussing with her mother's covers.

"Ada, I know this is hard to hear, but sit down, sweetie."

She returned to her chair, clutching her hands in her lap and staring at a stain on the floor in the shape of Florida.

Elaine tsked but continued. "As you know, Charlotte is a force. She had her first show, and her career just shot off like a rocket. No one expected it. I imagine it was quite like an aphrodisiac. Anyway, Paul felt just awful when he inevitably slept with her. He was still coming home every night to spend time with the boys, then trudging back to the gallery to sleep. For about a week, he couldn't look me in the eye. I figured out what was going on when Charlotte called the house one day looking for him. I could hear it in her voice. It's how I had felt about him in the beginning."

Ada pressed her palms against her temples, trying to keep her head from exploding. It was too much.

"We're getting there, dear. I won't go into all the sordid details, I promise." Elaine took another swig of water. "I'd guess it went on for almost a year. During that time, my MS went into remission, and I was able to do more with the kids, and it didn't hurt when Paul hugged me. One evening, after we put the boys to bed, we were doing the dishes, and our wedding song came on the radio. He grabbed me and we started dancing and, well, he spent the night. And the next one."

"Wait, so Charlotte is the one who got cheated on?" What a complete mind fuck.

"Yes, I suppose so. He told me he was going to break things off with her on a Wednesday night, and on Thursday, she told him she was pregnant."

It was hard to wrap her brain around. Correction: impossible.

"The time before you were born was the hardest for sure. Paul went back and forth, unsure what to do. We were still very much in love, and he wanted to be there for the boys, but he wasn't about to abandon his other child. He loved Charlotte too, and you, from the day he knew you existed. It was an impossible situation." She drained the rest of her water and held the empty bottle out to Ada. "Do you mind filling this for me, sweetie?"

"Of course." Ada went out into the hall, grateful for a break from this emotionally draining story. She found a water fountain and took a long drink before filling up the bottle. It was like everything she'd ever known was completely different from her initial perception. Back in the room, she handed Elaine the bottle and took her seat again.

"You hanging in there?" Elaine squeezed her hand.

Ada nodded.

"Okay, I'll try to wrap this up." She took another swallow of water before continuing. "Shortly after she told Paul about you, she took off to Eastport Beach. I made him go down there and make things right. I didn't want to risk losing you. You weren't even here yet and already I loved you. Pretty strange, huh? Maybe we should have gone on one of those talk shows?"

Ada snorted, the joke taking the edge off the emotion of the situation. "God, no."

"Yeah, I'll probably just do a best-selling memoir instead," Elaine teased.

She was full-on laughing now, tears leaking down her face. "I hope you get a giant book deal."

"Oo, then I can be more famous than your mother!"

Ada shook her head, wiping her cheeks, and feeling like a weight had lifted off her chest. "Is there more?"

"Yes, dear, another twenty some years." She smiled at Ada and tucked a stray hair behind her ear. "We couldn't risk losing you. As you can imagine, Charlotte's never been the settling-down type, so she didn't want to even discuss marriage, and honestly, that's not what Paul or I wanted anyway. We offered to raise you ourselves, so she could continue her traveling and general lifestyle, but she refused that. Basically, it came down to her terms, because we would have done anything to have you in our lives. After she came back to New York, she broke things off with Paul, and said we could help out with you as long as we didn't reveal who your father was. She didn't want you to think that he'd chosen us over you." She glanced over at Charlotte, a small smile on her face. "She really loved you, Ada. I know she wasn't very good at showing you, but she did, in her own way."

"And he stayed on as her manager? Wasn't that awkward?"

Elaine shook her head. "Part of Paul will always love your mother. Hell, I love her. She's vivacious and creative and a heck of a dancer." She must have clocked Ada's surprise, because she chuckled. "Oh yeah, your mom could cut a rug, as we called it back in the day."

Ada couldn't remember her mother ever dancing. She'd always assumed she got it from her father. In a flash, she had a realization. A matter-forming, big bang type of revelation. Paul always wanted her. He'd always loved her. "So, Charlotte never wanted me to know?" It was so much like her mother—her way or the highway.

"I like to think she would have told you when you got older, but now, it's hard to say." Elaine rose, and using her cane, crossed to the bed. "I miss her, Ada. It was like our own private little club, because no one knew the truth. I could speak freely with her and most visits, we talked about you the entire time. When your mom was painting, she ignored the world, and that wasn't fair to you. But she loved you, and we loved you."

Ada joined her beside the bed and took her free hand. "I've missed you so much."

"Aw, sweetie." Elaine turned and gathered her into a hug. "We've missed you too. Your father has been a mess. He's lost ten pounds."

"Maybe I could come by?"

"You better! Maybe you can get Paul to eat something before he wastes away."

As they parted, Charlotte opened her eyes and smiled. "Are you here to change my sheets?"

Chapter Forty-Six

Ada checked her watch for maybe the hundredth time since she sat down. This felt more like a first date than lunch with a man she'd known her entire life.

Her father.

She still couldn't quite grasp the concept. She'd always loved Paul. Looked up to him. Depended on him. Why was this new label so hard to comprehend? Her whole life she wanted to know her father. Now that she knew it was him, it was like rewiring every memory in her bank.

"Hey kiddo." Paul leaned down, kissing her on the top of the head as he'd done a million times before. This time it felt different though.

Tears sprang from her eyeballs like they were fleeing a burning building.

"Ah, Ada." He crouched beside her chair and wrapped his arms around her.

It didn't matter they were in the middle of a crowded diner. It didn't matter that she was now hiccupping huge sobs, drawing the attention of nearby New Yorkers shoveling food into their faces.

It'd been forty-eight days since her world imploded. Since she'd seen Paul. Since she'd left Trip without a word. Since she'd felt like Ada Maddox.

She clung to him—her father—like he'd vaporize if she let go. The last month and a half had felt like she was marooned on a distant planet. Nothing familiar, no one to love her. She'd been teaching ballroom at a studio in the city a few nights a week, but every time she danced her arms ached for Trip. She visited her mother every few days, but never once had the spark of recognition lit Charlotte's eyes. It was two strangers exchanging small talk, or Charlotte sleeping through the visit. Ada had hoped for something, some connection. But she felt more alone than ever.

"Do you want to leave?" Paul rubbed soothing circles on her back.

She choked down a sob, clearing her throat. "No, I'm okay." It was a lie. She hadn't been okay for a while now. Wiping angrily at her tears, she tried to pull herself together. "Please, sit. I ordered an appetizer for us."

Paul looked hesitant but took the chair across from her. "Ada, let's go to the gallery. Have a bit of privacy."

"No, honestly. It's fine." She'd chosen to meet in public so she wouldn't fall apart. Miserable failure.

The server arrived and set a platter in the middle of the table. He took Paul's drink order and left.

"Elaine wouldn't approve." Paul grinned at the giant plate full of fried foods—mozzarella sticks, onion rings, mac n cheese balls & zucchini fries.

Ada smiled and she felt it all the way to the edges of her face. "There's vegetables." She held up two fingers. "Besides, this was her idea."

He laughed. "I'll remind her of that when my cholesterol numbers come back." He dipped an onion ring in a giant side of ranch dressing.

When she was little, she and Paul would sometimes eat out when Elaine was feeling poorly and needed to rest. They'd always order something "naughty." Funnel cakes, cheese curds, anything Elaine would have deemed unhealthy. He'd called her his little partner in crime.

She'd forgotten about it until she was sitting in this diner, staring at the salad section of the menu.

They dug in, a frenzy of fried goodness and the comfort of memories. Ada had been remembering a lot the last few weeks, despite her efforts to stay mad at Paul for lying to her all these years.

"Did my mom really forbid you from telling me?"

He paused with a zucchini fry halfway to his mouth. A drop of ketchup fell from the fry to his plate. "Charlotte was used to getting her way." He set it down. "Ada, we would have done anything to stay in your life. Maybe I should have handled things differently, fought for you. We mostly just went along with what she wanted because it was easier. We got to see you often and most of the time Charlotte wasn't all that interested in raising you, so she was happy to let us step it. I didn't need the label. I knew there was love there." He sighed. "But I think you needed the label. And I'm sorry I didn't fight for that."

Tears threatened again. "Let's talk about something else."

"How's that fella you're seeing? Trip, is it?" He popped a mac n cheese ball in his mouth.

Ada shook her head, squeezing her eyes shut. *Not helping.* "I haven't spoken to him." She grabbed a napkin and pressed it against her eyes, attempting to keep the tears in.

"I don't understand. It seemed like you were a great fit. I appreciated how he stood up for you." Paul clasped her hand across the table. "What happened?"

His face became blurry as the tears finally won the battle. She didn't cry in public. Who had she become? "Can we go now?"

"Of course." Paul took out his wallet and threw some bills on the table, then helped Ada out of the booth. "Come on."

She kept her eyes on the pavement as they walked the three blocks to Paul's gallery. They bypassed the front door, and he entered a code on the keypad beside a nondescript entrance. Heading up the stairs, she waited without a word while he unlocked the door to the apartment above the gallery. She'd only been inside a few times—it hadn't made sense that he needed an apartment here when his and Elaine's townhouse was within walking distance.

Now she saw it in a whole new light. "Was this where you brought my mother?"

"I was living here when Elaine and I separated." He gestured at the sofa. "You want something to drink?"

"Water, please." She'd probably get dehydrated from all the stupid crying. The couch was different than she remembered, so maybe she didn't have to actually sit where Paul and her mother... She didn't want to complete that thought.

"I refurnished the place about a year ago. I let traveling artists use it."

She must have stared at the leather couch too long. "That's nice. Kind of like Heron House." Except this place was in the middle of a dirty, noisy city. Not the sweet, idyllic town of Eastport Beach. She sighed and flopped down, making the leather squeak. "I was an idiot. I was so upset about you that I left without telling him goodbye."

"Who, Trip?"

"Yeah. I really liked him. But it was all so complicated, and I didn't want to stay with him for the wrong reasons. I thought if I took some time, things would make more sense and then I could...But it's been too long now. And I'm still a complete mess."

"I think he really cared about you, Ada. You should try to reach out. He'd be a fool to say no." Paul handed her a bottle of water and sat beside her. "You're an amazing person, and I'm not just saying that because you have my DNA. You have a huge heart, despite a difficult upbringing and an emotionally distant mother. And you're so talented."

She raised her gaze from her lap to look into her father's eyes. Eyes she had seen so many times before, and as always, they were full of love. "Do you think he could forgive me?"

"Have you forgiven me?"

Her heart hurt. She couldn't lose everyone she loved. And she loved Paul. She gave a quick nod and then reached her arms around him.

He pulled her close, stroking her hair. "Thank you, kiddo. That means the world to me." When they pulled apart, he tucked her hair behind her ear. "Of course, he'll forgive you if he loves you. What I did was way worse. He'll understand, or he's not worth the effort."

This must be what it's like to get fatherly advice. But then it struck her that Paul had been doling out wisdom her whole life. The only difference was knowing. "I think he's worth the effort."

"Then go. It doesn't matter where you are, we'll always be around if you need us."

Part of her heart knit itself back together. But it wasn't whole yet. "What about Mom?"

"We've got your mother, Ada. Elaine and I will keep visiting and if anything changes, you'll be the first to know. Figure out who you want to be and who you want to be with. If it's meant to be, it will all come together."

She sure hoped so, because nothing had felt right since she drove away from Eastport Beach, North Carolina.

***

Her last class was set to start in thirty minutes, so she checked her email to see if the confirmation from Heron House had come through yet. She'd been too chicken shit to call Riley and ask if Trip was still around. So, she'd booked online and hoped her friends from North Carolina wouldn't hold her inexcusable behavior against her.

She scrolled through her messages, and one subject line jumped out at her. She clicked the email and scanned it quickly. It was from the head of the committee that originally approved her grant. Her heart practically stopped when she got to the last paragraph. Apparently, the program had regained its funding, and they were reaching out to the participants to see if they still had programs that could benefit from the grant.

Maybe she could go back to Virginia in a few months and restart the program if Susan reopened the studio in the spring.

She dialed Miranda, practically holding her breath.

"Well, hello stranger. Long time no talk." Miranda's voice held equal parts mirth and scorn. Ada deserved it. She'd been ignoring Randi's calls since her world came crashing down.

"I know, worst friend ever." She didn't have time to explain, because her first few students trickled in. "Did you hear about the grant funding?"

Her friend snorted. "Of course, it's been all over the news."

"The news? Why would a little arts grant make the news?"

"So, you haven't been just ignoring my calls. You've been living under a rock!"

More people were streaming into the room, and the volume was kicking up. She didn't have time for Randi's dramatics, as entertaining as they usually were. "Yeah, I checked out for a while, focused on my mom. What did I miss?"

Miranda sighed. "Sorry, I didn't mean to give you a hard time. Is she any better?"

"No, not really." She wished she had more time to fill her in on everything that happened, but it'd have to wait.

"Well, anyway, Senator Westinghouse had a massive coronary and kicked the bucket. I guess his son was planning to run for his seat anyway, but he knocked up some twenty-year-old, so that's not happening."

Ada felt lightheaded. Trip's grandfather died? After she just left without a word? She didn't deserve a second chance. The poor guy. As messed up as his family dynamics were, he still lost someone. "That's awful. What does it have to do with the grant?"

"So, his grandson, I guess, came in and insisted that the committee reconvene and look at the funding again. He, like, lobbied to make it happen. It was a pretty big deal on Capitol Hill, lots of juicy gossip and all that."

Ada covered her gasp. She couldn't believe it. Trip hated politics. He didn't want anything to do with Washington, D.C.

"Can you believe it?" Miranda laughed. "Ada, you still there?"

"Yeah, that's wild. Listen, I've got a class right now, but I can call you back after?"

"Of course. I got nothin' going on. Just driving Big Macs around until Susan's hip heals."

They signed off just as someone turned on some salsa music. As the beat reverberated through Ada's chest, she felt a faint flutter. Like maybe her heart knew how to work after all.

Chapter Forty-Seven

Trip's phone rang as he stepped into the sunlight. He'd been inside for hours, packing up his grandfather's office. He set the banker's box on a planter and swiped his screen without even looking at the caller ID. "Hello?"

"She just booked the Maddox suite for a month." Riley's declaration came out in one breath, her excitement evident.

He'd planned to give it two months. If Ada didn't reach out in sixty days, he'd track her down. Lucky for him, she was ahead of schedule. The timing couldn't be more perfect. He was finished in Washington and the place in Eastport Beach was almost ready. "Did she call you?"

Riley laughed. "No, she booked online. Cautious, just like you said."

Trip had only known Ada for a week before he fell in love with her. And before she left without a word. But he was confident she hadn't left because of him. It was her own family crap that sent her running off into the night. And Trip was a freaking expert on family drama.

On the Monday after the gala, Senator Carlton Westinghouse Sr had gotten his wish. Despite cancelling the appointment Robert had been trying to set the week before, Trip was forced to race to D.C. when his grandfather had a massive coronary on the Senate floor during a heated debate over oil drilling leases.

The old man had held on long enough for his family to surround him in Walter Reed National Medical Center. With his last breath, he reiterated his desire for his grandson to carry on in D.C. politics.

Trip didn't bother answering either way, because it was all over so quickly. One minute, Carlton Sr was wagging his finger disapprovingly, and the next his face was slack with his passing.

The family, well, his parents, at least, tried to put on a good show for the public, but Win's affair quickly came to light, and his campaign was put on an indefinite hold.

Trip stayed on in Washington, determined to make something good come from his grandfather's reign of power. He worked tirelessly to renew the funding to the arts program Ada had told him about. He knew it was a gamble, because if the program was renewed, she might stay in Virginia. He'd put all his eggs in the Eastport Beach basket, but he'd figure it out. He'd follow her anywhere at this point. The important thing was for her to follow her dreams.

She was his.

"When will she be there?" Trip squinted at his watch, the bright afternoon sun reflecting off the face. It was the one thing he'd kept from his grandfather's personal effects.

"Monday."

"I'll be back tomorrow. The contractors are supposed to finish by Saturday." For once, it felt like things were finally going his way. His grandfather couldn't control the family any longer, and his parents didn't have a leg to stand on when it came to dictating his life decisions.

His sister had flown back for the funeral, then promptly returned to Greece, where she was shacking up with a scooter mechanic.

Trip would be settled into his new home in Eastport Beach by Sunday, and hopefully Ada would join him shortly after. Why else would she return to North Carolina?

"It's all so romantic," Riley squealed. "You should have the wedding at Heron House!"

"Slow down, Tiger. Let's get through the reunion before you try to marry me off." The funny thing was the idea of marrying Ada didn't scare him one bit. In fact, he already knew how he would propose. But he knew Ada needed time to adjust to everything, so he was biding his time. He'd wait as long as she needed.

***

A light breeze tickled the back of his neck as he walked into The Landing. He'd just grab a quick drink and then get back to unpacking. It would be nice to have so many options within walking distance. No subways or crowded buses in Eastport Beach.

"Well, look what the crab dragged in!" Chesnee hopped off a stool and greeted his friend with a one-armed "bro" hug.

Sharkey was also seated at the bar, a mug of his own ale in front of him, if Trip had to guess. The bear of a man nodded at him, a slight smile somewhere under his dark beard.

"I was going to call, but I didn't want anyone to think I was just saying hi to get help hauling boxes." Trip gestured at the mug of dark brew in front of his quiet friend. "I'll have the same, Nic."

The bartender, a fit man in his forties, nodded and grabbed a clean mug from the rack. "I heard we're practically neighbors."

"Yeah, the contractors finished up today. I have a bed and everything." Trip grabbed the mug Nic slid toward him.

"And I heard you might have someone to share that bed with soon enough." Chesnee whooped and raised his glass.

His friend was entertaining, that was for sure. Trip chuckled and clinked glasses with him. "God willing."

"Is Ada back?" Sharkey joined in the congratulations with his own mug.

"Monday."

The brewer nodded, his eyes twinkling with merriment. "Cheers then. You got a plan?"

A plan. Did he have a plan? He'd only gone over it a million times in his mind. "I'm going to play it by ear. See how she's feeling before I go crazy."

Chesnee piped up. "Nah, brah. You need a big gesture, or some bullshit. Like sky writing, or a Jumbotron."

"He's not proposing, Ches." Sharkey stroked his beard. "Play it cool, Trip."

"Pretty sure it's a grand gesture. And Eastport Beach doesn't have sky writers or a major sports team." Trip took a swig of his beer. "Damn, Sharkey. Is this new?" The dark brew was equal parts rich and bitter, packing a surprising punch.

"Roasted Skate Stout. It's in the testing phase."

Trip took another taste, this time rolling the beer around in his mouth like a fine wine. "Is that caramel?"

Sharkey pointed at him. "Bingo."

"Enough about the beer. You've got to at least cover the bed with rose petals. Girls eat that shit up." Chesnee sipped his fruity mixed drink.

"It's hard to believe you're still single," Trip deadpanned.

His friend shrugged. "It's a conscious choice. I'm not ready to settle down."

"I'm sure it has nothing to do with Gina."

Sharkey chuckled.

Chesnee turned on the brewer. "At least I date. When was the last time you enjoyed the company of a woman?"

"The company of a woman? Exactly how old are you, Ches?" Trip teased.

"Younger than the old maid here." He gestured in Sharkey's direction.

"We prefer male spinster." Sharkey didn't seem the least bit ruffled by Chesnee's jabs.

Trip struggled to remember having seen the brewer with the opposite sex. He didn't know him well, and this was honestly the most words they'd ever exchanged. "Confirmed bachelor sounds more distinguished."

Sharkey tipped his head, thoughtful. "I can live with that."

"Spinster has a dried-up egg connotation."

"Don't got none of those." He drained his glass, slamming it on the bar and rising from the stool.

Trip was over six feet and the brewmaster towered over him.

"Well, gents." Sharkey added a fake accent as he tipped his imaginary hat. "My beer needs me."

"Beer can't keep you warm at night, old man." Chesnee slid his empty glass over to Nic. "Another Mai Tai, good man. Because I'm secure as hell in my masculinity."

"At least beer can give good head."

Trip choked on his brew. Who knew Sharkey had a killer sense of humor under all that fur?

The brewer shoved a twenty in Nic's tip jar. "Good luck, Trip." Then he ambled out of the bar like Bigfoot in a plaid shirt.

Chesnee sipped his fresh drink, staring into the pink depths as if it held the secrets to the universe.

"What, no more pithy comebacks?" Trip took the stool Sharkey had vacated.

His friend swirled the straw around his glass without looking up. "Gina left."

"Like moved?"

He nodded, looking like someone had run over his dog on the same day his house burned down.

Trip clapped him on the shoulder. "Wow, I'm sorry, man."

"It was the bass player from the gala."

The woman was truly obsessed with musicians. "Maybe you should learn to play an instrument."

Chesnee snorted. "I wish it was that easy."

"The two of you looked pretty cozy at the gala." Trip had never asked Chesnee about the morning after, when he'd seen him sneaking out of Gina's room and Gina later sneaking in. Between Ada's disappearing act and his grandfather's dramatic exit, he forgot all about it.

"I thought so too. But she packed up and left right after you." He continued to play with his straw. "Everyone left."

Trip felt awful. He'd been so wrapped up in his mess that he'd completely forgotten his friend. How long does it take to send a quick text? "Want to come see my place?"

Chesnee's face lit up. "Hell, yeah."

"Great. I've got this, Nic." He gestured at his friend's drink. "I've laid down a pretty penny, so I hope to be here for the long haul." It all depended on Ada at this point. But the look on Chesnee's face made Trip want to stay even more.

Chapter Forty-Eight

Riley was waiting when Ada pulled next to the heron fountain. She bounced on the balls of her feet, her whole body brimming with excitement. It was how Ada imagined it would feel to be greeted by a loyal pet. Of course, she wouldn't know because her mother had never allowed an animal in their home.

"Ada! It's so good to see you!" Riley launched herself at Ada the moment her feet hit the gravel driveway.

Returning the hug, Ada had to blink back tears. She'd missed this place, she'd missed her friend, but mostly, she'd missed feeling wanted. "It's so good to be back."

"I'm so happy the Maddox suite was available for you. We've been booked solid since the grand opening. I've even let a couple people rent rooms on the third floor because there's been such a demand."

Trip's room had been on the third floor. "Oh, did you add more rooms up there?"

Riley shook her head. "With both Gina and Trip moving out, it opened up two modest rooms, so I rent them for less. Right now, I've got a couple college students who are working on projects and have a small stipend."

Ada breathed deep, sucking in the fresh air laced with the salt from the nearby ocean. So, Trip was gone. Likely back to Virginia. A place she no longer had ties to. She'd cleaned out her rental and sublet it to a young couple. She was a woman without a home. "I'm glad I was able to secure a spot in such a happening place." She forced cheerfulness into her voice, despite the sorrow deep in her gut.

"Listen, I've got to answer some emails. So, you get settled and then I want to take you to lunch. They've changed up their menu at the Mermaid and you've got to try their chicken fried salad. It'll knock your socks off." Riley gave her another quick squeeze. "I'll meet you here at one. We can take the bikes down."

Ada wanted to bury her head under the covers and feel sorry for herself, but she also didn't want to disappoint Riley. They had become close during Ada's first stay at Heron House, and she truly had missed her while she was in New York. She was easy-going, naturally upbeat, and cared deeply for the people in her life. Maybe some of that effervescent happiness would rub off on Ada.

Riley hopped up the stairs, briefly speaking to an older couple that was seated on the porch swing before she disappeared into the house.

Ada popped her trunk and rearranged boxes and bags until she located the suitcase that hopefully contained the majority of her clothes and toiletries. She'd put most of her things in storage and hastily thrown her personal items into her trunk when she left Virginia. After her month here, she had no idea where she'd go. She never imagined she'd end up traveling around like her mother. Ada longed for roots, while Charlotte had spent her whole life fighting them like they were weeds in her artistic garden.

Movement down by the dock caught her attention. Someone had just pulled a kayak alongside the small wooden landing. Ada's heart jumped into her throat, and she dropped the suitcase at her feet. It was an eternity before the man disembarked and pulled the kayak up onto the shore. He was tall and well built, but when he yanked the baseball cap off his head and turned in her direction, Ada realized it was Ben. She gulped, her breath coming in short gasps, pain radiating through her chest. Why did she come here? This was too painful. Everything here reminded her of Trip. She was just torturing herself.

Unsure where she could go, Ada hesitated. Her belongings mocked her from the trunk of her car. How had this become her life? She was lifting her bag back into the trunk when Ben appeared beside her, pulling a shirt over his head.

"Ada, it's so good to see you. Can I help you with your bag?" Without waiting for a response, he grabbed the suitcase and hoisted it out of the trunk. "Riley has been talking non-stop about you coming back. She's made so many plans. I hope you weren't looking for peaceful solitude." He laughed at his joke as he carried her bag up the stairs of the porch.

Looks like I'm staying after all. It did feel good to be wanted, even if it wasn't by the man of her dreams. She grabbed a smaller bag and closed the trunk. Better to be miserable with friends than miserable and alone.

***

The women were cruising down River Road, the breeze they generated offering a little relief from the muggy day. It was late November and Ada had never lived this far south. "Is there no fall in North Carolina?"

Riley laughed. "We had fall in the mountains, for sure. Tourists flocked there like gnats to a bug zapper. This is my first year here at the coast, so I'm not sure when it's going to cool down. I'm still running the air conditioning in the house."

Luckily, most of Ada's wardrobe was in her car, so she'd been able to find a pair of shorts and a t-shirt that mostly matched. Tomorrow, she'd drag more stuff up to her room and get organized. Maybe if her belongings were in order, her life would follow. "I'm guessing you don't have to worry about snow, at least."

"Luckily my uncle was a clotheshorse, so he had a huge closet. I've got my cold weather gear way in the back, just in case, but I don't know what to expect." They slowed as they neared the stop sign at Main Street. "My lesson this year has been to enjoy the ride and not worry so much. I'm still figuring it out, though."

"With zero plans, I guess I need to try that too. Any tips?"

Traffic in town was light, so they crossed the street to the small park and chained their bikes up. Ada flashed back to this very park on her first date with Trip. She'd seen Eastport Beach for the first time with him. The memories were intricately bound together. There was no way she could stay here without him.

"For me, it was meeting Ben. Feeling secure in his love, I'm no longer scared of bad stuff happening, because I know we'll tackle it together. I never felt safe like that with my ex. He's not a bad guy, but he just wasn't there for me like Ben is."

Tears sprang to Ada's eyes, threatening to erupt in this extremely public place. The entire town of Eastport Beach would know about her breakdown in mere minutes. She was such an idiot. If she hadn't run away like a scared little girl, maybe they could still be together. Maybe her life would make sense.

Before she knew what was happening, Riley had her arms around her. "It's okay, Ada. I have a feeling this is all going to work out." She held her for a few more minutes, then patted her on the back before pulling away. "Now, tell me about your father."

Ada was grateful for the change in subject. A month ago, it would have been just as likely to make her cry, but she'd at least gotten some peace about the situation with Paul and Elaine. Things weren't quite back to normal, but she'd finally realized she was happy to discover that her father had been there all along, taking care of her and loving her. "It's a pretty wild story."

"I've got time."

The two started walking toward The Spicy Mermaid, Ada spilling all the dirt on her mother and Paul's "affair" and subsequent oddly functional co-parenting. She was finishing the story as they stopped across the street from the diner to let a car pass. Her attention was drawn to the building next door, where brown paper still lined the windows and the For Sale sign she'd seen when she was last there was now gone.

Light seeped around the edges of the paper, and she could hear the faint strains of music escaping from the front door, which was cracked open. "Did someone buy that building?"

Riley snickered, suddenly looking like a little girl who'd gotten caught playing with her mother's lipstick. "Yup."

"Do you know what they're doing with it?" Why was Riley acting so weird all of a sudden?

Her friend grabbed her hand and pulled her across the now-empty street. "Let's go see!"

Really weird. "Riley, what's going on?"

"Nothing! I swear!"

"So why does it sound like you are talking in all caps?"

Riley dissolved into a fit of nervous laughter. "I don't know what you're talking about." She yanked Ada closer to the vestibule of the historic building. The building that had haunted Ada's dreams the last few weeks. She knew exactly how she would turn it into a dance studio. She'd even sketched a logo out. But it was all a pipe dream. She couldn't stay in Eastport Beach. Not without Trip.

The music was clearer as they stood outside the door. It was Michael Bublé's "Save the Dance for Me." But it wasn't Michael Bublé's voice she heard. It was Trip's.

He appeared in the doorway, like a vision from a fever dream, which was appropriate because suddenly, the humidity became oppressive, and Ada felt like she could faint right here on Main Street for all of Eastport Beach to see. Trip held his hand out to her, his eyes sparkling with that magic gleam he got when they danced.

She was frozen to the spot, trying to comprehend what she was seeing. Was he really here or had she hallucinated him into existence?

Riley pushed her forward. "Trip bought the building. And there's no new menu at the diner. Bye!" Her friend fled the scene, leaving Ada within inches of the man she'd missed with every millimeter of her body.

Realization dawned, penetrating her thick skull. She should've known something was up. Riley was the worst liar on the planet. Slowly, she regained use of her limbs, her brain and finally, her heart. She placed her hand in Trip's, and he drew her into the cool interior of the building.

Everything fell into place as he tucked her into his hold and spun her around the room. They danced, Trip sang, and Ada finally felt whole again. He'd always be her last dance.

NEW YEAR'S EVE

DANCE PARTY

@ EASTPORT'S NEWEST
DANCE STUDIO!

 MAD ABOUT DANCING 

WED **12-31** 10 PM

8 MAIN ST, EASTPORT BEACH, NC

Epilogue
One Month Later

Ada sat at a small vanity, fussing with her hair. Every time she lifted her long locks off her neck, Trip wanted to grab her and kiss every inch of skin. The last few weeks had been blissful. They'd picked right back up where they left off after the gala, learning more about one another, growing as a couple and renovating the space on Main Street into Ada's dream dance studio.

When she finally settled on a high bun, he couldn't resist any longer. Jumping up from the bed, he stepped behind her, crouching low to place a kiss in the hollow between her neck and her shoulder. It was still warm in Eastport Beach, and she was taking full advantage of the mild weather with a backless gown of shimmering silver. It'd be a miracle if he made it through the night without whisking her back upstairs to their apartment for some naked alone time.

She smiled at him in the mirror, tilting her head for better access.

"We have some time, right?" he asked hopefully.

"I spent the last hour getting ready, so no, we don't have time for you to mess it all up." She spun on her stool and captured his face between her hands, drawing him down for a quick but intense kiss. "I can reapply my lipstick, though."

He took full advantage, diving back in, his hands roaming her bare skin as his mouth explored hers. He'd never get enough of this woman.

When his phone pealed from the bed, he groaned.

Ada pulled away, her pale cheeks flushed. "Get that while I fix my face."

Trip grumbled as he let go of his beautiful girlfriend and reached for his phone. "Sharkey's early. I'll see you downstairs." He kissed Ada on the head before hurrying out of the room, answering the phone as he walked. "I'll be down in a minute."

His friend grunted and hung up.

The caterers and beer were supposed to arrive an hour before the party. Trip had twelve more minutes to maul his girlfriend. He reached the bottom of the stairs and pushed outside to find Sharkey on the sidewalk with two kegs on a dolly.

"Getting an early start?" Trip unlocked the door to the dance studio and stepped aside so the brewer could push his wares inside.

"Good thing I did, because one of my tires was flat. I had to unload all the kegs from the truck and change the tire." He unloaded the cart and headed back outside. "I want to test them out. One of them felt light."

He must have really been early if he had time to change a tire. "You changed your tire in the dark? You could have called. I would have brought my truck."

Sharkey shrugged. He pulled two more kegs from the bed of his pickup and used bungee cords to strap them onto the dolly.

While he pushed them into the building, Trip lowered the tailgate and jumped into the bed of the truck. It wasn't his first time helping the brewer set up for an event. He slid the mobile bar, complete with taps, to the tailgate. Sharkey reappeared and helped him lift it down to the sidewalk. "Toss me your keys and I'll park your truck down at Ben's office." Trip hopped down and slammed the tailgate shut. A set of keys hit him in the chest and fell to the ground.

Sharkey just raised his eyebrows as he turned to push the mobile bar inside.

Trip chuckled, bending down to retrieve the keys. By the time he parked the truck and jogged back, Sharkey had all the taps attached and ready to dispense. The caterers weren't there yet, so Trip grabbed a plastic cup from the small office behind the studio and handed it to Sharkey, who was adjusting something under the bar.

"Moment of truth." He opened one of the taps and instead of a rich, foamy head, pee-colored water dribbled out. He shook his head, cursing under his breath.

The citizens of Eastport Beach would not appreciate a dry event, so Trip held his breath as the town's beer guru tried the other three taps. All looked normal and met with the brewer's silent approval.

Sharkey disconnected the compromised keg and held out his hand for his keys. "I checked all of these before I loaded the truck. Took a shower and came out to a flat tire and a flat beer." He narrowed his eyes, scrunching his face like he was trying to solve a calculus problem. "Can't be a coincidence."

"You think someone messed with your truck and your beer?" As far as Trip knew, the town revered Sharkey. He provided happiness for all the local events. None of the locals would destroy a perfectly good keg of beer.

"I've got time to grab a replacement. Be back." The big man stomped out the door as the caterers arrived to set up the food necessary to soak up all the booze.

Trip greeted them and showed them where to set up but was immediately distracted when Ada stepped through the doorway of the studio. She took his breath away every time he saw her, whether she was dolled up for New Year's Eve or wearing cozy pajamas on Christmas morning. Without thinking, he was at the door, taking her into his arms and spinning her around the room. There wasn't any audible music, but he didn't miss an opportunity to dance with his girl.

She laughed as he swept her across the gleaming wood floors. "You realize we're literally going to be dancing all night, right?"

"If I have my way, we're going to be dancing for the rest of our lives."

Ada's eyes went round, growing to the size of silver dollars. "That's an awfully long time. What if I'm crippled and in a wheelchair?"

"Then I'll pick you up and dance with you in my arms."

"What if I weigh two hundred pounds?"

Trip didn't hesitate in his steps or his words. "Then I'll train harder so I can still lift you."

She followed his lead, like she always did, the perfect partner in life and on the dance floor. "What if you can't walk from arthritis?"

"Then I'll sweep you onto my Hoveround and spin the night away." He steered them to the back of the room, pausing long enough to turn on some music before continuing their jaunt around the studio. "We'll be old and decrepit together. I love you, Ada. You're not getting rid of me."

"Well, you're not getting rid of me either. They have wheelchair dancing competitions, you know." She pressed up on her toes, planting a kiss near his mouth.

He slowed down, so she wouldn't miss the next time. "See, no problem then. Forever." Trip leaned down, kissing her properly and messing up her lipstick again.

"Well, I see West has finally learned how to stay on his feet during a kiss." Chesnee's voice boomed over the music. It seemed like he was back to his old, jovial self.

Reluctantly, Trip pulled back, wiping a smudge of red off Ada's skin. "To be continued," he whispered.

When he looked up, it wasn't just his boisterous friend that had arrived. It seemed like half the town was streaming through the door. Ada hurried to the back and turned off the overhead lights, letting the thousands of twinkle lights they'd strung along the ceiling provide ambiance. He'd even installed a couple small disco balls, which started spinning, sending sparks of silver bouncing off the mirrored walls.

Chesnee and a blonde woman Trip had never met appeared in front of him, beers already in their hands.

How long have we been dancing? Sharkey was at his post behind the mobile bar, happily filling plastic cups with his selection of beers and ciders.

"Great job on the studio. The lights are sick." Chesnee slapped Trip on the back.

"You're just happy I didn't ask you to help."

His friend nodded emphatically. "You got that right. Hey, this is Harmony. Harmony, my good friend, Trip."

"Are you a dancer?" Her voice was high-pitched like one of the Chipettes. Surely that couldn't be real.

Ada chose that moment to reappear, luckily. She slid her arm around Trip's waist, almost as if she was claiming him. *Fine by me.* "A little, but Ada here is the real deal."

"Trip is being humble. He's an excellent dancer."

He shrugged. "I'm just here in a supporting role. Ada will be teaching most of the classes. She even got a grant to teach underprivileged kids." All he did was get her application moved to the top of the pile. She did the rest.

"We're doing ballet, tap and modern dance for kids and teens. And ballroom for all ages. Trip will be helping me with that." Ada beamed up at him, her eyes twinkling. "He's the best partner I've ever had."

Warmth and pride filled his chest. He'd never felt so happy and settled. The crushing weight of his family's expectations was a distant memory. Those unrealistic obligations had died with his grandfather. His parents had finally split up and were too busy fighting over racehorses and ski condos to bother pressuring Trip. For the first time in his life, he was doing what made him happy, and that was taking care of Ada and helping her reach for her dreams. "She makes me look good." He squeezed her close and kissed her on the temple.

Chesnee's date of the week tittered, and they disappeared into the crowd. Riley and Ben showed up and raved over how nice the studio looked, then headed for the charcuterie table.

The evening was fun, full of dancing, good friends, delicious food and excellent beer. But the best part was having Ada by his side. Chesnee had offered to be Dick Clark for the night—apparently his grandma always made him watch old episodes of Dick Clark's New Year's Rockin' Eve. So, at a few minutes to midnight, he picked up a microphone and started an annoyingly long countdown.

Trip pulled Ada away from her conversation with Riley and swept her into a semi-private corner. "I'm so lucky to get to end this year with you and start a new one together. Being with you makes me happier than I've ever been. I love you so much, Ada." A few months ago, he never would have believed he'd be in love and not have to worry about his family ruining it.

She smiled sweetly up at him, her eyes already glossy with emotion. "I went looking for family and found you. Thank you for supporting my dreams and dancing through life with me."

Chesnee counted down from ten (finally) and as cheers erupted around the tightly packed room, Trip leaned down and kissed the woman he'd never dared dream of.

About the author

Tara grew up with her nose buried in a book, and not much has changed. She's a serial entrepreneur – doggie daycare owner, quilt shop owner, maker and, of course, author. Currently, she lives in the mountains of North Carolina with her #1 love, a shichon named Agador Spartacus. Her whole family lives nearby, including her two grown sons, who are inspirations for the "cool" things young people say.

If you enjoyed this book, please consider leaving a review on Goodreads or Amazon.com. Thanks!

Also by

Welcome to Heron House

Book 1 in the Eastport Beach series.

Meet Riley and Ben as they are each starting over and learning to love after loss.

Something's Brewing at Heron House (coming Feb 2026)

Book 3 in the Eastport Beach Series.

Sharkey & Hope navigate an opposites-attract romance in a hilarious and moving

way.

Turn the page for an excerpt!

Standalones

Above Average Girl (2022)

This is a sweet romance about a plus-sized girl trying to find her way in the dating

world with a little help from her friends.

The Things I Do For Her (2022)

Truly a story of friendship, this sweet romance is about growing up, finding love

and moving on.

For signed paperback copies, visit www.dreamingoftheseafabrics.com.

Something's Brewing at Heron House
Chapter 1

For most of his life, Seamus McLaughlin hadn't fit. He was bigger than his classmates in elementary school. In middle school, he was the only kid with facial hair. By high school, he'd become obsessed with chemistry, while most of the guys his age only cared about sports. Hell, his name didn't even fit and not a soul had used it since he was two years old and glued to Shark Week on the Discovery Channel. He'd been Sharkey ever since.

He certainly didn't fit in the dollhouse-sized shower inside his camper.

A stream of mumbled profanity stronger than the water pressure flowed from Sharkey's lips as he hit his funny bone for maybe the hundredth time. He was too damn big to live in a house on wheels. Turning the water off, he wrenched the shower curtain aside, popping several of the hooks off the top.

It was only temporary, he told himself again. And again. Once the brewery was finished, he could find a place with high ceilings and doorways he didn't bang his head on every other day.

The mantra started to work. He could feel his breath evening out and his muscles relaxing.

That's when he heard the racket outside.

Dammit! I'm going to catch those bastards once and for all. He raced to the door and flung it open, the cold January air hitting his naked, wet body and prompting him to pull the towel from around his neck and secure it at his waist. For weeks, someone had been making his life hell, basically undoing everything he did. Empty kegs, cut wires, an entire shipment of hops destroyed.

It was why he was living in this damn trailer. To keep an eye on things. To catch them in the act.

Barefoot, he slipped on the plastic steps, which he struggled with on a regular basis, because his feet were bigger than the treads. He nearly landed on his ass, but caught himself at the last second, by sheer will, determined not to make a fool of himself in front of his mortal enemy.

In his effort to save face, he lost the towel. Damn, it was cold.

A quick survey of the area between his camper and the container he would eventually use as the bar revealed no saboteurs. No one to see his pasty white ass. He quickly re-secured the towel and crept along the side of the giant metal shipping container.

For the last week, he'd been working inside the container, running plumbing and electrical. If someone was in there undoing everything he'd just done, there was going to be hell to pay. Sharkey was a pacifist, preferring quiet contemplation over confrontation any day of the week, but he'd make an exception. He was at the end of his rope. This project was already a month behind because of this mess.

When he poked his head around the corner, he didn't see anyone inside the container. Then movement closer to the riverbank drew his attention.

Atop one of his picnic tables stood a small, blonde woman waving her arms and...praying? It sounded like she was asking the Lord to rid her of the evil one.

Sharkey expected to find some punk kids messing with his property, not a possessed young woman dancing with the devil.

As he stepped closer, he finally saw the issue.

Damn gator.

He'd thought between the construction and more people frequenting the area that Stumpy wouldn't want to hang around. That alligator was too dumb for his own good.

Grabbing a stick, he rounded the corner fully and approached the table. Stumpy was acting a fool, snapping the air like he was actually going to eat the scared little waif.

Sharkey shook his head and puffed out his chest. When he was within six feet of the reptile, he slammed the stick into the ground and growled at the scaly interloper. The woman shrieked, and it appeared she didn't know who was scarier, man or beast.

Stumpy wobbled closer to the threat. He was missing most of his front right leg, but from the locals' experience, it didn't slow him down.

"I'm not playing with you today." Sharkey spoke low in tone and volume and banged the stick into the ground again. This time, the branch broke into two pieces. The animal took another step closer, jaws snapping like he was laughing.

The woman was hugging herself, repeating, "ohmygosh, ohmygosh, ohmygosh," over and over again.

It made it hard to concentrate. "Can you hush for a minute?"

She froze, her eyes growing to the size of sand dollars.

Sharkey tried to think, but between the cold breeze blowing through his partially open towel and the nine-foot gator stalking toward him, it was difficult. He wished it had been a couple punk kids instead.

Slowly, he backed toward the container, to the giant hole he'd cut in it to use as a serving bar. He reached his hand through the opening, keeping his eyes on Stumpy, trying to find anything he could use as a weapon. He had plenty of options in the camper—although right now he was wishing he'd grabbed pants.

Finally, his fingers wrapped around the handle of a cordless drill. He lifted it and was relieved to feel the weight. He hadn't put the battery on the charger last night. Throwing up a prayer that it still had juice, he brandished it at the gator.

Whirrlllll.

Stumpy took a step back.

Sharkey advanced, waving the power tool through the air.

The beast turned toward the woman on the table, snapped his jaws, and then fully turned around, heading back to the river. Just as he slid into the water, the drill died.

The blonde pixie started back up with her "ohmygosh" chant, looking from the river to Sharkey and back again.

"Ma'am, you can get down now."

Arms flailing, she shook her head, her short bob swishing from side to side. She muttered something incoherent. Just what he needed. A woman with the vapors.

Sighing, he set the drill down and reached his hand out.

"He probably won't come back today." He didn't want to lie to the woman, but he also wanted her to get off his table before she fell and broke her neck and held him liable. Of course, getting eaten by an alligator could also cause liability issues. He made a mental note to check with his insurance company about coverage for wildlife attacks.

The woman looked like she was struggling to choose between being eaten alive or canoodling with King Kong. Sharkey had heard the comparison before. Just because he was big, hairy, and grunted a lot, people compared him to an ape. Whatever, let people think what they want. It didn't keep anyone from buying his beer.

"I need you to get off the table, please." He spoke slowly, hoping the words would penetrate her fear, and she'd see that this particular ape was literate.

Clutching her chest with one hand, she reached toward him with the other, a look of sheer terror on her face. She was lovely, really, once you got past the horror. Delicate features, striking hazel eyes, full lips.

Well, hell.

He tried to soften his face—appear less threatening—but he was a big dude, and she was a tiny thing that he could crush just by hugging her too tight. Not that there would be any hugging. Or kissing, despite the kissable lips. He still didn't have a good reason why she was there in the first place. On his property.

"I'm not going to hurt you." Sharkey wasn't used to doing the talking. Usually, he left that to other people, preferring to only speak when necessary.

Finally, she placed her hand in his, and his heart stilled. It was tiny, almost fitting in his palm, the fingers slender and delicate, the skin almost as pale as his Irish complexion. Carefully, he pulled her off the table, to the bench, then down to the ground. As her feet hit the dirt, she stumbled.

He caught her as she fell against him, and that's when his towel hit the ground for the second time.